"I've got to brin

She knew it. "Please. I'm telling you the truth. I work as a stunt driver."

"But you don't own this car," Ben said.

"No, but I work for the people who do. I can't get arrested. I need to get these back to where they belong."

"Let me guess. Nobody knows you and your buddy are out here for a little joyride, do they?"

"No," she admitted. "But that's why you've got to cut me a break. I know you don't owe me anything, but please help a girl out."

Ben rubbed the back of his neck while he thought it over. He glanced back at the second police car, then put his hands on his hips. "I can't. What's your friend's name?"

Of course he couldn't. *Wouldn't*. She had burned this bridge.

Dear Reader,

I have always been the good girl. I follow the rules and try my best to do what is expected. Shelby Young is the complete opposite of me, and that made her more fun to write. Shelby has had a tough life, mostly due to things outside her control, but she blames herself anyway.

Ben Harper is more like me. He plays by the rules and tries to do the right thing even when that's not the easiest thing to do. When Shelby returns home after ten long years, he isn't sure what the right thing is anymore.

These two have a lot to work through and some pretty big obstacles to overcome to finally see that we all deserve happiness, whether we're like Ben, with a heart of gold, or like Shelby—a little bit of trouble. I hope you enjoy this Valentine's story of love, loss and redemption.

I love to connect with readers on social media. Please find me online at amyvastine.com, on Facebook at Facebook.com/amyvastineauthor or Twitter, @vastine7.

xoxo,

Amy Vastine

HEARTWARMING

The Sheriff's Valentine

—

Amy Vastine

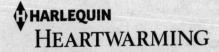

HARLEQUIN®
HEARTWARMING™

ISBN-13: 978-1-335-42659-8

The Sheriff's Valentine

Copyright © 2022 by Amy Vastine

This edition published by arrangement with Harlequin Books S.A.

For questions and comments about the quality of this book, please contact us at CustomerService@Harlequin.com.

Harlequin Enterprises ULC
22 Adelaide St. West, 41st Floor
Toronto, Ontario M5H 4E3, Canada
www.Harlequin.com

Printed in U.S.A.

Recycling programs for this product may not exist in your area.

Amy Vastine has been plotting stories in her head for as long as she can remember. An eternal optimist, she studied social work, hoping to teach others how to find their silver lining. Now she enjoys creating happily-ever-afters for all to read. Amy lives outside Chicago with her high-school-sweetheart husband, three teenagers who keep her on her toes and their two sweet but mischievous pups. Visit her at amyvastine.com.

Books by Amy Vastine

Harlequin Heartwarming

Stop the Wedding!

A Bridesmaid to Remember
His Brother's Bride
A Marriage of Inconvenience

Return of the Blackwell Brothers

The Rancher's Fake Fiancée

Grace Note Records

The Girl He Used to Love
Catch a Fallen Star
Love Songs and Lullabies
Falling for Her Bodyguard

Visit the Author Profile page
at Harlequin.com for more titles.

To all those troublemakers out there who just want to be loved.

PROLOGUE

February 14—Twelve Years Ago

HEART RACING, SIXTEEN-YEAR-OLD Benjamin Harper slid into the passenger's seat of his dad's cherry red 1970 Dodge Chevelle. His dad's prized possession. His pride and joy. Every weekend, the man religiously pulled it out of the garage and sat in it. He didn't drive it. He just sat at the wheel or polished it but mostly simply admired it.

"Buckle up, Harper," Shelby said, readjusting her grip on the steering wheel. "This is going to be one heck of a ride."

"Swear to me that we will put this car back in my garage without a scratch on it," he begged as he clicked the seat belt into place. Shelby just smirked as she revved the engine. It was the opposite of reassuring. "I'm serious, Shelby. If my dad finds out we took this car, we're dead."

"If you don't want to do this, tell me now

because once I put this baby in Drive, no one is going to stop me until we run out of road."

It was Valentine's Day, and in Goodfield, Georgia, Valentine's Day was a big deal. As soon as Christmas ended, the whole town's focus shifted to the holiday dedicated to love and romance. Ben always thought it was sort of a lame holiday until Shelby moved in with Mrs. Wallace next door. Today was the anniversary of her arrival in Goodfield.

If he was honest, Ben had fallen in love with Shelby the moment he saw her. He'd spent the last four years convincing her to be his friend, which he felt he had accomplished. They were inseparable most days. Ben had finally worked up the courage to tell her how he really felt, to confess he didn't want to be just friends anymore.

At first, he considered giving her flowers or maybe a bracelet with a heart charm, but Ben knew better than to waste his money on that kind of stuff. The things other girls thought were sweet or romantic didn't impress Shelby. He needed to be more creative than that.

Shelby loved cars and speed. She loved breaking the rules. She loved taking risks and the thrill of a good chase. That was why he was sitting in his dad's newly renovated classic car on a deserted back road. Ben had hoped this gesture would make her realize that he was the guy who would do anything for her. He wouldn't be able to use words like *girlfriend* or *boyfriend*. She wouldn't like those labels, but maybe she wouldn't mind letting him kiss her, because all he ever thought about these days was kissing her.

Ben had been chasing after Shelby since the day they met. He couldn't help but wonder what would happen if she'd slow down so he could catch her. What would it be like to hold her hand? He wouldn't know until he was honest with Shelby about how he felt. He was definitely in love with her.

Shelby pulled her gaze from the wide-open road ahead of them. With her brown hair pulled up in a ponytail, she turned those emerald green eyes on him. "What's it going to be, Harper? Are we doing this or not?"

"You know I've never been able to say no to you. Why would I start now?" He braced himself. "Show me what this thing's got."

The smile that broke across her face was worth all the fear he felt the second she put that car in Drive and slammed down on the gas. Ben's body pressed hard against the seat from the force of the acceleration. Shelby was in her glory.

Out the window, the world was flying by at a speed Ben had never experienced before. Everything was a blur as they flew down the road, a mix of colors with no definite shape. Ben kept his eyes forward. The two black stripes on the hood matched the color of the asphalt road ahead.

Shelby shifted gears again. "Do you feel that?" she asked. "I heard your dad tell Mr. Klobucher this thing pushes 675 horsepower thanks to the engine rebuild he did two years ago. Why have we never taken this baby for a drive before? This thing is a monster!"

Ben knew she had more experience driving than most kids their age. She had taken Maggie's car for a joyride more than a couple times last summer even though she had only turned sixteen last month. The Chevelle was way different than Miss Maggie's car. If his dad found out they took his car out, licensed or not, Ben was a dead man.

He glanced at the speedometer, which said she was already pushing ninety-five miles an hour. He would have been more afraid if her smile wasn't so big. Being the one who did that, who made Shelby Young beyond happy, meant everything to him. Emotions were something she usually kept contained. She was the best at acting like she didn't care. He knew that was a defense mechanism so people couldn't use her feelings against her.

They were coming up fast on a tractor. On the other side of the road was a 16-wheeler. How did the road go from deserted to crowded all at once? Just as he had started to relax, his anxiety spiked again. Surely, Shelby would slow down until the truck passed.

"Hang on, Harper. This is going to be close."

Before he could scream at her to slow down, Shelby shifted gears, pushed on the gas and pulled into the left lane to pass the tractor. Ben could only watch in horror as the truck came barreling toward them. They were going to die. He was about to be splattered all over this rural highway.

As he braced for impact, Shelby slid past the tractor and slipped back into the right-hand lane allowing the truck to fly by, the horn still blaring in warning. Ben's heart had stopped beating. His life had definitely flashed before his eyes. He had to be dead. There was no way they had made it.

Shelby put her hand on his knee and he

was very aware of being alive. "Holy moly, Harper! Did you see that? That was…amazing! This car is incredible!"

"Pull over, Shelby."

"What?"

"Pull. Over."

"Oh come on, Harper. That was a little scary, but I had everything under control."

"Pull over right now!" Ben wasn't a yeller. He didn't lose his cool or raise his voice. He fancied himself one of the most easygoing people on the planet. That was probably the only reason Shelby did as he said.

When the car came to a complete stop, Ben opened the door. He climbed out, needing to have both feet on the ground and in control of how fast or slow his body was moving. He felt like he was about to throw up.

"Are you okay?" Shelby asked, coming around to his side of the car. She actually sounded concerned.

"No, Shelby. I'm not okay. You almost got us killed back there!"

"No, I didn't," she argued. Her nose scrunched up like he had accused her of something ridiculous. "I had everything under control. I knew I could make it and I did."

Ben laced his fingers behind his head and

tried to take some deep breaths like he did after running sprints at the end of basketball practice. When he finally caught his breath, he dropped his hands to his sides.

"All I wanted to do was make you happy. I wanted to give you something no one else could give you for Valentine's Day. It couldn't be boring like a box of chocolates or a dumb charm bracelet. A ride in my dad's car was perfect. Only I didn't expect you to try to get us run over by a semitruck!"

There was a definite crease between her eyebrows. "Driving your dad's car was my Valentine's Day gift?"

Ben should have known she wouldn't have made the connection.

"Forget it. We need to go home." He stalked over to the driver's side. She was not driving this car for another second.

"You've got to chill out, Harper. You're wound so tight, one day you're going to snap."

He was about to snap, but it wasn't because he wasn't "chill" enough. The only reason he was going to lose it was because she was out of control.

"Sometimes I have myself convinced that no one gets you like I do. Other times, especially when you go out of your way to give me a heart attack, I feel like I don't know you at all."

"What is that supposed to mean? Since when is being willing to take a risk not who I am?"

"This wasn't taking some meaningless risk. This was putting your life and my life on the line like that for…what? A stupid thrill?"

Shelby stared hard at the ground, unable to look him in the eye as he finally set her straight. He waited for her to say something. Anything to explain herself. At least offer an apology for being so reckless. When she had nothing to say, he felt completely defeated.

"I love you, Shelby, but I guess you don't care if I live or die."

Her head snapped up and her eyes locked on his. "Excuse me?"

"It's obvious that you don't care about me."

"Not that part. Did you just say you love me?"

Ben scrubbed his face with his hand. That wasn't exactly how he planned to tell her he was in love with her. It kind of annoyed him that she was somehow that surprised. Didn't he spend every moment of free time with her? Wasn't she the one he went to first when he had good news or bad news? She had to have noticed the way he looked at her because sometimes he couldn't tear his eyes away.

"Come on, Shelby. I've been in love with you for a long time. Don't act like you haven't noticed. The point is you obviously don't feel the same."

She had almost killed him and clearly felt no remorse about it either. She thought it was "amazing" to put their lives in danger like that. Ben had to face the facts: there was never going to be more between him and Shelby than this.

"A long time? Like how long?" she asked, moving slowly in his direction.

"I'm pretty sure that doesn't matter."

She gently bit down on her bottom lip and nodded. "It kinda does."

"If you don't care about me, why would it matter if I've been in love with you for four years or four minutes?"

Shelby stood in front of him now. She was so close their bodies were almost touching. His breath hitched and his heart began to race again.

"I would never let anything happen to you, Ben." She placed her hand on his cheek. Her thumb brushed his cheekbone ever so softly. "You're probably the only one I truly care about in this whole stupid world. I never imagined someone like you could love someone like me. Something that good doesn't happen in my world."

It wasn't "I love you," but Shelby had never been someone who used those words to describe her feelings about anything. Ben felt a flutter in his stomach. She didn't tell him she loved him, but she did push up on her tiptoes and kiss him.

Ben's heart exploded right there on the side of the road. He could feel the joy spread through his body like a wildfire in a dry forest. Shelby didn't need to say those three words. He felt them. It was the best Valentine's Day ever.

May 14—Ten Years Ago

SHELBY YOUNG WASN'T sure which was louder— the sound of her heart beating like a drum inside her chest or the scraping noise the old wood-framed windowpane had made when she pushed it open. Everything sounded so much noisier at night, from the creak of the bedsprings when she stepped on her mattress for a boost to the thud of her backpack hitting the ground outside. It all seemed capable of waking the dead.

Not that Shelby was worried about the dead; she was much more concerned about the living. Maggie Wallace might have been old, but she was definitely very much alive. Thankfully, as long as Shelby used the window in her room instead of the front door, Maggie wouldn't hear a thing.

The window in the Harpers' house directly across from Shelby's was closed. The room was dark. No one was sleeping in that room tonight. Ben was still in the hospital. Maggie swore that she'd heard from his mom that he would make a full recovery. Still, Shelby worried.

The winds off the lake picked up and blew between the two houses. There were curtains that hung inside that other window, bright red with a black stripe at the bottom. The Georgia Bulldogs had been Ben's obsession since he was a toddler. If he really did make a full recovery, he could go to school in Athens in the fall. There was nothing holding him back once Shelby left town.

She placed the folded up piece of notebook paper with Maggie's name scrawled across it on her pillow and scanned the moonlit room one more time for anything she might want to take with her. Her gaze fell on the photograph Mrs. Harper had given her as a birthday gift in January. It was of her and Ben sitting on the dock last summer. Shelby's head rested on his shoulder and his arm wrapped around her waist. It was the best gift anyone had ever given her. She shoved it into her duffel bag before climbing out the window and closing it behind her.

There were no signs of life at the Harpers'. Mrs. Harper had been staying at the hospital with Ben while his dad came home at night to be with Nicky, Ben's little brother. Mr. Harper had made it clear the other day that there was no place for her in Ben's life anymore. She really couldn't disagree. She pulled another folded piece of notebook paper from her back pocket and ran a finger over his name.

Ben.

Her first friend. Her first boyfriend. Her first love. Her first heartbreak. She had no one to blame for the last one except herself. She had been behind the wheel of his dad's Chevelle on prom night and hit a deer going too fast. Ben had been ejected and was lucky to be alive. The sooner she got out of Goodfield, the better for him.

She folded the goodbye note again, making it square instead of a rectangle. She had written and rewritten it a dozen times. There were so many things she wanted to tell him and so many more she couldn't. She took a step toward his window. He always went to the window in the morning. Always waited for her to show her face. Always reminded her to smile. *Good morning, Trouble*, he'd say.

Trouble was his nickname for her, a name she'd happily lived up to until today. The note would be the only thing to greet him when he returned home, though. He'd have no more trouble in his life after tonight. It was better that way.

Shelby tried to steady her racing heart as she got closer to the window. Hopefully he'd see why she had to go. He'd understand.

Someday.

Probably.

Maybe not.

She held the note against her chest. She thought about all the times he had told her he loved her. How he had made promises to never leave her behind. It was going to be them against the world. He thought he could protect her from a world that always managed to do her wrong. Little did he know he really needed to protect himself from her.

She shoved the note back in her pocket. It was pointless to leave him nothing but a bunch of excuses and apologies. Better to leave without saying goodbye. He would need a clean break.

Shelby heaved her backpack over her shoulder and resisted the temptation to steal one more glance at Ben's window. There was no more looking back, only forward.

CHAPTER ONE

January 17—Present Day

SHERIFF BEN HARPER loved his job. Except on the nights he had a 12-gauge shotgun pointed at his face. He was new to the job, but he had to believe this wasn't a usual occurrence.

"Sir, I need you to put the gun down," Ben said, showing the man his hands. "I'm with the sheriff's office, responding to your call about trespassers."

Dressed in black-and-red-plaid pajama pants and a white undershirt, the old man stood on the front porch of his dilapidated farmhouse in untied boots. The porch light's yellow glow illuminated the scowl on his face. He didn't lower his weapon an inch. "I heard someone messing around behind my garage."

The sound of breaking glass prompted the man to shoot his gun in the direction of the noise and thankfully not at Ben's head. Ben drew his gun. "I need you to put your weapon down, sir, so I can do my job. No one has to get hurt."

Another loud crash came from behind the garage. "You bastards picked the wrong guy to mess with! The police are here! If they don't shoot you, I will!"

Not having control of the situation made Ben tense. "No one needs to shoot anyone," he reminded the angry man. When people didn't listen to the police, people got hurt. It also wasn't clear who he should be more concerned about—whoever was trespassing or the trigger-happy homeowner. "If you could put your gun away that would be really helpful while we check out what's going on over there, Mr....?"

"Carson. Mel Carson," the man responded. "I know you. You're the guy who stole the election from Sheriff Bowden."

Ben still had some constituents to win over. Not everyone was happy to have fresh blood in the sheriff's office after November's election. Some people preferred things to stay the same. Change was scary.

"Well, if by 'stole the election from Sheriff Bowden' you mean earned more votes than him, then yes, I am that guy. Now, if you'll let me get to the bottom of this, I'll take care of whoever's back there."

Mr. Carson brought his gun down and put his arm through the strap. "I don't ask for trouble, but I will give it to anyone who tries to mess with me."

"I completely understand, Mr. Carson," Ben assured him.

He radioed for an ETA on his backup, which arrived seconds later in the form of Deputy Kevin Mitchell, a veteran officer and also a proud supporter of the former sheriff. He had no issue with voicing his concerns about Ben's lack of experience and sensationalized heroics. Not exactly the guy Ben wanted to have his back tonight.

He gave Deputy Mitchell a rundown of what had happened and the two of them carefully made their way around the dilapidated garage. Ben heard rustling noises coming from behind three overflowing garbage cans. It was frustratingly dark in these rural parts of Georgia this time of night. He turned his flashlight on the trespasser's hiding spot, praying whoever was there would simply give themselves up.

"Police," he announced. "We need you to

come out with your hands up so we can see them."

No one moved and it got real quiet. Maybe they were contemplating their options, which were limited to coming out and giving themselves up or making a run for it. Adrenaline flowed through Ben's body, so he took a deep breath to stay calm. All of his senses were on high alert.

"Trust us," Mitchell said. "We're your safest option right now."

Ben had to agree. Mr. Carson didn't seem to be kidding about shooting whoever was destroying his property.

Mitchell motioned for Ben to go left while he went right. If the trespasser wasn't going to come out, they would have to get him. Ben moved cautiously, keeping his flashlight and gun aimed at the cans. His bad shoulder began to ache. *Tough it out*, he told himself.

Expecting a teenager or maybe two, Ben stepped around to the other side of the oversize black plastic cans. It wasn't teenagers, though. Instead, a beady-eyed possum shot forward making a noise that sounded more like an enraged pig than a scared rodent. Ben jumped back and let out an embarrassingly high-pitched shriek.

The large possum ran off followed by her five babies. Ben clutched his chest as his heart raced. He slid his gun back into its holster. No one was getting shot or going to jail tonight. He relaxed until the loud click of a shotgun racking made every muscle in his body tense. He whirled around as Mr. Carson took aim.

"Don't shoot!" Ben shouted. "It's all clear. You had possums. That's all. Just critters, sir."

"You screamed like you guys needed some help." Mr. Carson lowered his gun.

"I'm fine," Mitchell said. He tipped his head in Ben's direction. "He's the one who thought the tiny animals were going to kill him."

Ben stood a little taller, straightened his shoulders. "They startled me, that's all."

"You screamed like a little kid," Mitchell added.

"Sure did." Mr. Carson nodded.

Mitchell clicked his tongue. "Not very sheriff-like if you ask me."

"Okay, I get it." Ben had to stop them from humiliating him any further. "Why don't you—" He wanted to tell both Mitchell and Mr. Carson where they could shove their observations, but two cars came flying down the road at speeds that rivaled light and sound.

They came to a stop just past Mr. Carson's house. One pulled alongside the other.

"You finish up here and I'll go check that out," Ben said, taking off for his police cruiser. As soon as he pulled out into the street, the two vehicles took off. He flipped on his lights and sirens and began his chase. The vehicles ahead of him were side by side on the two-lane road, engaged in some sort of perilous drag race. They were moving so fast they traveled a couple of miles before he got close enough for the drivers to realize he was in pursuit. The bright yellow car on the left slowed first and pulled behind the other on the shoulder of the road.

"Is that a Maserati?" Ben asked himself in disbelief. He'd never seen one in person. That was the kind of car people around these parts only saw on television or in the movies.

The second car, a silver Aston Martin, was just as rare. Neither one had plates, so there was no telling who these people were. He called dispatch, knowing it would take Mitchell a few minutes to catch up. Minutes that would surely increase the anxiety in the drivers. Minutes that would allow them to consider their next move. Ben took a deep breath to regain his focus. They could have outrun him if they had really wanted to, but they stopped. Hopefully that meant they planned to cooperate rather than resist.

The driver door of the Maserati opened, and Ben reached for his radio. "Please stay in your vehicle," he said through the car's PA system. "Do *not* exit your vehicle."

The driver closed his door and opted to wave a hand out the window instead. Was this a diversion? Ben's view of the first car was slightly obscured. He didn't detect any movement, but the darkness felt horribly ominous. He scanned his surroundings, searching for any sign of danger.

"I can explain everything if you just come talk to me!" the driver, a female, shouted out the window. Her voice was so familiar it gave him pause.

Deputy Mitchell finally pulled up behind him. "What do we have here?" he asked over the radio.

"No tags. The driver in front of me tried to get out, but I stopped her."

"Her? Interesting. I think I should talk to this one," Mitchell said.

Ben stopped him. "I'm primary, Deputy Mitchell. I've got it. You keep an eye on the driver of the other car while I talk to this one." If there was one thing Ben was confident about, it was his understanding of procedure. There was no way he was giving this one up. His curiosity had been piqued.

Stepping out of his vehicle, Ben approached the Maserati with his flashlight in hand. From what he could tell, the woman inside was the only occupant. She reached up to tighten her ponytail.

"Hands on the steering wheel," he instructed. People did things to distract officers all the time. A simple move this way or that was meant to keep him from staying focused. He scanned the areas around the car one more time for anything out of the norm.

The woman turned her head to the left, attempting to glance back at him. "I can explain what happened and who these cars belong to," she said.

Ben didn't need her to explain what had been going on. "What happened is you and your friend up there were drag racing and putting yourself and anyone else on this road in grave danger. I could arrest you for that alone."

"Come on, Officer. If you'd just let me talk, I could clear everything up. This is all a big misunderstanding."

"I'm sure it is, miss, but—"

"Would it help to know I'm good friends with Sheriff Harper? He and I go way back. You wouldn't arrest someone who's friends with the sheriff, would you?"

Ben stepped forward, his skin prickling with anticipation. He lifted his flashlight, shining it directly in her face. She quickly shielded her big green eyes. Even with her hand blocking his view, he knew exactly who was using his name to get herself out of trouble.

Trouble herself—Shelby Young.

CHAPTER TWO

SHE KNEW IT was wrong. *So* wrong. Mentioning Ben hadn't been her plan, but if she and Walker didn't get these stunt cars back on the set before Hector realized they were missing, he was going to fire them both. If they got arrested, Walker was going to kill her for convincing him no one would catch them. Seriously, how many times had she raced this highway as a teenager in Maggie's car?

It was a long shot, but she hoped knowing Mr. Hometown Hero could get her out of a ticket. Deputy Do-Right didn't seem too impressed with her connection to his sheriff, though. He practically blinded her with his flashlight.

"Geez! Mind shining that thing somewhere other than straight in my retinas? Being able to see is kind of necessary in my line of work."

He didn't let up. The blinding beam of light stayed pointed at her face. "Step out of the car," he said without the authority that had been there a minute ago. His voice sounded different, strangely...wounded.

Shelby pushed open the door and climbed out. "Listen, I'm part of the stunt team for *Ready, Set, Go 4*." When all else failed, Shelby always pulled out the Hollywood card. "These cars are in the movie. It's our job to make sure they're ready to perform. If you let us go, maybe we can get you on the set."

"Did you seriously just try to bribe an officer of the law?" the cop asked, a tad harsher than she thought necessary. He blew out a frustrated laugh. "Some things never change. Do they, Trouble?"

The beam of light dropped to the road and her heart sank. It took her eyes a few seconds to adjust, but she knew she was standing in front of Ben Harper himself. No longer the gangly boy she had been infatuated with, he had definitely filled out. His hair was cut short, no more shaggy locks to run her fingers through. His face was shadowed, but she knew those eyes made even the bluest skies envious.

"I don't know, Harper. Are you gonna cover for me like you used to?" She tried playing it casual, like this wasn't the most gut-wrenching moment of her life. Seeing his name on an old election billboard had been tough. Being close enough to touch him was terrifying.

Ben shook his head and ran a hand down his face. That wasn't a good sign. The angel on one shoulder was debating with the devil on the other. Shelby used to be good at getting him to give in to his dark side, but that was a long time ago, before she ruined his life. Something told her the angel had been winning a lot more these days.

"I've got to bring you in, Shelby."

She knew it. "Please. I'm telling you the truth. I work as a stunt driver."

"But you don't own this car."

"No, but I work for the people who do. I can't get arrested. I need to get these back to where they belong."

"Let me guess. Nobody knows you and your buddy are out here for a little joyride, do they?"

"No," she admitted. "But that's why you've got to cut me a break. I know you don't owe me anything but please help a girl out."

Ben rubbed the back of his neck while he thought it over. He glanced back at the second police car, then put his hands on his hips. "I can't. What's your friend's name?"

Of course he couldn't. *Wouldn't.* She had burned this bridge. "Walker. Walker Reed."

"Stay put," he said as if he really believed she might take off on him. He approached the Aston Martin and asked Walker to exit the vehicle. "Either one of you have ID?"

Shelby had no identification. She wasn't planning on getting caught. Walker handed over his license and glared at Shelby like he wished he had heat vision. Before she knew it, the two of them were handcuffed and in the back of Ben's car.

Shelby hated herself for the way things had ended. She had often wondered how he was doing. She still worried about the long-term damage the accident may have caused him. The only way to stop the guilt from over-whelming her was to push it away and to act like nothing bothered her. It was how she had survived all the bad stuff she'd experienced as a kid.

"You really should have taken my bribe, Harper. We've got some amazing cars on set. Even better than the ones you saw tonight."

"Stop talking, Shelby." The man driving her to the police station was not the same boy she'd left behind. This Ben didn't tolerate her nonsense. She had broken him in more ways than one.

Once inside the station, Ben motioned for her and Walker to take a seat on a bench outside one of the offices.

"I am never listening to you again," Walker said, turning slightly away from her. He was the closest thing she had to a friend these days. There weren't a lot of stunt drivers in the world and even fewer working ones. Having a friend or two in the business was important. The two of them had ventured into the world of friends with benefits about a year ago, but Walker wanted more and Shelby didn't have more to give. He dropped the benefits and their friendship had been on unstable ground since then. Hopefully getting him arrested wouldn't put an end to it for good.

"Oh please," she said, trying to cajole him. "Like I had to twist your arm. You should be happy we got stopped because I was going to win that race."

Walker laughed. "Dream on! I had you beat by a mile."

"You had nothing and know it."

He shook his head and turned serious. "Yeah, well, you better hope we have a job after this or we'll both have nothing."

Shelby leaned back, resting her head against the wall. Losing this job would mean she'd have a much harder time getting another one. She'd have to go back to driving in lame car commercials, which was much less profitable. She began counting the ceiling tiles to keep the negative thoughts at bay.

Seven, eight, nine, ten...

"You two want to make your call?" The sound of Ben's voice caused her to lose count.

He was the main reason why she wanted to crawl out of her skin. Thanks to the well-lit station, Shelby could see exactly how good the last ten years had been to him. His neck was thick and his body lean and strong. A light stubble graced the sharp edge of his jaw. And those eyes... Ben Harper was drop-dead gorgeous.

"We only need one and I should make it," Walker said. He was right, of course. Hector would at least listen to what Walker had to say. The movie's stunt coordinator thought Shelby was a skilled driver but a little too impulsive when the cameras weren't rolling, and this evening's events would only strengthen that opinion.

"You sure you don't want to call anyone?"

Ben asked her. His eyes held her prisoner better than the handcuffs ever could.

"I'm sure." She bit her lip, wishing he would look away so she could, too. It seemed like he wanted to ask her something else but his lips never moved. They sat in a straight line. Nothing like the lips that belonged to the Ben she knew. Her Ben had smiled all the time. Day or night. Rain or shine. Win or lose. There had always been a grin permanently attached to his face. Sometimes it was wider, made his eyes crinkle or his nose wrinkle, but it had always been there.

This Ben wore an unreadable expression. Was he still angry with her? Was he surprised to see her? He had to still hate her. Maybe he had forgotten how much until tonight.

Maybe he didn't care. Maybe he said nothing because there was nothing to say. There were things Shelby wanted to know. Was he married? Did he have a family? What happened after she left? But her mouth remained shut like his.

When production moved south of Atlanta a couple nights ago, she feared this might happen. When she found out that he was still in Goodfield and sheriff, she'd laughed. Not because it was unexpected but because it made perfect sense. There was no one more suited to make the world a better place than Ben. If she was honest with herself, knowing he was near was probably the reason for her recklessness. Pushing the boundaries was the best way to shut off her feelings. And Ben Harper made Shelby feel.

"When he gets done, we'll take inventory of your personal property," Ben finally said. "Then, we'll take you to Booking."

"Boy, maybe I should call a lawyer."

Ben started to go but paused. "Maybe you should grow up and be responsible, Shelby," he said over his shoulder.

Anger quickly replaced the anxiety, but she bit her tongue and didn't snap a retort.

Shelby's head fell back again, her eyes searching for the last ceiling tile she'd counted. Ben had known her better than anyone else. She never let anyone get as close as she had let him. Of course, letting people in only gave her an opportunity to hurt them. Hurt them she had.

Eleven, twelve, thirteen, fourteen...

Walker got ahold of a very irate Hector, who made no promises about not pressing charges. When he showed up at the sheriff's office, he bailed out Walker but not Shelby.

It was frustrating that he assumed all of this was her fault, even though he was right. It had been her idea, but Walker was a grown man. She hadn't put a gun to his head.

"He said he thought you needed a night in jail to get your head on straight," Ben explained to her when he came to retrieve Walker from the holding cell.

"Seriously?" Shelby threw her hands in the air. "Walker, can you talk some sense into him? I can't stay here."

Walker shrugged. "I don't think I'm going to change his mind tonight, Shelbs. But if he won't come get you in the morning, I will."

Shelby stopped pacing inside the cage. "You won't come back tonight? I can't stay here all night. You know I don't like being without an escape plan."

Ben and Walker laughed at the same time. "I'm not pushing my luck tonight," Walker said. "I'll see you in the morning, I promise."

"Walker, please!" Shelby gripped the bars and shook, but her plea went unanswered. She resumed her pacing and chewed on her thumbnail.

Had anyone other than Ben pulled her over, she probably wouldn't be locked up right now. If another deputy had heard she was friends with Ben and was offered a set visit, she would have gotten a warning and been sent on her way. This was all Ben's fault. At least that was what she tried to tell herself. She sat down on the cold metal bench. Maybe he was right. Maybe it was time she took responsibility for her choices. She had no one to blame for being locked up but herself.

After what felt like an eternity, Ben reappeared with keys in his hand. "Come on, Shelby. Time to go."

Relief flooded her body. "Thank God! I knew Walker wouldn't leave me here." She could not get out of that holding cell fast enough.

"Walker isn't the one who bailed you out." Ben unlocked the door and led her out of the holding area.

"Hector came back for me?"

He shook his head. "Nope."

Maybe Walker sent one of the other guys so he'd stay out of trouble with Hector. As she came around the corner, she expected to see Gary or Johnny. Instead, she noticed the woman with the bright red-orange hair and matching lipstick. Maggie Wallace was Shelby's former foster mom. The last one and the only one who had put up with Shelby's shenanigans for more than a couple of weeks. She was a truly kindhearted and patient woman.

Shelby stopped and glared at the back of Ben's head. "What did you do?"

Ben turned and shrugged. "What was I supposed to do?"

"Not wake her up and tell her to come here. Are you crazy?" She did not understand him. It was bad enough she had to face him in this situation, but did he really need to make matters worse by humiliating her in front of Maggie?

"You said you weren't going to make it through the night," he replied. "I didn't want you to have a panic attack. I thought I was doing you a favor."

Maggie sat on a chair by the main entrance with her ankles crossed, hands folded in her lap and eyes closed. She was either asleep or dead. Seeing how she was pushing close to eighty years old, either was truly a possibility.

"Maggie?"

The old woman startled. Her wide eyes took in her surroundings. She had clearly forgotten where she was for a moment. When her gaze landed on Shelby, her face lit up. "Shelby Rae! It really is you."

"It's really me. I'm so sorry Ben bothered you."

"Bothered me?" Maggie got to her feet and opened her arms. "Oh, sugar plum! This is a bonus for me. I thought I was only going to get one day in Atlanta with you."

Shelby was not a fan of public displays of affection, but gave Maggie a hug anyway. It was the least she could do for the only person who'd ever attempted to give her a real home.

"All right, Mr. Harper, take us home," Maggie said, letting go and snatching her purse off the bench.

Ben avoided Shelby's glare. She couldn't believe he'd done this. "You picked her up and drove her here?"

"No." Curtis Harper pushed off the wall by the exit. Shelby hadn't noticed him until he spoke. "I did." Ben's father was the reason she had planned to meet with Maggie in Atlanta instead of coming to Goodfield, which was about an hour south of there. His hair was a little thinner since the last time she had seen him, but he was as intimidating as ever. It was clear by his frown that he was disappointed she had dared to show her face in town again.

SHELBY THOUGHT BETTER of asking Mr. Harper to drop her off at the hotel where the rest of the crew was staying. It was thirty minutes away, halfway between Atlanta and Good-field. The man was clearly in no mood to take her anywhere but Maggie's. She texted Walker, begging him to meet her at the house, but received no reply.

Maggie was a chatterbox the whole drive. She must have been trying to stay awake because her tolerance for silence had been something Shelby appreciated about her.

"I thought I was dreaming when Benjamin called and said we needed to bail you out of jail. You didn't mention anything about being outside of the city the last time we talked."

"I didn't realize we were doing some filming south of Atlanta until right before we left," Shelby said. She couldn't tell Maggie that she had been unable to visit. She had made Mr. Harper a promise a long time ago she'd never come back. Keeping her word had been the only way she knew to make up for what she had done.

Mr. Harper's eyes met hers in the rearview mirror. He didn't want her here. She had not only severely injured his son, but she had destroyed the man's prized possession when she hit a deer on prom night with his Chevelle. He hadn't been a fan before that happened and certainly wasn't after.

"Well, I can't wait to catch you up on all the things happening around here," Maggie enthused. "You won't believe it."

The only people in Goodfield that Shelby cared about were Maggie and Ben. Maggie probably knew everything that was going on with Ben, but it was a rule between the two of them—Shelby didn't ask about him and Maggie didn't tell.

Mr. Harper pulled into Maggie's driveway. "Have a good night, ladies. Or morning, I should say."

"Thank you for the ride. Tell your wife I owe you two dinner. My treat at The Village Inn whenever you're both free."

"You don't have to do that."

"But I'm going to do it anyway," Maggie said, giving his arm a pat. "Thanks again, Curtis."

Shelby wanted to get out of the car almost as much as she had wanted to get out of that holding cell. She escaped the back seat but had to wait for Maggie to climb out the front.

Mr. Harper dipped his head so he could see her through the open door. Ben used to call her Trouble, but it was Mr. Harper who actually believed she was. "Welcome home, Shelby."

"Thanks. I, uh, appreciate your help tonight. Sorry we got you involved in this little misunderstanding."

His laugh was the same as his son's. "Is that what you're still calling the trouble you get yourself into?"

Yep, still hated her.

"Thanks again for the ride." She shut the door with a little extra zip.

Shelby checked her phone for a message from Walker. Nothing. She sent him another text. Maggie unlocked the front door and motioned for Shelby to come inside.

"Your bed has sheets on it," Maggie said as Shelby took in the familiar sights and smells of the house.

The old grandfather clock that used to drive her nuts was still in the foyer along with the Go Jump in the Lake sign. Adjacent to the foyer on the right was the sitting room, where no one ever really sat. It was more of a museum for Maggie's eclectic treasures. She still had her forest green velvet couch in there as well as the stone elephant she said she had shipped all the way from Thailand after she and her husband had traveled there for their ten-year anniversary. African masks hung on the wall above the couch, and pottery Maggie made in a class at the community center was displayed on the end tables.

To the left was the hall that led to the bedrooms. From where Shelby stood, she could see straight through to the fireplace on the far wall of the family room. In between the foyer and the family room was the kitchen and breakfast nook where Shelby remembered sharing some of her favorite times with Maggie. Whether it was chowing down on Maggie's famous baked ziti or having a late-night ice cream snack together, the kitchen was where they connected after school and had their most important conversations.

"There are some bins in your closet full of things you left behind. I have to believe you can find something to sleep in."

"Oh, I'm not sleeping here."

Maggie frowned. "Where else are you going to sleep?"

"The crew is staying at the Starlight. My buddy will come get me." The hotel, which had seemed too close to Goodfield when she first arrived, now seemed so far away.

"Oh nonsense! It's two in the morning. You can sleep here tonight and he can pick you up at a less godforsaken time."

Glancing down at her phone, Shelby knew

there was little hope of getting Walker out here before dawn and no way Maggie would let her go if he did.

"I'll stay. Thank you. Please go back to bed and get some sleep," Shelby said. "I'll see you in the morning."

"Promise?" Maggie seemed genuinely concerned that Shelby might leave before she woke. It was a gut punch that Maggie felt she had to worry about that. Of course, given the way Shelby left last time she was under this roof, it shouldn't have been an unexpected fear.

Shelby tried to reassure her, although she wasn't sure her words would be trusted. "I'll be here when you wake up. I promise. I'm also going to pay you back the money you put up for bail."

Maggie waved her off. "Pfft! Don't worry about it."

"I do worry. You bailed me out, let me stay in your home. I owe you."

Maggie smiled and placed a hand on Shelby's cheek. "This will always be your home, too, sweetheart."

Home. That was never a word Shelby put much stock in. She grew up in a lot of houses, not homes. Maggie's was the exception.

Shelby wished her a good night and retreated to her old bedroom. She didn't know what to expect, so she held her breath as she pushed the door open. When she flipped on the light, it was like stepping back in time. Memories she had locked up in the deep, dark corners of her mind came forward.

Sitting down on the bed, she ran her hand over the comforter. It was one of the first things Maggie had bought for her. She had even let Shelby pick it out. Solid black. It had been Shelby's way of expressing her distrust. She wouldn't get comfortable. Not if it could all be taken away at a moment's notice like it had before.

Maybe the black had been a tad overdramatic. It was a wonder Maggie had put up with her. At twelve years old, she had been a foster parent's nightmare. Shelby's mom had died when she was five. Her dad managed to be a single parent for six months before he decided he was incapable of caring for a kid on his own. Those early losses made her moody, rebellious and completely incapable of getting along with anyone her age or in authority.

Shelby kicked off her shoes. She wasn't much different from the girl she had been all those years ago. She still had a wild streak.

Some might say her mood was unpredictable. Rules were meant to be broken. Making friends would always be a challenge. Shelby didn't like many people. Had it not been for Ben, she might never have believed she could have a real friend.

Unfortunately, their friendship had not endured. There was nothing left. She had seen to that when she took off all those years ago.

Shelby got off the bed and opened the closet. Inside were the bins Maggie had said would be there. Everything Shelby had left behind had fit into three containers. The first one was a painful high school flashback. Class notebooks Maggie could have burned, the yearbook only three people signed, the graduation gown she never wore.

The second box, filled with clothes, seemed less emotionally charged until digging through it revealed the T-shirt with HARPER printed on the back. It was stolen goods, really. He had given it to her after one of their late-night make-out sessions down by the lake ended with her shirt accidentally falling in the water. The T-shirt had smelled like him, so she'd kept it instead of giving it back.

Clutching it in both hands, she lifted it to her nose and inhaled. She felt stupid for thinking it might still carry his scent. But the feelings that had been kicked up thanks to her encounter with Ben tonight made her take off her shirt and put his on.

For old times' sake, she told herself. Nothing more.

CHAPTER THREE

BEN HANDED THE grocery clerk forty dollars and helped bag the items he had purchased. He had picked her up all the essentials—bread, eggs, half gallon of milk, brown sugar ham, a few fruits and vegetables, and a package of her favorite frosted lemon cookies. Hopefully, it was enough to get Maggie through the next few days.

"I can do that for you, Sheriff." Sue Gibson, who had been the store manager for as long as Ben could remember, came over to bag up his order.

"It's no trouble," Ben insisted.

"You deserve the same level of service that you provide this town, young man." She covered his hand with hers to stop him from bagging. "I live down the street from the Kellys, and I can't imagine how Rosemary would have maintained her sanity if she had lost her kids *and* her husband. I think you should know you didn't just save those kids, you saved Rose, too."

The enormous lump in Ben's throat prevented him from responding. He let Sue bag up the groceries and took his change from the clerk. With a nod and a tight-lipped smile, he grabbed his bags and left. His feet couldn't move fast enough even though he wished his heart would slow down.

It confounded him that so many in the town thought he was some kind of hero when the whole situation made him feel more like a failure than anything. He had saved those kids from drowning but not their father. The Kelly family still suffered an immeasurable loss.

He rubbed his tired eyes, exhaustion setting in after a more than eventful night shift. Shelby was back in Goodfield. He never thought he'd see the day. She was the same but different. The rules still didn't apply to her. She certainly didn't like being caged in. She was unbelievably beautiful.

Ben knew he shouldn't be thinking about how incredible she looked, but anything was better than rehashing the Kelly accident. He couldn't stop comparing the woman he saw last night with the image in his head of the girl he had once foolishly been in love with. She had those same get-lost-in-them green eyes, same dusting of freckles across the bridge of her nose. The differences were subtle but significant. Gone were the black skater shorts and angry-girl T-shirts. The skinny jeans and low-cut, clingy tank top she wore last night showed off curves he didn't remember her having.

It didn't matter what she looked like. At least that was what he told himself. Shelby had no plans to stick around. Based on her reaction to seeing Maggie, staying in town wasn't her plan. That was fine by Ben. He had more important things to think about. There was no room for trouble, and that was Shelby's nickname for a reason.

A nondescript black sedan sat in Maggie's driveway as he came around the bend. He pulled in behind it as the door opened and Walker Reed climbed out. Ben checked the time. It was almost eight-thirty. He had convinced himself there was no way Shelby had stuck around all night and morning, although there was a tiny part of him that had hoped. Walker's presence was completely unexpected, however. He hated that he had wondered how close those two really were.

Walker held his hands up when Ben got out of his patrol car. He was almost the complete opposite of Ben. Tall, dark and dangerous. Probably everything Shelby was looking for in a man. "I obeyed all of the traffic laws on my way here, Sheriff. I swear."

"All of them?"

He dropped his hands and grinned. "Almost all. Speed limits sure are low in this town. Something tells me last night wasn't the first time Shelby's gotten picked up for speeding around here."

"She used to be pretty good at not getting caught," he replied, pulling open the back door to retrieve the groceries. Ben winced as a sharp pain shot through his bad arm. Some days, it was easy to forget that he had several screws in his shoulder. Other days, it hurt almost as much as his heart did when he thought about the accident that led to those screws a decade ago.

Ben had allowed Shelby to drive his dad's Chevelle two times. The first time, she had nearly crashed the car but kissed him after he confessed his love for her. The next time he let her drive, Shelby did crash the car and abandoned him while he was stuck in the hospital.

"You need some help?" Walker took one of the bags from Ben. "I bet Shelby got away with a lot. That's the only reason I can come up with for why she still thinks she can."

This guy knew her well. Ben forced himself not to think about how well. He decided to focus on the fact that the man seemed much nicer than his first impression suggested.

"You two knew each other when she lived here?" Walker asked.

Ben closed the door with his foot and nodded in the direction of his parents' place. "Grew up next door."

"No way. She must have been a real pain in your butt."

"What makes you say that?"

"Well, you're obviously some kind of Boy Scout and Shelby's nothing but trouble," Walker said like someone who had played with fire and gotten burned. "I also noticed how you were completely unfazed by those darn puppy dog eyes of hers. I struggle to say no when she looks at me like that. She makes me believe that all I have to do is give her what she wants and she'll let me care about her."

Ben would never claim to be unfazed by what he saw in her eyes. He didn't give in last night because he had learned the hard way that giving Shelby what she wanted didn't make her any more willing to let someone in.

"Does she?" Ben had to ask. It was clear there was something more than a working relationship between the two of them.

"Does she what?"

"Let you care about her?"

"She can't really stop me." Walker let out a humorless chuckle. "But she sure tries."

Ben nodded in understanding and wondered how Shelby would feel about her past and present colliding on Maggie's porch. Before they got the chance to ring the bell and find out, Maggie opened the door. Dressed in purple with an emerald green turban on her head, she covered her heart with her hand.

"Sheriff Harper, you are too good to me and now you've got your friends in on it as well?"

"This is a friend of Shelby's, Maggie. We just happened to get here at the same time."

Maggie took a good long look at Walker. "A friend of Shelby's?" she asked as if it was almost inconceivable.

"Yes, ma'am." Walker introduced himself and explained why he was there. "I had some messages on my phone to come get her in the middle of the night, but the boss wouldn't let me do that until now. I tried calling her back but her phone must be dead."

"Well, come on in and let me get you something to drink. Shelby's sleeping like the dead. Makes me wonder if the poor thing hasn't had one good night's sleep in the ten years she's been gone."

Maggie led the men inside and insisted they sit while she unpacked the groceries. Ben was pleased to see color back in her cheeks. The last time he had visited, she had seemed a bit down in the dumps. Today, there was a lightness to her. She hummed a happy tune as she slid the lemon cookies into her secret spot in the cupboard.

Ben needed to leave. His only reason for stopping by was to make sure Maggie was all right and to see to it that she had a few things in her refrigerator. He told himself it was for the best that Shelby was still sleeping. Seeing her again would only complicate things and he was too tired to deal with complications.

Just as he got to his feet, Shelby shuffled into the kitchen. "Please tell me you have coffee, Mags. I cannot function without coffee." She lifted her head and she must have caught sight of the clock on the microwave. "Oh my gosh, is that the actual time? Why didn't you wake me up?"

Ben felt like a cartoon character whose jaw dropped and eyes bugged out of his head. His gaze traveled up her long, tanned legs to the hem of the T-shirt, which barely covered the black short shorts she was wearing.

His eyes flew to hers. She was possibly more mortified than he was. She tugged the shirt down and ran out of the room without a word. Ben noticed his name on her back and sat down until he was sure he could stand without falling over.

"What are you doing here?" Shelby shouted from the hall. Out of sight but not earshot.

Ben couldn't speak. He couldn't think straight. Why was she wearing his shirt?

"You texted me to come get you," Walker replied, apparently not as thrown as Ben was by seeing her half-naked. "Hector told me I couldn't bail you out until you spent the whole night in jail. I let him believe you were still in lockup so he thinks you suffered."

A mix of emotions kept Ben frozen in his seat. They were all overshadowed by desire until the hurt settled back in. He should not be here. He needed to leave.

"Oh my gosh! I'm not talking to you,

Walker!" Shelby screamed from farther away. She must have gone back to her room. He hoped to put on more clothes.

"I should go," Ben said, finally finding his voice. "I've been up for more hours than I can count. My bed is calling my name."

Maggie didn't argue. She had always been respectful of his feelings. She had let him vent when he was angry, cry when he was sad and leave when he got overwhelmed. It had taken a long time for him to come to terms with Shelby's disappearance, and Maggie didn't judge or think he should put time limits on his pain like some other people in his life.

"Thank you again for stopping at the store for me. You spoil me, Benjamin."

"Someone's got to," he said, giving her a kiss on the cheek. "Stay out of trouble, Mr. Reed."

"I'll do my best, Sheriff."

Ben was halfway out the door when Shelby stepped out of her bedroom in yesterday's clothes, asking him to hold up. Watching her walk toward him sent his heart into overdrive. How many times had he been standing in this exact spot, waiting to walk with her to school, watching her wrangle her backpack while shoving breakfast in her mouth, or listening to her shout her goodbyes to Maggie before they took off for a day on the lake?

It felt like a million.

"Were you here to make sure I didn't jump bail or something?" She joined him outside and shut the door behind her. The wind off the lake picked up and blew her hair around her face in an angry swirl. She was the perfect picture of outrage and misplaced angst, a mirror image of her teenage self. "I wouldn't do that to Maggie."

He wanted to laugh. She wouldn't disappear? He wasn't buying it. History told a much different story. "I wasn't here to check on you. I was here to check on Maggie like I do every Saturday. Sometimes I drive her to the store, sometimes I bring her some groceries like I did this morning. My being here has nothing to do with you."

She tried to tame her hair and her temper. "You do that for her?"

"She has no one to take care of her. Someone has to do it." It came out harsher than he intended it.

Shelby's jaw clenched like it used to right before she'd unleash a string of words that would make a sailor blush. She shut her eyes and took a breath before opening them again. "Should I apologize for being able to cut the apron strings?" she retaliated. "I'm not the only person in the world to grow up and move away, Ben. People do it all the time."

"You're right, but you didn't move away. You disappeared, Shelby. There's a difference. If something had happened to her those first few years, I don't even know how we would have let you know. You didn't cut the apron strings, you vanished."

Ben's hurt was masked by anger at the moment. He was acting like he had felt bad for Maggie, but the truth was Shelby had not only left Maggie, she had abandoned him and all the plans they had made. They were supposed to stick together. He'd been sure they would get married someday. He'd believed without a doubt that they were going to be together forever.

"I sent Maggie postcards from the road. She knew I was okay."

"At least her peace of mind mattered to you. We know mine didn't. What am I talking about? I didn't matter period."

The muscles in Shelby's jaw flexed again, but it was the pain in her eyes that made him take a step back. He couldn't feel bad for her.

Not when she was the one who had created this chasm between them.

"Whatever," she said with a sigh. It was her signature way to end a conversation she didn't want to have any longer. Ben hadn't noticed the shirt in her hand until she held it out to him. "This is yours. Maggie accidentally packed it up with my stuff."

"I don't want it," he said stubbornly. She had been wearing it two minutes ago. He wasn't taking it back now.

"Well, I don't want it. It's yours. Take it." She pressed it against his chest, so he snatched it from her before she could feel how hard and fast his heart was beating.

"I'd say see you around, but I doubt I will," he quipped.

"Probably not."

"Great."

"Super."

He turned his back to her and strode toward his car. "Have a nice life, Trouble."

"You, too, Harper."

She really was a pain in the butt. He was glad she wasn't going to show her face around here anymore. Ben yanked open the door to his patrol car, climbed in and slammed it shut. He was so done with her. Shelby Young was no one to him anymore. She hadn't been for a very long time.

She stood on Maggie's front porch, arms folded across her chest like a defiant child. What had he ever seen in her? There was no one better at pushing people away than her. Shelby reached up to wipe her cheek before turning to go back inside and he felt that familiar tug at his heart. She had once been a sad little girl who hid behind her anger. She may have tried her best to scare everyone away, but the truth was she simply believed everyone would eventually give up on her. Better to run than be told to leave.

ALL BEN WANTED to do when he got home was get some sleep. Nick, his younger brother/roommate, and his fiancée had other ideas. Tiffani was on the phone and Nick sat at the kitchen table filling out the newspaper's crossword puzzle. Tiffani didn't live there but was a regular guest. She was there so often, Ben thought she should pay part of the mortgage.

"You're late," Nick said, setting his pencil down.

Ben furrowed his brow. "Late for what?"

Tiffani snapped her fingers and mouthed

for them to be quiet. "We can look at those new listings whenever you have some time," she said to whoever was on the phone. "I have an open house next Saturday until noon, but after that, I'm free."

Tiffani Lyons sold more properties in Goodfield and the surrounding areas than any other Realtor in the county did. Three years ago, she had been the one to sell Ben this house. Ben had gotten a home and Nick had gotten a girlfriend out of the deal.

"Great, I'll see you then." Tiffani said her goodbyes to her client before turning her glare on Ben. "We were supposed to talk about the wedding plans this morning at eight. You said you would be here."

Ben winced. He had completely forgotten about it. Their wedding was four weeks away and sometimes it felt like it was all the two of them had talked about for the past year. Honestly, Ben wasn't sure how he felt about Nick's choice in a bride. Ben had known Tiffani practically his whole life since they were the same age and were in school together all the way through high school.

His brother and Tiffani were so different. She always had to be in control and image was everything. Nick, on the other hand, was a super genius. He had skipped a grade in school, and growing up always had his nose in a book. He was also one of the most well-adjusted people Ben knew. He didn't stress about the little things and didn't care what other people thought. Ben feared that Tiffani might suck the easygoingness out of Nick. Her intensity was bound to rub off on him in some way. It would change him and not for the better.

"It was a rough night. I got out of work late and then I dropped off some groceries at Maggie's."

It was best to leave out the part about arresting Shelby, helping bail out Shelby and seeing Shelby wearing one of his old T-shirts. Nick would have too many unwelcome opinions. He had always had too many opinions about Shelby. From what Ben could remember, the two girls had not gotten along. At all. Of course, Shelby's list of friends had been very short—so short, calling it a list was pretty much an exaggeration.

"How's Maggie?" Nick asked.

"Good. Same as always." Truth was he was a bit worried about her. She was the only person who had truly understood how he felt when Shelby left. They had both leaned on the other to deal with the loss. He wondered how she would handle Shelby disappearing again.

Ben didn't want to think about Shelby. He also didn't want to think about this wedding. He wanted to go to bed and get some sleep.

Tiffani held a manila folder out for him. "Here are the final best man duties. There are a lot of things you're responsible for several days before the wedding and, obviously, the day of the wedding as well. With all the Valentine's Day events going on in town, there will be so many things to work around that day. I need you to make sure you have all this handled."

Ben tossed the old shirt Shelby had given him on the kitchen chair next to Nick and grabbed his to-do file. It was more of a packet than a list. He scanned the first two pages. This seemed a tad over-the-top.

"Because you're late, I don't have time to go over it all with you now," Tiffani said. "I'll trust you and Nick to read it over, and you can ask me questions later."

That was a great idea. Ben would be sure not to have any questions.

"Sounds good," he said. "Nick and I will

talk about it as soon as I get a couple hours of sleep."

He placed his list of duties on the table and picked up the T-shirt.

"What's that?" Nick asked.

Ben threw it over his shoulder. "Nothing," he said, trying to sound unaffected, but moving it closer to his face made him aware that it still smelled like Shelby. "I mean, it's an old shirt Mom found buried in a box somewhere. It needs to be washed or thrown away."

Tiffani frowned. "You stopped at your parents', too?"

"No. I only went to Maggie's. The shirt has been in the car," Ben lied.

"Babe." Nick reached for Tiffani's hand. "Don't give him such a hard time. It's nice that he helps Maggie out."

"You're right. The poor lady has no family. I can't imagine."

Ben's shoulders tensed. "She has family."

Tiffani barked a laugh. "Please tell me you aren't counting Shelby Young. God only knows what happened to her. She's probably dead or in jail."

"She's not, and don't talk about her like that," he snapped, feeling more defensive of Shelby than she probably deserved. She had been in jail a few hours ago after all. Exhaustion made it too difficult to manage any of his feelings at this point. "And for your information, Maggie has been in regular contact with Shelby since she left."

Tiffani huffed. "You have always been too nice to her. We all know the kind of person that girl was. She had some major issues. You're lucky you got out of that friendship with your life. Literally."

Friendship. That was what most everyone in town thought they'd shared. Sometimes he wished that was all he and Shelby had been to one another. Friends. Maybe it would have hurt less when she left. People also assumed that because they were only friends, all his pain and suffering was from the physical injuries. Few knew that it was the heartbreak that almost killed him.

"We all have issues, Tiff. Shelby was braver than the rest of us who liked to pretend we didn't."

Nick stood up and stepped in between his brother and his fiancée. "Okay, you two. You're both right. Shelby had a traumatic childhood that made her who she was. She also didn't apologize for being who she was because of that trauma. She owned it. Lots of other people pretend their lives are perfect even though they aren't."

"Can we talk about something else?" Ben asked. Thoughts of Shelby had been running through his head since he pulled her over. He was trying to push her out and this wasn't helping. "I don't know why we're talking about Shelby anyway. Can we move on?"

Tiffani couldn't let it go. "Well, I hope none of us, including Maggie, ever cross paths with Shelby Young again, which should be easy since Maggie is putting her place on the market. I'm heading over there right now, as a matter of fact."

Ben's stomach dropped. He had to tell them right away or it would look bad. "You might not be able to avoid crossing paths with Shelby, then."

Tiffani's right eyebrow arched. "What?"

"She's at Maggie's. Well, she was. She's a stunt driver for that movie that's filming nearby."

Ben shifted his gaze to Nick, hoping to catch his initial reaction to the news. His brother knew how strong Ben's feelings had been.

"Funny you didn't mention that first," Nick said, staring at him with concern. "All the messages from Mom and Dad asking me to tell you to call them make so much sense now."

Ben had been avoiding his parents' texts and calls all morning. "It's not a big deal. She stopped in to say hello to Maggie, and I'm sure she won't be around again."

"Did she say that?" Tiffani asked.

"I didn't really talk to her, but I assume so based on the fact that she's the same old Shelby she's always been."

Tiffani nodded, satisfied with Ben's assessment. Nick, on the other hand, didn't look so sure. "Well, I'm happy for Maggie. I bet she's ecstatic to have Shelby home even though it might be hard to see her go again," he said, but Ben knew he was more worried about how that would be for him.

"I don't know why she'd have a hard time letting her go," Tiffani said, oblivious to all the nonverbal communication going on between the brothers. "Shelby certainly didn't care about her feelings when she ran away a few days before graduation." She kissed Nick's cheek. "I have to go now but I'll see you later. Please review the list, Ben. Best man is a lot of responsibility."

"Right."

Tiffani was out the door, leaving the two brothers alone.

"You saw Shelby this morning?"

"I can't talk about it right now, Nick."

"Oh, we're going to talk about it. I have been preparing for this day for a long time. I know you aren't going to stand here and act like this is no big deal."

Ben heaved a sigh. "Of course it's a big deal. I'm just not talking about it right now. I need some sleep, man. Can you allow me a few hours of sleep before you try to dig into my psyche?"

"I'll be here when you wake up." Nick's words were more of a warning than anything else. This wasn't going to be the last conversation they had about Shelby.

Ben retreated to his bedroom, throwing his old T-shirt into the overflowing hamper in his closet. He undressed and got in bed, hopeful sleep would come quickly. He stared up at the ceiling and began the arduous task of swatting away the annoying thoughts of Shelby and her return that were buzzing in his brain.

Ben tossed and turned, losing the battle. He imagined all the different things he could have said or done last night and this morning. He should have come off less affected. Maybe he shouldn't have acted so hurt. Ten years was a long time and "time heals all wounds" or so the saying went.

Ben's wounds had become scars, physical and emotional ones. Those first few years after she left, he had imagined a thousand different ways a reunion would go down. None of them came close to what really happened.

Shelby seemed like the same person he knew all those years ago. She loved living on the edge. She hated it that he played it so safe. She liked guys like Walker. Guys who would push her limits, not ones who would set them. He rolled on his side, and his gaze fell on the shirt perched at the peak of his Mount Everest pile of laundry. The memory of Shelby wearing it this morning came rushing back.

He got up and grabbed the shirt, determined to throw it away. Before he got the chance, the scent of roses hit him again. Shelby's one girly indulgence was a lotion that made her smell like a rose garden. Ben had noticed it last night and had to ignore the way it made him want to bury his nose in the crook of her neck.

Instead of tossing the shirt in the garbage,

Ben folded it up and put it in his dresser drawer. It was probably a bad idea, but as soon as his head hit the pillow, he was out like a light.

CHAPTER FOUR

"I PROMISE I'M still going to take you out to dinner before I head back to California," Shelby said, letting Maggie give her one more hug.

"You better or else I'm going to have Curtis drive me to your movie set to see you."

The last thing Shelby wanted was to see Curtis Harper ever again. "I said I promise. I'll call you in a couple days."

"Thank you again for the breakfast," Walker said, giving his belly a pat. Maggie had extended this little visit another hour by offering to make Shelby's favorite—eggs Benedict. Thanks to Sheriff Harper, she had all the ingredients.

Shelby couldn't think about Ben. She couldn't risk the rush of emotion that threatened to overwhelm her if she did. He was alive. He could walk. He had a job. He was probably very happy. She hadn't completely ruined his life. All of that was proof that the best decision she'd ever made was to leave this town no matter how much it hurt her to do so.

"It was my pleasure," Maggie replied. "It's been a long time since I've been able to cook for someone other than myself."

Shelby tried to ignore the way that made her heart ache. Leaving had been the only option. It had to have made things easier on Maggie. She didn't need the trouble that seemed to follow Shelby around.

"I'll talk to you soon." Shelby reached for the doorknob just as the doorbell rang. "Expecting someone?"

"Oh, I completely forgot!" Surprisingly strong for an old lady, Maggie nudged Shelby out of the way with her hip. "This wasn't the way I wanted you to find out."

"Find out what?"

Maggie opened the door and the voice Shelby heard next was like nails on a chalkboard.

"Well, good morning to you, Miss Maggie. Your landscaping alone could be the reason someone buys this house. It is just breathtaking."

That voice. Shelby could never forget it. Tiffani Lyons had used her voice plenty of times over the years to talk down to anyone she thought was beneath her. She had believed Shelby was *way* beneath her.

Maggie stepped aside to allow Tiffani in the house. Shelby's childhood nemesis hadn't changed much in ten years. Her blond hair was shorter, but otherwise, she looked the same. Too primped, too proper, too perfect. Even as a kid, Tiffani had this overcontrolled persona. Her image had been everything to her. Shelby could have overlooked that particular flaw, but Tiffani had also thought it was her job to judge everyone else for everything they did, said, wore, thought. Far too many people at Goodfield High had obsessed over what Tiffani Lyons thought about them.

Tiffani's attention was quick to shift from Maggie's trees and bushes to Shelby. Not one iota of surprise registered on her face. It was as if she fully expected to see Shelby there.

"Good morning, Shelby." Her eyes scanned Shelby from head to toe. "Welcome back. It's been a long time."

"And yet somehow not long enough."

Tiffani laughed. "Ben wasn't wrong when he said you were the same as always."

She had talked to Ben this morning? About

Shelby? Hearing her say his name shoved Shelby off-balance.

"What's going on, Mags?" Shelby didn't feel like pretending she had any interest in catching up with Tiffani.

Maggie grimaced. "I'm putting the house on the market."

"You're selling the house?"

"It's time for me to downsize. This is a lot of house to keep up. I'm hoping a nice, young family will move in and fill it with love and happiness."

"Don't you worry, Miss Maggie. I'm going to make sure the right people find this place. They will be my future in-laws' neighbors after all."

The room spun. All the air had been sucked out and Shelby couldn't breathe. Her brain had quickly put two and two together. Ben marrying Tiffani was more than she could stomach.

"We have to go. Walker, we have to go."

"Is this your boyfriend?" Tiffani asked, her gaze fixed on Walker. Shelby could almost hear her judging him inside her head.

"Friend." Walker added with a wink, "When she's nice to me."

Shelby groaned. "I'll call you later to talk

about this, Mags." "This" being selling the house with the help of Tiffani and how in the world Tiffani got her hooks in Ben.

Maggie opened her arms and Shelby gave the old woman a hug. "I love you, Shelby. It was nice to have you home. Even if it was for one night."

Once she was outside, Shelby forced the air in her lungs with a deep breath. Of all the scenarios that she had imagined when she thought about coming back here, never in a million years did she picture Ben with Tiffani.

"You good?" Walker asked as he unlocked the car.

"We need to get out of here. As far away from here as possible."

Walker chuckled. "I see you're a big fan of the real estate agent."

"We are not talking about her. We will never talk about her."

"Oh boy, can't wait to hear that story from the good sheriff. Sounds like he knows both of you pretty well."

Shelby could only see red as she jerked the car door open. No way was Walker ever talking to Ben again. The urge to leave Georgia right this second was strong. Shelby could go back to LA, pretend she was never here. Of course, she would ruin her career. Finding another stunt coordinator to hire her when she left this one high and dry would be difficult. Walking out on Hector would get her blacklisted for sure.

Leaving wasn't an option, which meant she only had one thing she could do.

As Walker began to pull out of Maggie's driveway, Shelby did something she had sworn she would never do. She googled Ben.

"If I were you, I would avoid Hector today," Walker said. "Give him one more day to cool off. Check in with Brian when we get back and be as helpful as possible until the drivers' meeting Monday morning."

"We need to make a quick stop before we head back," Shelby said, putting the address she found into the map app on her phone.

Walker squinted at her in confusion. "Stop where? For what?"

"Turn left up here," she said, refusing to answer any of his questions.

Walker stopped at the intersection. "I'm not going anywhere unless you talk to me."

"I think it's a great idea for me to not see Hector until the drivers' meeting on Monday. I appreciate you looking out for me."

Walker's head fell back and he let out a deep sigh. "Come on, Shelby."

"Turn left here," she repeated.

His head lolled to the side and he stared at her. Walker knew her well enough to know that she only did what she wanted to do. He had to know it was pointless to fight her on this or to force her to explain herself. He turned left.

Shelby chewed on her thumbnail as they made their way across town. She had no idea how she would start the conversation, she only knew she had to say something. There was no way Ben could spend the rest of his life with Tiffani. Anyone but Tiffani.

Her heart beat hard in her chest as they turned onto his street. This was a bad idea. She should mind her business and go back to the hotel. Ben was a grown man. He could marry whomever he wanted.

"Straight?" Walker asked as they came to a stop sign.

"Do you think that I'm a bad friend?"

Walker frowned. "You're not a bad friend."

"I'm not a good friend, though."

He put his hand on her knee. "You are a good friend. You took me in when I needed somewhere to stay after the wildfires forced me out of my place last summer. You've helped me get jobs. You make sure I get home safe when I have too much to drink at the bar. You're a terrible girlfriend, but you're a good friend."

Shelby placed her hand on his and let out a laugh. "I've always been a terrible girlfriend. That's why I try to avoid being one at all costs."

"You've always been there for me when I needed you. I'm trying to do the same, but what are we doing right now? Where are we and where are we headed?"

Shelby looked at her phone. Ben's house was three down on the right. Would she be a good friend or a bad friend if she told him not to marry Tiffani Lyons? The Ben she knew definitely would want her to talk him out of this.

"The white house on the right," she said, lifting her chin in that direction. "I need to say something to someone. At least get it off my chest even if it doesn't make a difference."

Walker gave her knee a quick squeeze. "Okay, then. Here we go."

Ben's house was perfectly Ben. It was a white brick ranch home with black shutters and a two-car garage. The landscaping was well maintained and there was an American flag hanging from the flagpole on the front porch. An all-American house for an all-American guy.

"You going in? Do you want me to come with you?"

"No," Shelby replied hastily. She did not want Walker to witness her making a fool of herself. "I'm going. Alone."

One more deep breath and she opened the car door. Her stomach was in knots and her feet felt like they were cement blocks. It was a chore to get to the front door. She would say her piece and then leave. She wouldn't let herself spend more time than she should with him. That wouldn't be good for either of them.

Shelby rang the doorbell before she could talk herself out of doing this. While she waited, she paced. Back and forth across the small front porch. What was she doing there? A short while ago, he had accused her of not caring about him period, and she hadn't even denied it. She should have denied it because nothing was farther from the truth. Ben mattered more than anyone, but telling him that wouldn't change anything. She had already broken their bond.

Shelby was milliseconds away from running back to the car when the door opened. "Shelby?" the man said. He had the same color hair as Ben but light brown eyes instead of blue. There was something familiar about him.

"Nicky?" The last time Shelby saw Nicky Harper, he was a skinny fifteen-year-old bookworm who was smart enough to skip a grade in elementary school and used words like *indubitably* and *veracious*. Shelby still didn't know what either of those words meant, but she did know that Nicky was not a little kid anymore.

"It's me," he said, his smile broad like his shoulders. "I go by Nick now."

"Right. Of course. You're all grown-up. I'm surprised you don't go by Nicholas."

"Someone once told me I should because it would be more professional, but Nicholas was the name my mom called me when I was in trouble. It makes me feel like a little kid, which I'm not anymore. I work with kids and they call me Dr. Harper, so it really doesn't matter what my first name is if you ask me."

"Dr. Harper? Wow. I knew you were smart. No surprise you're a doctor. Probably trying to cure cancer or something like that."

"I'm a clinical psychologist actually. I counsel and treat kids with emotional and behavioral issues."

Shelby nodded. She had known several psychologists as a kid. She was also an expert on emotional and behavioral issues. She still had a few.

"Not to be rude, but what are you doing here?" Nick asked, leaning against the door-jamb.

"Yeah, not rude. I get it. I came to talk to Ben. This is Ben's house, right?"

The way Nick stared at her made her feel like that eleven-year-old girl sitting in the doctor's office with the psychologist who desperately wanted to know why she was such a bad kid. No one wanted to adopt bad kids. Bad kids had to go from foster home to foster home because no one could ever love them.

"This is Ben's house. I mean, we both live here, but it's his house. He's sleeping. He had the late shift last night."

This was a bad idea. Nick and Shelby had gotten along back in the day, but surely none of the Harpers wanted her anywhere near Ben after what happened ten years ago. She didn't blame them. She had almost killed him.

"Right. Okay. Well, I should probably just

go, then. It was good to see you, Nicky."
Shelby backed away and almost tripped down
the steps. "I mean, Nick."

Nick stepped out onto the porch. "Shelby,
you don't have to leave. I don't decide who
Ben talks to. Actually, he'd be mad at me if
I let you leave without telling him you were
here. I don't think you realize what it meant
to him to see you this morning. Having you
back is a big deal. I mean, I know you're not
back for good or anything, but please, give
me a second to get him up. Do you want to
come in?"

Shelby's heart soared for a second before
reality came crashing in on the party. As
much as it mattered that Ben was affected
by her return, the way Nick made it sound,
there were some major expectations attached
to her being in Goodfield. She didn't need
that kind of pressure. She also wasn't sure if
Nick meant it was a big deal to Ben because
he had missed her or because he was marrying Tiffani and he knew Shelby would have
this reaction if she found out. Shelby didn't
want to know which was true.

She backpedaled. "No, no. I—I should go.
You don't have to wake him up. I don't want
to bother him."

"Just hang on one second. Okay? Don't run away." Nick disappeared back inside the house.

His choice of words was not lost on her. She stopped and stood still. She wanted to kick herself for coming here and putting herself in this position. She should have told Walker what she was doing so he could have talked her out of it.

Ben was the Harper brother to return to the front porch. He closed the front door and came down the porch steps. He scratched at the back of his neck. "What are you doing here, Shelby? How did you find me?"

His guess was as good as hers as to why she was there. She had no idea anymore, but seeing him again felt like walking into the sunlight after a long, dark night. She knew if she stood here too long, though, she'd get burned.

"I googled you," she said, feeling like an idiot.

"Why?"

"How could you ask Tiffani Lyons to marry you?"

Ben's brows furrowed. He had sleep lines on his face from his pillowcase and his hair was matted down on one side. "What are you talking about?"

"Tiffani came over to Maggie's and said that she would make sure that her future in-laws had good neighbors when she sells Maggie's house. I need to know if you really are marrying Tiffani, because I can't believe that you would, because I know who she was in high school and I know who you are and that just doesn't make sense."

"Ten years is a long time, Shelby. People change a lot in ten years," he replied, stepping closer to her. His feet were bare just like they always were when they were younger. Shoes had always been optional because Ben loved the water and anything that had to do with the lake. Every day he could, he had sat on the dock or gone out fishing on the boat or swam for hours. During the summer, he had lived in nothing but board shorts and a hat.

Shelby snapped herself out of her memories. She couldn't think about shirtless Ben Harper right now. The fully shirted Ben standing before her was about to make the biggest mistake of his life. She had to know how that happened. "That doesn't answer my question, Harper."

"Tiffani is going to be my parents' daughter-in-law this Valentine's Day when she walks down the aisle and marries..." His dramatic pause was not appreciated. Shelby was about to scream when he finally said "...my brother."

A rush of relief flowed through her body. *Hallelujah*, Ben was not marrying Tiffani. She pressed a hand against her chest. "I knew you wouldn't do that. I didn't even think about Nicky. I almost didn't recognize him when he came to the door. When did he get old enough to get married?"

Ben folded his arms across his chest. "Like I said, people change a lot in ten years."

His forearms were so much bigger than she remembered. He had been tall and athletic as a kid. As a man, though, Ben had filled out. His neck was wider. His shoulders were broader. His arms and legs looked stronger. He wasn't wrong. People did change in ten years. He seemed to have changed in all the ways that made her heart beat a little faster.

"Did you really come all this way because you thought I was getting married?" he asked, interrupting her admiration of the way time had treated him.

Shelby shrugged one shoulder. "Pretty much."

Now that he wasn't, it seemed silly that she had gone out of her way to bother him. Seeing him standing there in front of her made it worth all the embarrassment. Shelby didn't miss people. When she was little and her mom died, she hadn't been allowed to miss her mom because the caseworker told her nobody would want to adopt a sad girl who cried all the time. After that, Shelby didn't allow herself to get attached to anyone. That made it much easier not to miss anyone. Of course, Ben and Maggie changed all that. Running away had seemed like an easy thing to do until she did it and her heart broke. Seeing him was a twisted combination of pain and pleasure.

"You could have saved yourself a lot of trouble by just asking Tiffani which Harper she was marrying."

She answered sheepishly, "I didn't ask Tiffani because you were the only option I considered. In my mind, Nicky was still some little kid, not a grown man ready to marry someone."

"I used to think you knew me so well."

"So did I. That's why it didn't make sense that someone like you could have sold your soul to someone like her. People might change. They get taller or they grow a beard. People can mature some, settle down a bit, but people don't change who they are at their core. I came to ask you to explain it to me. Not that I deserve an explanation. I was just hoping you'd provide one."

He sighed and dropped his arms to his sides. "If you had given her the chance, she would have shown you she's not the high school bully you used to know."

Once again, he validated that he was the same guy. Still trying to convince Shelby to give people the benefit of the doubt, to trust that not everyone was out to get her. She had almost believed him once, but that was a long time ago. "I'll have to take your word for it, I guess."

An awkward silence settled between them. It made Shelby sad because one of the things she had loved most about Ben was that it had never been awkward between the two of them. They used to sit together and not say a word for hours. He simply had known that being social took a lot out of her and there were times she had needed to be in her head. Now, everything felt off-kilter, like there were so many unsaid things that a giant wall had grown up between them.

"Is there anything else you want to know?" he asked.

There were plenty of other questions she wanted to ask but knew she shouldn't. She shook her head.

For the first time, he looked past her and took notice of Walker sitting in the car. "Looks like your chauffeur is ready to go, then."

Shelby glanced over her shoulder. Walker gave a wave to Ben, who waved back. It was time to leave.

"Yeah. Sorry to wake you up. I'll let you get back to bed." She began to back away.

"Topher is supposed to get into town today," Ben said just as she turned to go. She swung back around to look at him. His beautiful face made her knees weak. He seemed nervous. "His sister had another baby and they're having the christening tomorrow. We're getting together tonight at Buck's. I'm sure he'd love to see you. You know, if you and Walker wanted to get out and play some pool or something. That's where we'll be around eight."

Christopher "Topher" Harris was the only other person from Goodfield that Shelby might have been able to consider a friend.

He had been Ben's best friend before Shelby had come to town and kind of stolen that title. For some reason, Topher had never resented how close Ben and Shelby had been. He had treated her like one of the guys.

Shocked by the invitation, she couldn't make any words come out of her mouth. She nodded and continued her retreat. Once safe in the car, she quietly cursed under her breath.

"That looked like it went…well?" Walker guessed.

"I don't know what that was." She glanced back as Walker pulled away from the curb. Ben gave her a wave before heading back in the house. "He invited us for drinks tonight."

"Sheriff Harper invited us for drinks?" Clearly as stunned as she was, Walker clarified, "The two people he arrested last night? He wants to hang out with us?"

"We probably shouldn't go," Shelby replied, back to worrying her thumbnail.

"I'll do whatever you want."

"He probably just asked to be nice. Probably feels guilty for arresting us."

"Do you want to go?"

"It would be awkward. Ben probably regrets saying anything to me about it."

"I'm still not hearing you say you don't want to go. Maybe that means we should go."

He was right and he was wrong. There was a part of her that would have gone to Buck's right now if Ben had asked her to, but why was she going to torture herself? There was no reason to spend time with Ben or Topher. They didn't need her in their lives, even if it was only for a night.

Walker let her stay in her head a little longer as they headed back to the hotel and farther away from Ben. Shelby tried to ignore the way it felt like her heart had gotten snagged on something back at Ben's and couldn't get loose. There was a tug-of-war going on inside her that was at a complete standstill. One part wanted to be in Goodfield and one part wanted to get as far away as possible. It was unclear which would give up first.

"I don't need to know how things went bad because it's obvious things ended badly between you two, but can you explain to me how you and the good sheriff became friends in the first place?" Walker asked, breaking the silence.

"We were kids. Didn't you have a friend when you were little that wouldn't make any sense now that you're all grown-up?"

"Of course. You get older, you have different interests and you lose touch. But you and the sheriff were close as teenagers. That means you had more in common than you're telling me. Is he one of those reformed bad boys?"

Shelby laughed. "No! Lord, Ben's been too good his whole life."

"I didn't think that was it. He seems like the type that was voted Most Likely to Help an Old Lady across the Street, and I know you are more likely to run that old lady over going sixty-five in a twenty-five, so you have to explain it to me."

The thought of hitting a person made Shelby want to throw up. It had been traumatic enough to hit an animal. She couldn't remember the accident, but she did remember what Ben looked like after it and that still gave her nightmares. "We better get back to the hotel. Can you stop driving like an old lady?"

"Don't deflect." Walker refused to take her argument bait. "Spill."

Shelby sighed and reclined her seat all the way back. She put her feet up on the dash.

"What are you doing?" Walker asked with a chuckle.

"If you're going to psychoanalyze me, I need to be lying down. That's how all the shrinks got me to talk. It all started when I was twelve years old, Doc. I was sent to live with Maggie after being kicked out of my one hundredth foster home."

"You were kicked out of one hundred foster homes?"

"Give or take a few."

Walker shook his head. "Right. A few. So you moved in next door to the soon-to-be sheriff."

"And his parents made him walk me to school my first day. Valentine's Day, which is kind of a big deal in this town." Shelby remembered that day like it was yesterday. Ben had shown up at Maggie's dressed in his khaki shorts and a red polo shirt ready to show her the ropes. When she'd told him she had been to a million schools and was pretty sure she could figure out that room 107 was next to room 108, he had quickly corrected her that they were actually across the hall from one another because odd-numbered rooms were on one side and even-numbered rooms were on the other.

"I thought he was annoying, and since I never stuck around anywhere long enough to make friends, I didn't work too hard to get to know him. That didn't faze Ben, though."

By lunchtime that first day, a rumor that Shelby had been in jail for murder was spreading like wildfire across the middle school. Ben had decided he wasn't afraid of her, though, and sat with her at lunch.

"I may have told some girl in PE class that my appendectomy scar was from getting shanked in the bathroom when I was in juvie. It was the easiest way to get people to leave me alone. It worked on everyone except Ben."

Walker was entertained by the story. "Of course Sheriff Ben isn't scared of criminals. I don't know why you thought that would work."

"He actually called me out on my tough girl act, so I dared him to play hooky the rest of the day."

"No way did the good sheriff play hooky."

"Oh, he did."

The two of them had snuck out of school and gone to the lake. Ben had showed her this small, secluded inlet that had a rickety old dock he liked to fish off of with his friends. Large trees had lined the shore, their branches stretched out over the water. They had offered

Shelby a much more death-defying way of jumping in than the dock had, so she stripped down to nothing but her underwear and T-shirt.

"We went to the lake and all I wanted to do was jump in. It was the middle of February and I thought because it was warm out that day, the lake would be warm, too. Ben tried to explain that no one went swimming in the lake until spring, but I thought I was so cool, so I climbed one of the trees along the shore and jumped off into water that was a little too shallow and absolutely freezing. I cracked my head open on a rock. Luckily, Ben waded in fully dressed and saved me. He got help and I got a couple stitches."

"Sheriff never ditched another day of school in his life, did he?"

Shelby couldn't help but laugh. "He did not. Ben pretty much played by the rules after that."

Walker nodded. "At least your friends learn from your mistakes."

Ben had become her friend that day. It had been a game changer for Shelby. Up until then, she had never believed anyone truly cared about her well-being. Ben had been the first person to ever treat her like her life meant something, like she was worth saving.

Her throat tightened as the memory of their first day together was replaced with their last. Their relationship started off with him saving her life and ended with her almost taking his.

Why in the world would he want her to spend one more second in his life? Shelby had proven she wasn't worth the effort.

CHAPTER FIVE

"You did what?" Nick followed Ben into his bedroom.

"I asked her to join us at Buck's tonight. I thought maybe Topher would want to see her again," Ben explained, but Nick tipped his chin down and gave him that look—the one that said he didn't think his brother was thinking straight. "Don't look at me like that. I know what you're thinking, but I am not getting myself into any trouble. Knowing Shelby, she won't show up anyway. Being social has always been too exhausting for her."

"And if she does?"

"She won't." Ben had to keep telling himself that so it wouldn't sting when she didn't. He wasn't even sure what possessed him to ask her. He had been so thrown and slightly amused by the fact that she stalked him that he hadn't been thinking straight.

Nick sat on the bed. "We need to talk about this."

Ben groaned. "I really need to go back to bed. I told you that you could do your head shrinking when I get up."

"You're up."

"Not if you get off my bed."

"Listen, I've missed Shelby. I would love to hang out and catch up, but I know what her leaving did to you. Don't act like I have no reason to worry about you now that she's back."

"She's not back. She probably never would have shown her face in town if I hadn't pulled her over last night."

"I might have believed that if last night was the only contact you had with her." Nick shook his head. "But now? She didn't come to the house by accident, Ben. Why was she here? What did she want?"

Ben couldn't help but feel a little amused that Shelby was worried he was engaged to Tiffani. At the same time, he didn't dare think it meant she cared more than she led on earlier today.

"Tiffani got to Maggie's before Shelby left. She heard Tiffani say something about Mom and Dad being her future in-laws."

"And that made her come looking for you why?"

Ben decided it best not to share Shelby's opinions on Tiffani with Nick or the fact that maybe he'd once had those same thoughts himself. Nick saw something in Tiffani that Ben couldn't and Shelby never would. How Ben and Shelby felt about Tiffani really didn't matter anyway.

"So she sort of assumed that Tiffani was marrying *me*."

Nick's eyes went wide. "She thought you were marrying Tiffani so she hunted you down and what? Wanted to congratulate you?"

"Not exactly…"

"Oh come on. What did she say?"

"She just wanted to know if I was the one getting married. Once she found out I wasn't, that was pretty much the end of the conversation."

Nick nodded. "Interesting."

His brother surely had some thoughts about Shelby's motives. Nick was constantly analyzing people, situations, life. "What's so interesting about it?"

Nick shrugged.

"You're going to insinuate that I'm being evasive and then be just as evasive?"

"Fair." Nick stood, took off his glasses and

cleaned the lenses with his T-shirt. "From what I remember about Shelby, she was never very trusting. She probably needed to hear it from you because she knows you'll tell her the truth and nothing but the truth." He put his glasses back on. "But it makes me wonder what she would have done if you were the one marrying Tiffani."

It was Ben's turn to shrug. "She probably wouldn't have done anything."

"Maybe she still cares about you."

"Pfft! No, she doesn't!" he argued. Ben rubbed his aching shoulder. It hurt more when he was anxious.

"Why else would she need to know if you were marrying Tiffani?"

Ben didn't have the heart to explain it was the who, not the engagement, she had been worried about. Shelby's arrival on their front porch had more to do with Tiffani than it did Ben. That was the sad reality.

"Don't confuse curiosity for caring, brother. Shelby is in Georgia to make a movie and then she will go back to California and no one but Maggie will hear from her again."

"So you're trying to be rational about this? Come on, man. I know how long you wished she would come back. I don't want this surprise visit to give you false hope, but you can't tell me you're not having some kind of emotional response to this."

"You want emotional?" Ben asked, getting back in bed. "How about hopeless? I have no false hopes. I'm hopeless when it comes to Shelby."

"I'm sorry, brother. It has to be hard seeing her and talking to her after all these years. It's got to bring up a lot of mixed emotions." Nick sounded like the counselor he was. "I want you to know I am here for you whenever you need me."

Ben pulled the covers up and rolled to his side. "Right now, all I need from you is to leave so I can go back to bed."

"What if she docs come to Buck's? Because she's still curious, let's say?"

Ben returned to his back and stared hard at the ceiling. "We'll have a few drinks, reminisce with Topher and wish each other well. I'm not going to fall apart like I did when she left. I'll be fine. I promise."

"I'm not judging you or how this could affect you. I only want you to be thinking about it so you can be prepared for how it might feel. Emotions can come on strong and when we least expect them."

Ben shifted his gaze to his brother. Nick had Ben's best interests at heart. He had seen firsthand what losing Shelby had done to his big brother's life. No one who cared about Ben wanted to see him go through that again.

"I'm prepared. I can handle this. I'm not that eighteen-year-old kid who was broken inside and out. I'm a strong and much wiser man now."

Nick nodded as he moved toward the door. "I know you are."

"How would you feel if she came to Buck's tonight?" Ben asked, wondering what kind of reception she might get if she did show.

"Like I said, I missed Shelby. I'd like to find out what she's been up to. The little Maggie's been able to share over the years makes it seem like she's doing well. I'd like to hear about her job. I hope she's happy."

"Me, too," Ben said. He had those same thoughts. He wanted to know for sure that Shelby was okay. There was also a selfish part of him that hoped maybe she hadn't always been okay. That she had regrets about leaving him behind.

"I guess we'll see what happens," Nick said before he left the room.

Ben rolled over like he was going to sleep.

Of course, it didn't matter how tired he was, there was no way he could fall asleep, because all he could think about was what might happen. Would Shelby be curious enough to come to Buck's? Would she blow him off because it was all too much? Or worse, because she didn't care? There was no predicting what she would do because Shelby had always been unpredictable.

Ben closed his eyes and was transported back to the first time he'd ever laid eyes on Shelby Young. It had been Valentine's Day, her first full day in Goodfield.

Ben's mom and Maggie had arranged it so Ben would walk her to school and show her around Goodfield Middle School. He had arrived on Maggie's doorstep bright and early.

Ben had never really been interested in girls before that day, but his jaw dropped when a beautiful brown-haired girl emerged from her bedroom, complaining that she had a stomachache and couldn't go to school. She had been a little on the skinny side but seemed strong. Her dark hair had almost hidden her face when she had bent over in fake pain. When Maggie made it clear she was going to school regardless of a stomachache, Shelby righted herself and pushed her hair behind her ears. That had been the moment when Ben fell in love with those eyes of hers.

Maggie would have made Shelby go to school kicking and screaming, but thankfully Shelby had given up the act pretty quick. Ben believed that one of Shelby's superpowers was knowing who she could manipulate and who she couldn't.

Ben had stood in Maggie's front hall like a dolt as Shelby took off, slamming the front door behind her. Maggie had warned him that day to be careful: Shelby's bite was even worse than her bark. He hadn't understood what she meant by that since he had always heard people say it the other way around. Maggie had been right, though. It was easy to think that Shelby was all tough talk, no action. Ben had spent the next six years believing she was harmless, but when Shelby wanted to break a heart, she smashed it to smithereens and then took off without looking back.

"BENJAMIN HARPER, LOOK at you. I can't believe it's been, what? Two years?" Topher held his arms out and waited for his friend to come in for the hug.

Ben moved in for the man hug and gave

Topher a few pats on the back. "Two years sounds about right. I think the last time you were home it was for your nephew's christening."

"Man, I really need to come home for something other than my sister's babies' religious ceremonies. Nick! How are you, my little brother from a different mother?" Topher wrapped his arms around Nick and lifted him off the ground like he used to when Nick was much smaller.

"Put me down, geez."

Topher's laughter was deep and contagious. He had the kind of carefree attitude that Ben envied. Topher didn't sweat the small stuff. To be honest, he didn't sweat the big stuff either.

"I had no idea how much I've missed the Harper brothers until right this moment."

"We miss you, too, big guy," Ben said, signaling the bartender over. "First round is on me."

"Another reason to love you."

Buck's had a huge bar in the front with a jukebox and a small dance floor. Neon beer signs hung on the walls. The floors were always sticky and it smelled like cigarette smoke even though there was no smoking allowed inside the bar. Like every other establishment in Goodfield, Buck's bar was decked out in hearts and cutout cupids for Valentine's Day. The schedule of town Valentine events was posted on the wall by the entrance. In the back, there were a half dozen billiards tables and another smaller bar. It was a popular hangout for Goodfield locals.

The three friends caught up and took turns buying drinks. Topher regaled them with a colorful account of his latest travels. He was a commercial airline pilot and often flew overseas. He had been all over Europe more times than Ben had been to Atlanta.

"Have you guys ever had steak tartare? It seriously looks like uncooked hamburger on a plate. Then they put an egg on top. A *raw* egg! On raw meat. I can't even explain how—" Topher set his drink down and rubbed his eyes. "What did you put in my drink because it is messing with my mind. I swear the woman that just walked in looks exactly like Shelby Young."

Ben's heart stopped. He leaned to the right so he could see around Nick. Standing by the door, biting her bottom lip as she scanned the room was Shelby. She had on black jeans and an emerald green shirt that immediately reminded him of her eyes. To her left stood Walker, who spotted Ben before she did.

Ben waved them over. "Your drink isn't as strong as you think. That woman is actually…Shelby! You guys made it." Ben shook hands with Walker. "Good to see you again, Mr. Reed."

"I wasn't going to pass up a night on the town with the sheriff. I figured we can't get into too much trouble when we're hanging with the big man."

"Is this for real? Are you for real?" Topher's eyes locked on Shelby.

"How's it going, Topher?"

"How's it going? Are you kidding me? Get over here! I can't believe it's really you." Shelby let Topher give her a hug even though Ben suspected her anxiety was sky-high.

"I heard you were coming to town and I couldn't stay away any longer."

"Did you know about this?" Topher asked Ben.

"I may have had the pleasure of arresting these two for drag racing on County Road D in the middle of the night in a Maserati and an Aston Martin."

Topher's eyes nearly popped out of his head. "You own a Maserati?"

"How did you know she was driving the Maserati?" Walker asked.

Topher rolled his eyes. "A Maserati GranTurismo has only been Shelby's dream car since it first came out in 2007."

Shelby flashed him a killer grin. "Good memory. I don't own a Maserati, though. I'm a stunt driver for the new *Ready, Set, Go* movie. We're filming just outside of Atlanta and Walker and I thought we should take the cars out for a test run."

"That is so cool! Leave it to you to find the perfect job. I always thought you'd end up driving for NASCAR or something, but stunt driving is even better."

Ben had thought the same thing. Shelby had managed to find a way to make a living doing what she loved. He was happy for her, but admittedly surprised that she wasn't a bit more cautious behind the wheel after what happened to them. Of course, maybe the accident didn't have the same impact on her that it did him. Being in a car used to cause Ben quite a bit of anxiety.

Shelby introduced Walker to Topher and Nick, and Topher was quick to buy them both a drink.

"You two have some catching up to do.

We've been here for an hour. In fact, I thought it was time to call it quits when I saw you walk in. I was sure I was hallucinating."

"I'm real," Shelby said, glancing at Ben for a quick second.

Ben took a swig from his bottle. She was real. After ten years, she was standing just a foot away. He could smell her rose-scented lotion. He could hear her satisfied sigh after taking a drink. He could feel how warm her skin was when she brushed against his arm as she moved out of Nick's way so he could go to the men's room. It was unbelievable and a little overwhelming.

"Do you guys remember that time we camped up near Jacks River Falls?" Topher asked. "We hiked like ten miles and it was so hot. I thought I was going to melt."

Ben remembered that trip. It had been the three of them and their friend Noah. It had been the summer before senior year. They spent a weekend up near Blue Ridge and hiked both Jacks Falls and Beech Bottom Trail. Summers in Georgia were warm in general, but that summer, the heat was off the charts.

"I remember how you were looking for a tree branch to use as a walking stick and came across the smallest snake in the world but screamed like it was some kind of king cobra about to poison you," Shelby said, laughing at the memory.

Topher pushed her shoulder. "Smallest snake in the world? That thing was huge. And I swear it was venomous and was definitely thinking about biting me."

"Oh, you were a snake mind reader, huh?" Shelby teased.

Ben was envious of how easily the two of them could reminisce. He didn't remember there being a snake. He remembered that he and Shelby shared a tent and, unbeknownst to Noah and Topher, made out all night long. Even their closest friends were unaware of the romantic nature of their relationship. At least that was what Ben thought.

"I remember that was the weekend you two started carrying on your secret love affair," Topher said, causing Ben to choke on his drink.

"What?"

"Oh please. Did you really think that Noah and I were idiots? We could hear you guys slobbering all over each other when you were in the tent. I mean I had my suspicions before then, but you guys were pretty obvious on the trip."

"Well, if you think we started our so-called love affair that night, you are an idiot because we had already been together over a year by then," Shelby replied to Ben's surprise.

"Hold on a second." Topher sat down on the barstool next to him. "You're telling me that you two were together all junior year?" He pointed his beer bottle at Shelby and then Ben as he spoke.

Shelby glanced at Ben and cleared her throat. "Valentine's Day sophomore year."

Topher held his head in his hands, his mind blown. "Sophomore year? How did I not know this?"

Nick returned and announced there was an open billiards table. Walker ordered another round of drinks for everyone and they headed to the back room to play some pool.

"Did you know that your brother and Shelby were dating behind everyone's back most of high school?" Topher asked Nick.

Nick nodded. "I was probably the only one besides Maggie."

"Maggie didn't know," Shelby said.

Nick smirked. "There isn't much Maggie doesn't know, Shelby. She may not have known how you snuck into Ben's room late at night, but she knew you and Ben were more than just friends."

"You snuck into his room at night?" Topher grabbed Ben's arm. "How did you keep this information to yourself? The day after I got to first base with Trina Blake, I told you. You knew every crush I had, everyone I was going to ask out before they got asked out."

Shelby jumped to Ben's defense. "Don't be so hard on him, Toph. He kept it quiet because I asked him to. You know what would have happened if he broke a promise to me."

She would have never talked to him again. There had been no way Ben would ever risk that. As much as he wanted to shout it from the mountaintop, he kept his mouth shut because being with Shelby in secret was better than not being with Shelby at all.

"You were much scarier than me. Those are facts," Topher acknowledged.

"Who's sitting out the first round?" Walker asked, grabbing a pool cue. "Sheriff, want to be on my team?"

Ben was surprised by the invitation. "Sure."

"Then it's me and Shelby," Nick said. "We'll let Topher sit this one out while he comes to grips with his two best friends kissing each other back in high school."

Ben would do anything to get everyone to stop talking about how he used to kiss Shelby. Of all the things they could spend time catching up on, that was not the topic he wanted to revisit.

Walker racked up the balls and offered to let Shelby break. The two of them bantered back and forth, putting a genuine smile on her face.

It was clear they were good friends. Their ease around one another reminded Ben of what it used to be like between him and Shelby back in the day. Did she make out with Walker behind closed doors? Did she swear him to secrecy? Ben didn't really want to know the answer to those questions. He had to shove the feelings of jealousy aside before they overwhelmed him. She wasn't his girlfriend anymore. She wasn't anything to him anymore. She could make out with whomever she wanted.

Shelby knocked in two solids. Nick high-fived her and she smirked at Walker. Ben felt like the outsider of the group.

"I like stripes better anyway," Walker quipped.

"Good to know," Shelby said, lining up her next shot. "I'll be sure to leave them all here for you when I'm done." She knocked another ball into the corner pocket.

A group of six guys took over the table next to them. They were loud and obnoxious. Shelby was visibly annoyed by their presence. Two of the men started singing along with the song playing throughout the bar right before she took her next shot. She missed and scowled at her distracters.

"Well, that was quick," Walker said. "You want to go first, Sheriff, or shall I?"

"It's all yours."

A waitress came over to make sure they all had something to drink. The biggest guy in the group next to them sat on a barstool with another bearded guy in a black leather jacket. When he noticed the waitress, he shouted, "What's a guy got to do to get some service around here? Don't you like tips, sweet cheeks?"

"Don't call her that," Shelby snapped.

The guy stood and hitched up his pants. "Excuse me?"

Shelby wasn't at all intimidated. "I said, don't call her that."

He seemed amused. "Aren't you feisty?"

"Oh, you don't want to see me feisty."

Ben didn't like where this was headed. He walked around the table and stood next to Shelby. "Nobody needs to get feisty. I'm sure everyone can behave themselves, right?"

The big guy held his hands up. "I was simply trying to get a drink. Your little lady friend is the one who needs to mind her business."

Shelby didn't back down. "Don't be a jerk and I'll happily mind my business."

"What did you call me?"

"You gonna let her talk to you like that, Freddy?" the guy's bearded friend asked.

Walker, Nick and Topher were now flanking Shelby on her other side while Freddy's buddies backed him. Ben needed to put the deescalation skills he learned in his police training to use.

"Hey, everybody needs to calm down. We're all here to have some drinks, play some pool and hang out with our friends. Let's not start something that's going to end with me arresting everyone for disrupting the peace."

"You're a cop?" the bearded guy asked.

"He's the *sheriff*," Walker retorted.

"The sheriff?" Freddy crossed his arms over his chest. "Are we supposed to be scared because you're the sheriff? Does being the sheriff mean your friends get to harass people and call them names?"

"It means I'm asking you guys to go back to enjoying your night and let us do the same."

Freddy and Shelby were staring each other down. Neither of them wanted to be the first to give in. Ben tried to get Shelby's attention. "How about you and I take a walk?"

She looked away from Freddy and turned her glare on Ben. "You're okay with him talking to the waitress like that?"

"Walk with me and we can talk about it."

Her look of disgust was almost too much. She bumped shoulders with him as she walked away. Ben followed her to the front of the bar.

"Shelby, wait."

She stopped and turned on him. "That guy is a jerk and I'm not scared of him. I didn't need you to step in."

"Oh trust me, I could tell you weren't scared. I'm sure you'd have no problem putting him in his place, but at what cost? Are you ready to start a brawl over a guy being rude to a waitress?"

"If that's what it takes to teach him a lesson."

She hadn't changed one bit. Her temper

was short and her foresight was nonexistent. "Getting yourself in trouble isn't going to teach him anything, but it is going to ruin our night and make things harder for that wait-ress, who will be the one who has to clean up your mess."

The fire in her eyes flared for a second and then died down. "Fine. You're right."

The tension in his shoulders relaxed a smidge. "Thank you."

"I had a foster dad who talked to women like that." Shelby's gaze dropped to the floor. "It brings back bad memories."

Ben forgot how often her response to a cur-rent situation was based on her past. Shelby had been in horrible foster home after hor-rible foster home until she ended up with Maggie. She had seen more ugliness than he had, even as an adult working for the sheriff's department.

"I'm sorry. I know there are things from your past that trigger you. I only want you to be safe, and picking a fight with that guy wouldn't end well for any of us because you know your friends back there were ready to throw down with you. And for the record, my brother can't punch to save his life. He'd probably end up with a broken face, and then you'd have to answer to Tiffani."

"Point made. I do not want to deal with Tiffani." Her lips twitched like she was fighting a smile.

"Good. Now, let's go finish our game of pool because I'm pretty sure Walker and I were about to win."

She rolled her eyes. "Dream on, Harper."

Things appeared to have cooled down when Ben and Shelby returned to finish their game. Everyone had retreated to their respective pool tables. Walker pulled Shelby aside and seemed to be checking to make sure she was okay. Ben tried to focus on something else, anything but the way their friendship reminded him of the one he used to have with Shelby.

"All good?" Nick asked.

"Let's hope so." Ben glanced over at Freddy, who gave him a wink. "But the faster we finish this round of pool, the better."

"Don't worry, brother. Shelby and I will beat you in no time."

"You're hilarious."

Walker was saying something in Shelby's ear and she nodded. She put her hand on his shoulder and he put his hand over hers.

"Are we ready to play?" Ben asked, hoping to bring an end to their intimate moment.

"I'm ready, Sheriff. Let's get this game over with." Walker lined up his shot.

Shelby took her cue stick from Topher and looked in Freddy's direction. He was busy talking and laughing with his bearded buddy. She turned her attention to the pool table where Walker knocked two striped balls in at once.

"Lucky," Shelby scoffed.

"I learned that little trick from you." Walker took another shot and the ball rolled right to the edge of the side pocket. "No! Ugh!"

"You didn't learn *that* from me," Shelby said with a grin. "You're up, Nicky."

The waitress brought a tray of drinks to Freddy and his pals. Shelby paid close attention. The waitress placed Freddy's drink on the small high-top table between him and the bearded guy. When she reached out to remove the empty peanut bowl, she knocked over the bearded guy's beer bottle and what was left in it spilled.

"You owe me a drink. I wasn't finished with that!" he yelled.

She apologized and grabbed some napkins

to clean it up. "I won't charge you for the new one," she said.

"You're darn right you won't charge him. Man, you're lucky you're cute because your looks are all you have going for ya," Freddy said, giving her a shove.

That was all it took for Shelby to break. Ben didn't have time to react. There was no way to stop her. Freddy didn't even know what hit him. He was knocked out with one punch. The six-foot-plus guy fell right off his stool and onto the floor.

That was when everything got completely out of control.

CHAPTER SIX

THE HANDCUFFS AROUND Shelby's wrists were tighter than she would have liked. She tried not to move so the metal wouldn't press so hard against the skin. With her hands cuffed behind her back, she rested her cheek on her knee. Ben and his deputy had sat her and Walker on the curb of the sidewalk just outside of Buck's.

"Who would have thought we'd manage getting arrested twice in two days?" Walker mused. The right side of his face was red and his eye was swollen. He was going to have a black eye tomorrow.

"Never a dull moment when you hang out with me, right?"

Walker's laugh relieved some of her worry. "Ain't that the truth."

Two police cars were parked in front of the entrance of the bar, their lights still flashing. A red and blue glow was cast on everything around them, including Ben, who was talking to a couple officers and the owner of the bar. She couldn't hear what he was saying, but he didn't look happy.

One of the paramedics on the scene tried to interrupt, pointing to the cut on Ben's head. Someone had hit him with a beer bottle when he jumped in and tried to break up the melee. He waved the guy off. Topher had left to follow Nick, who had been transported to the hospital. His face wasn't broken, but his hand might not have been as lucky. Ben had been wrong about his little brother's ability to fight. Nick could punch with the best of them. Shelby prayed that his injury wasn't as bad as the paramedics thought. The last thing she needed was an angry Tiffani to come after her for putting her fiancé in a cast right before their wedding.

"I'm not sure the good sheriff is going to be able to get us out of this one," Walker said, stretching his legs out in front of him.

"I couldn't just stand there and watch him put his hands on that woman. I don't care what my punishment is. I would do it again."

"I don't blame you. The guy had it coming. I do wish you had knocked him out when he didn't have a huge posse of friends hanging around. That would have made it much easier on all of us."

"Yeah, Ben sort of mentioned that as one of the reasons not to fight when he took me to cool off."

Walker wouldn't blame her for what happened, but Ben would. He had warned her, and she didn't listen. If he hadn't regretted asking her to join them earlier, he sure did now.

The waitress at the center of this entire debacle was escorted over to Ben, the other cops and the bar owner. They asked her a couple questions and she answered, gesturing toward Shelby. Ben said something and the owner of the bar nodded. Ben shook the bar owner's hand. He seemed relieved. That had to be good.

Ben and one of the cops made their way over to Shelby and Walker. "Uncuff them," Ben said to the officer.

Shelby rubbed her wrist as soon as she was free of those things. "What's going to happen?"

"The waitress corroborated our story that Freddy had been harassing her and assaulted her. They're going to take him down to the station and charge him with disorderly conduct."

"We're not under arrest?" Walker asked to be sure.

"Everyone else is just asked to disperse."

"Even the guy who hit you with a bottle?" Shelby asked.

Ben touched his forehead and grimaced. "If I charge him, I have to charge Walker for breaking that cue stick on that other guy's back."

"Thanks for not doing that, I appreciate not having to go to jail two nights in a row."

Ben nodded. "You guys should get out of here before the officer in charge changes his mind."

"You don't have to tell me twice," Walker said, digging his phone out of his pocket. "I'll get us a ride."

Walker wandered off to order a car. Shelby wasn't sorry she'd knocked Freddy out, but she was sorry she'd caused all this trouble for Ben. His jaw was tight and his eyes were tired.

"Thanks for whatever you said to get us cut loose."

"Yeah, well, no one likes doing more paperwork than they have to."

She knew he had to be angry with her. The fact that he was so calm was almost worse than if he was lecturing her.

"I hope Nick is okay."

With his hands on his hips, Ben averted his eyes and kicked at something on the ground. "I'm sure he'll be fine. Topher texted me that he's getting his hand x-rayed right now."

"I'm sorry I ruined your night with Topher. I bet you wish I hadn't taken you up on your offer to join you two tonight."

Ben's eyes met hers. "When you invite trouble, that's usually what you get. It's my own fault."

Shelby swallowed hard and nodded. "I'm sorry anyway. I should probably get out of here."

"That's a good idea. Good night, Shelby."

"Goodbye, Ben."

The use of his first name seemed to take him aback. All through middle school and high school, she had called him Harper in front of other people. It had been how she separated their public friendship from their private, more intimate relationship. It was only when they had been alone and she had felt safe enough to express how she really felt about him that she would call him Ben. It was the only name she whispered when she had lain in his arms after climbing through his bedroom window late at night or when she'd wanted him to kiss her in the back seat of his car.

"This isn't the last time I'm going to see you, is it?" he asked as she started to back away.

"You don't need trouble in your life, do you?" He hesitated, so before he could answer she said, "Don't say anything. We'll see what happens."

Walker reappeared. "I got a car picking us up in two minutes. Good night, Sheriff. Thanks again."

"I'd tell you to stay out of trouble, but I don't think I'd believe you if you told me you would."

"That's fair," Walker replied with a chuckle. "I do promise to try at least."

"Good enough."

Ben rejoined the other officers as they finished taking statements. Shelby couldn't stop herself from staring at him until her ride showed up. How many times would she let herself hurt him when all he ever did was try to keep her out of harm's way?

"Do me a favor," she said when they got

in the back seat of the ride. "Talk me out of anything that has to do with spending time with him. I can't do it anymore."

"Shelby—"

"I'm serious, Walker. All I ever do is make the man miserable. Keep me away from him."

"I'll try, but based on what I heard tonight, you two have a long history of not being able to stay away from each other. I don't see how that's changed one bit."

THE NEXT MORNING, Shelby called Maggie and against her better judgment asked for Ben's phone number. She hadn't forgotten that she was supposed to stay away from him, but she did want to check on Nick and make sure she wasn't going to get a surprise visit from Tiffani.

"Thanks, Maggie." Shelby swallowed her anxiety down. She owed Maggie so much. Her former foster mother deserved more than one accidental visit. "I was also wondering if you would want to come to the set one of these days and see what it's like to make a movie? Maybe you could even watch me do my stunts."

"I would absolutely love that, sweetheart! You know, I used to do a little acting myself back in the day. I played Eliza in the community center's production of *My Fair Lady* when I was in my twenties."

"I bet your accent was dead-on."

"Oh, ya beah it was," she replied in a cockney accent.

Shelby laughed. How she had missed Maggie's sense of humor. "I'll set up your visit. We'll get you a ride out here and a special behind-the-scenes VIP pass."

"You don't have to get me a ride. I'm sure I can talk Benjamin into bringing me out there. Now that you two have reconnected, I'm sure he'd love to see what you do for a living."

Shelby couldn't think of a way to explain why that would be a bad idea without causing Maggie to have a million questions. "Ben's a busy guy, Mags. I don't want to bother him."

"Why don't you ask him when you call him? If he says no, you can find me another ride."

That was an easy way out. She would tell Maggie he said he couldn't make it. She wouldn't even have to bring it up with him. "Will do. I'll talk to you soon."

Shelby ended the call and sprawled out on the hotel bed. She had gotten a room with one king-size bed instead of the usual two queens. It was kind of fun to have a bed she could lie on in any direction and no part of her body hung off it. She had made herself a pot of coffee, but it didn't taste very good. She had to decide if she was going to go buy some real coffee downstairs before or after she texted Ben to see how Nick was.

The knock on her door answered that question. She pulled it open to find Hector on the other side.

"Good morning, Boss."

"Don't good morning me, Shelby. It has been nothing short of a nightmare trying to get my cars out of impound. We need to have a serious talk." He pushed past her and into her room. "When I hired you on, I thought I knew what I was getting. I never imagined you'd end up costing me an arm and a leg."

"Hector, you have every right to be—"

He cut her off. "You know I have to fire someone over this. I've narrowed it down to either you or Brent for giving you access to my cars in the first place. Walker is an idiot for listening to you, but I know it was your idea."

Shelby didn't want to be the reason someone else lost their job. She had used the fact that Brent had a massive crush on her to get those keys. "I get it. I would understand if you had to let me go. It was a stupid thing to do and I was arrogant for thinking I could get away with it."

"You're darn right you were! Those cars are worth more money than you're going to make on this job. I also could have had the cops charge you with grand theft auto. You could have been looking at doing time, and good luck getting another job driving cars with that on your record."

"Well, actually, we weren't intending on keeping them, so it would have only been a joyriding charge…" Shelby quickly noticed the bulging vein in Hector's neck. "But I know you could have had them throw the book at me and I appreciate that you didn't. I take full responsibility for what happened."

"It should be you that I fire. And if you weren't the best female stunt driver I know, it would be you. I don't know what you did to charm the pants off that guy, but it was his responsibility to secure those cars and he didn't do his job. Saying no to a pretty lady shouldn't have been that hard."

Shelby's shoulders fell. There was no way to save Brent's job. "I'm sorry. I'm really sorry."

"I hope you are, because you are the best at what you do, Shelby. This movie is going to give you the exposure you need in this business. You won't get another shot like this."

"I know. I appreciate you taking me on and keeping me on."

"Be smarter," he said before leaving the room. "And don't even think about getting behind the wheel of any of my cars again unless I am standing right there." He slammed the door on his way out, causing Shelby to jump.

Making not-so-smart decisions was becoming a bad habit lately. She needed to break it and fast. She went to her suitcase and pulled out the photograph that she had carried around with her for the last ten years. It was the picture Mrs. Harper had given her for her eighteenth birthday. The edges were a little worn and there was a crease in the center from when she had folded it so it would fit in her back pocket when she'd auditioned for her first stunt driving job to remind her to be safe.

As painful as it was to think about Ben over the years, looking at this picture reminded her that what they had had been real. It also helped her to remember her actions had consequences.

She decided to text Ben and make sure Nick wasn't paying too dearly for her stupidity like poor Brent.

She waited, chewing on her thumbnail, for Ben to reply. Maybe he wouldn't answer her. He had every right to ignore her, but the way he'd sounded disappointed when he assumed her goodbye last night was permanent made her hopeful he wouldn't.

Broke his hand in two places. 4th and 5th metacarpal.

Shelby winced.

Cast?

Just a splint. But will take 6 to 8 weeks to heal. Tiffani is NOT happy.

Of course she wasn't. Tiffani liked things to look a certain way. A bar fight injury would taint her perfect wedding photos. Shelby struggled to hold back a grin. If she had to ruin someone's wedding photos, it wouldn't bother her much if it was Tiffani Lyons's. It was petty, but she couldn't help it.

Please tell Nicky that I'm really sorry.

Not that her apology would change anything. What was done was done.

I will.

This was where Maggie would have wanted her to ask him if he'd bring her to the set, but Shelby couldn't ask him that. It was better for the two of them to just be done. He didn't need to see her again or take time out of his life to help her out. He deserved to go on with his life and forget she was ever a part of it.

Her phone rang in her hand. Ben was calling her. She froze even though her heart began to race. By the fourth ring, she knew she had to do something or it would go to voice mail. She answered it.

"Hello?"

"Sorry, I sometimes feel like texting is a little too impersonal. I'm always afraid of writing too much, so then I write too little. I didn't want you to think I was being short with you."

"I didn't think that." She was glad he was willing to say anything to her.

"Now I made it weird by calling, didn't I?"

Shelby smiled. "No," she lied. "It's not weird."

"My brother, who spends his days telling troubled kids not to lose their cool and get into fights, has spent the day bragging to anyone who will listen about how he got in a bar fight and broke his hand on a guy's head. I think I may need to take him back to the hospital and get an MRI. He must have a head injury, too."

"Sounds like Nicky has always dreamed about living on the wild side," Shelby said with a laugh. Thank goodness Nick wasn't angry about what happened. "I can only imagine how that's going over with Tiffani."

"Not well. They got into a little argument about it. She told him that she thought she was marrying a man who uses his brains not his brawn to handle conflicts. Nick promised to avoid fighting in public but told her he's thinking about taking up boxing as a hobby. You should have seen the look on her face. I was sure she was going to blow a gasket."

"I wish I could have seen that."

"Better you didn't. She totally blames you for being a bad influence. I would try not to cross paths with her if I were you."

"I hear you, but if Freddy the Waitress

Bully doesn't scare me, why would I be scared of Mean Girl Tiffani?"

"I knew you'd say that."

"I actually can't believe Tiffani got her hooks in Nicky. He's so smart. How did that happen?"

"Be nice," he said in that familiar tone of his. "She sold me my house. Since Nick was going to room with me, he used to come along to look at places. The two of them hit it off pretty much right away."

Shelby couldn't believe it. What could those two possibly have in common? Nicky was a nice kid. She remembered him as super-intelligent and quirky. Tiffani cared about one thing and one thing only—her image. "Of course now that he's not a nerdy-looking brainiac, she's willing to give him the time of day."

"Maybe that's true. He is still a brainiac, but he definitely blossomed in college. Puberty finally had its way with him."

"It sure did. He had a major glow up. I'd dare to say he's almost cuter than you now," she teased. Ben would always be the handsomer Harper, but it was fun to give him a hard time.

"Ouch! I take a lot of pride in being the

better-looking older brother. Don't take that away from me."

"Okay, okay. I said *almost*. You win best-looking brother and he wins smartest. You both have something to brag about."

"You know I've always been jealous of how smart he is," Ben said. "I always felt like he was special and I was always falling just short of what my dad wanted me to be."

Shelby didn't remember it that way at all. Ben was the golden child in her eyes. Plenty smart, handsome, star athlete. He was a leader, not a follower. He'd been popular even though he chose to spend his time with the troubled foster kid next door.

"First of all, in school, you were *the* Ben Harper. Basketball superstar. Class vice president. Today, you're Sheriff Benjamin Harper. That's a pretty big deal. You don't need to be jealous of anyone, and your dad should be proud."

"Yeah, well." He paused. "Sometimes, I don't really feel like I'm good enough."

Shelby couldn't imagine why he would feel like that. Ben was the epitome of good. He was more than enough in her eyes.

"Not good enough for what? To be sheriff?

The people of this county clearly disagree," she argued.

"The people of this county elected some-one they thought was some big hero. My dad convinced me to run on that platform and it never felt right."

Shelby had noticed the billboard with his picture on it and the Hometown Hero tag-line. She didn't know the story behind it, but it made sense. Ben was the best person she knew, so of course he was heroic.

"What am I missing? When have you ever acted in a way that would make people think you're unheroic?"

"I didn't mean to bring all this up. Forget I said anything. We were joking around and I turned things serious."

"Too late," Shelby said, unable to move on from this glimpse into his life. "I'm invested now. I need to know what happened."

Ben sighed but relented. "There was a ter-rible accident last summer. A man and his two little girls were in a car that ended up in the lake. I wasn't even on duty that day. I was fishing nearby when the accident happened. I jumped out of my boat and was able to pull the two girls out alive."

That was not surprising. It was what Ben

did—he saved those who needed saving. "Sounds like hero material to me."

"Yeah, that's what most people say."

"But?" She could sense there was something that didn't sit right with him.

"But they forget that there was a man in the water, too."

"You saved two out of three people from drowning and you're stuck on the fact that one didn't make it? If it wasn't for you, none of them would have made it."

"It wasn't as simple as that. After I got the girls out, I swam back to him. He was flailing, barely keeping his head above water. I had this adrenaline rush when I first jumped in, but by the time I got to him, I was tired."

"No doubt. You were one guy under some pretty extreme conditions."

"All I remember is the chaos. I tried getting my arms around his chest, but he was in such a panic. He started to pull us both under. I tried to calm him down so I could help him, but he was struggling so much that I had to let him go. I had to push him away, Shelby, and he drowned. That's not what a hero does, is it?"

Shelby pressed her hand to her chest. The thought of Ben dying while trying to save

these strangers made her heart hurt. The fact
that he thought he wasn't a hero because he
saved his own life made her want to shake
him.

"Ben, he would have killed you if you
didn't let him go. You tried to help him and
he couldn't cooperate. I get that it's sad, but
you are still very much a hero."

"I should have grabbed some life jackets
out of my boat before I jumped in. It's such
a simple, obvious thing. When I think about
all the mistakes I made, it makes me so frustrated."

"I get it. Hindsight is twenty-twenty, as
they say. No one is perfect. You were in a
crisis situation and you reacted. Your objec-
tive was always to help. In the end, you had to
save yourself. There is nothing wrong with a
little self-preservation. How would the world
have been a better place if both of you had
lost your lives that day?"

"You sound like Nick."

"Well, I might not have skipped a grade
in school, but I've always been smarter than
your average troublemaker."

Ben laughed on the other end of the line.
She was glad she could lighten the mood.
"No one would ever call you average, Shelby."

He'd always had this way of making her feel like she was special and important. "I don't know anyone more worthy of being called a hero than you, Harper. You deserve to be sheriff."

"I appreciate your kind words. I do. I'm sorry for spilling my guts. You've always had a way of getting me to talk about stuff I never talk to anyone else about. I'm sure the last thing you need is to hear about my problems."

It had been a long time since she felt like she was doing right by Ben. Knowing she could still be that person for him made her heart feel close to bursting. She had to talk around the lump in her throat. "Maybe I like hearing about other people's problems because it makes me feel like I'm not the only one who has 'em."

"You are not alone, Shelby."

Those words caused the tears to well up in her eyes and fall down her cheeks. Sometimes alone was all she felt. Being back in Georgia, seeing and speaking to Ben again, made her realize how much she missed him. It was an ache that went all the way to her core.

She wiped her face and cleared her throat. "Hey, I was wondering if you weren't busy sometime, maybe you could drive Maggie to where we're filming next week so she could see me in action? I mean, I can get her a ride if it's too much for you. I know you're busy being sheriff. She just thought maybe you could come with her. I told her it probably wasn't possible, but I promised her I would ask. You have—"

"Shelby, stop. I would absolutely love to bring Maggie to the set. Why don't you text me some days and times, and I can figure something out."

Her heart did a backflip. "Really?"

"You think I want to miss out on seeing *Ready, Set, Go 4* being made? I've watched the first three movies a million times."

She loved that he was excited. It felt good to do that for him, too. "Cool. I'll text you."

"I'll be waiting," he said before letting her go.

Shelby ended the call and let it all sink in. So much for keeping her distance from the good sheriff. Walker was right, the two of them had a hard time staying away from each other. She swore this time, she wouldn't let herself do any permanent damage.

CHAPTER SEVEN

BEN WALKED INTO the sheriff's office on Monday morning a bit more apprehensively than usual. Surely, the whole department had heard about the bar fight Saturday night. He greeted the front desk sergeant and headed back toward his office. He made a quick stop in the break room and poured himself a cup of coffee. Maybe the deputies on scene at Buck's Saturday night had kept quiet about his involvement. Everyone was going about their business as usual.

On his way out of the break room, he almost ran into one of his deputies.

"Watch out, Russo, I heard the sheriff has been known to knock people out when they spill his drink," Deputy Mitchell called from his desk.

"Hilarious, Mitchell."

"I heard it was his lady friend who had the mean right hook. She's the one you have to look out for," Lieutenant Larry Frye chimed in.

"Same lady friend who stole the Maserati and was drag racing on County D Friday night?" Mitchell asked, playing dumb. "Should we be concerned our fearless leader is cavorting around town with a known criminal?"

"I'm glad you guys can amuse yourselves this morning. I'll see you all in roll call in ten minutes." Ben retreated to his office and shut the door. The two interior walls were half windows with mini blinds that could be closed for privacy. He could almost see the whole department from his desk. The men and women under his command were good, hardworking officers of the law. They expected a lot of their sheriff, and Ben was determined to be the leader they wanted and needed. That meant he needed to be his best on and off duty.

He reviewed the activity logs from overnight and checked in with the previous shift's commander. Lieutenant Frye ran the majority of the roll call meeting while Ben typically started and ended them with some words of encouragement. He gathered his notes and headed to the room down the hall.

Everyone was seated in rows when he arrived. A couple of the guys were joking around and another group was discussing the basketball game last night. Atlanta had won big over Milwaukee.

"All right, let's get started," Ben said, placing his papers on the podium at the front of the room. He took attendance and reviewed the events that had occurred overnight. Nothing too exciting. Sunday nights were generally the quietest in these parts. "I'm going to turn it over to Lieutenant Frye to go over assignments this week."

"Sheriff?" Mitchell raised his hand. "Is anyone going to be assigned to keep an eye on the newest troublemaker in town or were you going to take care of that one personally since you two seem to be old friends?"

It was one thing to joke around before the shift began, it was another to disrespect him in front of the department. "If you've decided to become a stand-up comic instead of a law enforcement officer, I'll happily accept your resignation and let you go get your laughs. If that's not your plan, you can keep your mouth shut. Are we clear?"

Mitchell's smug smirk was quickly extinguished. "Yes, sir."

Lieutenant Frye took over and Ben stood back. How was he going to gain his deputies' respect if he gave them a reason to cast doubt on his ability as their leader? He hated that Shelby was being weaponized against him. He didn't want his connection to her, however fleeting, to jeopardize what he was trying to achieve at work. Why did trouble have to follow her wherever she went? And when would he learn his lesson?

Ben had paperwork to complete and he spent the rest of his morning stuck at his desk, filling out forms and handling things like vacation requests and signing off on purchase orders. He didn't realize it was lunchtime until there was a knock on his door.

"Any chance the sheriff's mom can take her son out for lunch this afternoon?" Ben's mom stood in his doorway with her purse on her shoulder and a smile on her face.

"Mom, why didn't you call first? We didn't have plans, did we?" Things had been so chaotic lately, he feared he had forgotten something.

"No, I was running errands nearby and I thought I would pop in and see if I could treat you to a sandwich down the street at our favorite deli."

Ben didn't believe for a second that she had been running errands nearby. This was about what happened on the weekend. The return of Shelby Young had everyone in his family a bit concerned.

He logged off his computer and grabbed his jacket. Avoiding the issue wouldn't make it go away. "I would love to join you for lunch, Mom, but only if I can treat you."

"Whatever it takes to get some time with you, honey."

January in Goodfield wasn't the warmest time of year. Ben was happy to have a jacket. All the Christmas holiday decorations had been taken down and replaced with giant red and pink hearts. The words *Love*, *XOXO* and *Be Mine* were everywhere. Goodfield hosted a Valentine's Day Fest kicked off by the Sweetheart 5K Run and Walk the weekend before Valentine's Day. The rest of the week, the main drag was closed to vehicle traffic for a huge block party. There were food vendors, craft booths, and more chocolate and roses were sold than anywhere else in the world. Regardless of the day Valentine's Day fell on, a pageant was held and the Goodfield Sweetheart was crowned.

Ben and his mom walked down to The Happy Pig, a small delicatessen that served the best pastrami sandwich Ben had ever eaten. Whenever he was working from the office, he stopped in to get a sandwich and their homemade potato chips.

"How's the day going so far?" his mom asked when they sat down to wait for their order to come up. "You looked busy when I got there."

"Mondays are heavy on the administrative side of things. I would much rather be out in the community, connecting with people than behind a desk all day."

"Speaking of connecting with people..." She somehow perfectly segued into the real subject she wanted to broach.

"Yes, I have reconnected with Shelby. And I know what you're going to say."

"I wasn't going to say anything," she said with her hand up like she was under oath. "I only want to know that you are okay. I am very concerned that she's back in your life for twenty-four hours and she's already brought quite a bit of trouble into it."

Ben rubbed the back of his neck. "Mom, it's not a big deal."

"Tell that to your brother's hand."

"Nick made the decision to punch a guy in the head. He has no one to blame for his broken hand other than himself."

"I wasn't blaming her," she asserted. He gave her a pointed look. "Fine, I'm blaming her a little bit. But can you blame me? Your brother has never been in a fight in his entire life. Shelby Young goes out for drinks with you guys and he's fighting a gang of hooligans that she provoked."

"Whoa, whoa, whoa. Shelby didn't provoke those guys. They provoked her. One of them was seriously harassing the waitress. Shelby was standing up for her. Did Nick say that she started it?"

His mom shook her head. "Tiffani called me yesterday, crying over the whole thing."

Leave it to Tiffani, who wasn't even there, to be spreading false rumors about what happened. "Well, Tiffani doesn't have the whole story, I guess. Shelby wasn't arrested at the end of the night, but the other guy was."

His mom pulled some napkins from the dispenser on the table. "Well, we both know why that was," she mumbled.

"Mom!" Ben had to rein in his frustration. He lowered his voice. "I did not help Shelby avoid arrest. I am the sheriff. It is my job to serve and protect. I can't play favorites. Shelby, along with everyone else who was part of the fight, including your youngest son, was let go. The only one who was arrested was the guy who harassed and assaulted the waitress in the first place."

"Okay, I get it. Tiffani thought maybe you pulled some strings like you did on Friday."

"I didn't pull any strings on Friday either. I was the arresting officer. I brought her in instead of letting her go, which I could have done. The only thing I did do was call Maggie for her, so she wouldn't have to spend the night in jail."

She reached across the table and put her hand on his. "Okay, I believe you. I apologize. I didn't mean to make you feel defensive. If you would have answered any of my calls this weekend, I could have heard everything from you instead of secondhand from Tiffani."

"I'm sorry for not being more in touch this weekend. It was pretty emotional for me."

Concern etched his mother's face. "That's why I've been worried. Shelby's return must have thrown you for a loop like it did the rest of us."

"Honestly, I can't figure out how I feel. She's back and there are moments when she's standing in front of me and it's like she was never gone. It never takes long for the memory of when she left to smack me in the face. It's like she ripped off a Band-Aid I forgot was still stuck to my skin. That sucker had been on so long, it was basically glued there. When it came off, it made a brand-new wound."

"I'm so sorry, honey." Ben's mom hadn't known how much in love Ben had been with Shelby back then. It didn't take long for her to figure out after Shelby left that she had been much more than a friend. "I heard she's just here for work. Nick said you're taking Maggie to see her in action."

"Shelby invited me to tag along. Who would pass up the opportunity to visit a real movie set?"

"I can't believe that girl gets behind the wheel of dangerous cars as a profession after what happened."

The accident he and Shelby had been in had turned his mom into a reluctant driver. And she wouldn't allow his father to buy another muscle car.

"People shouldn't be ruled by fear. I'm sure she got back in the driver's seat like people who get thrown off horses get back in the saddle."

"Well, she's not planning on staying longer than it takes to finish filming her little movie, right?"

Ben wished that knowing she'd be leaving again would somehow make it hurt less, but it didn't. "I assume she'll go back to her life in California. Why wouldn't she?"

"I guess I worry what seeing you has done to her."

"What do you mean?"

"I'm assuming you weren't the only one with a bandage that was covering a decade-old wound, sweetheart."

The young woman behind the counter called their number, and Ben went to retrieve their lunch. He didn't know how to explain to his mother that Shelby wasn't like everyone else. She had an armor that was impenetrable most of the time.

They ate their sandwiches, changing their conversation to the kitchen remodel that was going on at his parents' house. His mom was nervous things wouldn't be ready by the wedding. They were going to be hosting some of the extended family who were coming from out of town and had to have a functioning kitchen.

"So the man from Kitchens Plus says the fancy corner cabinet, the upper one that I liked the best, is on back order until the end of February. Obviously, that doesn't fit in our timeline."

Ben was happy to talk about anything other than Shelby. He listened to his mother fret and offered support where he could. When they were finished, Ben accompanied her to her car.

"Thanks for getting me out of the office for a little bit. I hope things get finished up in the kitchen before Aunt Laurie gets in town. We both know she will have lots to say either way."

"My sister has always been full of opinions." She fixed the collar on his jacket. "I'm glad we could catch up. I've been worried about you."

"I'll be fine, Mom. Don't worry about me."

"I wish it were that easy," she replied with a sigh.

"I'm not a naive kid anymore. I have a much better idea of how the world works. I have no illusions about how things are going to end this time."

"You're right. I'm sorry that you have to revisit those sad memories, though."

"Not all of my memories are sad."

One corner of her mouth curved up. "I'm sure that's true."

Ben's memories of Shelby were mostly good ones. Some were the best memories of his life. Only one hurt so bad that he tried to keep it buried. He remembered the way she used to come over to his house and inhale a whole bag of sour cream and onion potato chips. They were her absolute favorite and his mom started buying them just for her. He remembered how she learned to water-ski off the back of his parents' boat and had absolutely no fear. She mastered slalom skiing before he did.

There were little moments, too. Things that only happened once, but that he would never forget. The time the two of them took a quart of ice cream out of Maggie's freezer and ate as much as they could on the dock before it became a melted mess. He remembered when she broke her finger while they were playing two-on-two basketball against a couple of his varsity teammates. She refused to quit and hit two three-pointers to help them win.

Then there were the fuzzy memories. The ones that were flashes of images instead of a movie in his head. The way her hair shined in the summer sun. The sound of her laughing hysterically at something Topher did or said. The salty taste of her skin when he kissed her neck.

It wasn't the memories that haunted him. They had happened. He got to go back and revisit those moments when he wanted to. It was the dreams he'd had for the future that stung. The ones that never came true because she left. It was his dashed hopes and dreams that had hurt. Still hurt. Would possibly always hurt.

BEN HAD TO take the following Thursday afternoon off from work in order to drive Maggie to Shelby's movie set. The production had taken over a shipping yard about twenty miles south of Atlanta. One half of the giant lot was filled with row after row of storage/shipping containers while the other half was littered with tents, movie equipment, cars and trailers. The place was swarming with people. Maggie was fascinated by the cameras set up on cranes that were attached to the top of the SUVs.

"Is that how they film the cars racing?"

Ben shrugged. He had no idea. "I'm sure Shelby will show us how they do it. Those things are pretty cool, though."

Ben texted Shelby that they were there. They had checked in with Security and got their passes, but Ben hadn't a clue where to find her.

"You made it!" Shelby greeted Maggie first and then thanked Ben for taking time out of his day to drive her there. They hadn't spoken since the day he'd called her, but they had texted back and forth a few times. Shelby had been superfluous with her thanks each and every time.

"It's not a problem. Is that who I think it is?" Ben took off his sunglasses to get a better look.

The star of the *Ready, Set, Go* franchise came out of one of the trailers. Hugh Levi was built like a Mack Truck. He had muscles in places Ben was pretty sure no other man had.

"That's him. Looks like he's heading toward the hospitality tent. Do you want me to introduce you guys?"

"I don't want to bother him while he's eating. We can wait."

"If Hugh isn't doing a scene, he's eating. Do you have any idea how many calories he has to ingest to keep his body looking like that? I heard he once ate three whole chick-

ens in one sitting. There's no better time to
chitchat than when he's hunkered down at a
table."

"Oh come on, Ben. Let's go rub elbows
with some famous people. It'll be fun," Maggie said. Today, she was dressed as if she had
just stepped off the pages of a fashion maga-
zine. She had on a deep purple jumpsuit with
a bright multicolored silk scarf around her
neck and cat-eye sunglasses. She was sure to
attract some of Hugh's attention.

Shelby, on the other hand, was in a black
tank top, layered over a white one and some
dark denim jeans. Her dark hair was pulled
back into a high ponytail. She looked the way
he remembered her—no frills, laid-back, un-
complicated. Vanessa Howard, the actress
from the three previous movies, walked right
past them and was dressed exactly the same
as Shelby. Even their black tennis shoes were
identical.

"Is that who you're pretending to be? Vanessa Howard?"

Shelby nodded. "Today, there might be
shots where you can see me in the car, so I
have to look like her. Other times, the driver
won't be seen and I don't have to worry about
wardrobe or hair and makeup."

"Oh, can I see what the hair and makeup trailer looks like?" Maggie asked.

"Sure. We can see it all. Whatever you want to check out, let me know. You, too, Harper."

"I want to see you in action. Is that going to happen today?"

"They wouldn't have dressed me up like Nessa if it wasn't," she said, giving him a nudge with her elbow.

When they reached the hospitality tent, Shelby waved her arm like one of those models on game shows pointing out a prize. "One thing you learn fast about a movie set, there's always food. Tons and tons of food. They like to keep everyone well nourished, I guess. What you see here is mostly the crew. Crew eats while the actors typically steer clear. The talent, as they're called, tend to hang out in their private trailers. Hugh is an exception."

Hugh sat at one of the long tables with three plates of food in front of him. One was completely filled with meat. He had a cheeseburger, ribs, some kind of Italian sausage and three strips of bacon. The other was nothing but carbs—bread, pasta and rice. The third plate was clearly his dessert plate. There was a stack of chocolate chip cookies, two muffins and a slice of peach pie with a scoop of vanilla ice cream on top. Ben didn't eat that much in a day, never mind in one meal.

"Hugh, can I introduce you to a couple of my friends?" Shelby asked as they approached.

Hugh wordlessly waved her over since his mouth was full of food. Ben was a bit starstruck.

"This is my friend Ben, he's a local sheriff in the area, and this is my Maggie."

"Oh, this is Maggie?" Hugh stood up and reached for Maggie's hand. "I have heard stories about you, Miss Maggie."

"I hope only the good ones," Maggie said with a wink.

"Are there any other kind?"

Maggie pretended to zip her lips. Hugh chuckled and turned his attention to Ben. "Sheriff Ben, nice to meet you."

Ben shook hands with this monster of a man. His hand was large enough to grip a basketball the way Ben held a baseball. "I'm a big fan."

"Well, thank you. Fans are the reason I still get to do this for a living, so I appreciate every single one of you."

"What's good here?" Ben asked. "Looks like everything."

Hugh's laugh was as hearty as the rest of him. "It is all good, but I gotta say, my favorite is the peach pie. Can't get peach pie like this anywhere else. Georgia peaches are the best."

"Can you handle a little pie before you watch me do my thing, Mags?" Shelby asked, throwing her arm over Maggie's shoulders.

"You know I never say no to pie, Shelby dear."

The three of them left Hugh to his feast and each grabbed a slice of pie. It was amazing to see Shelby in this environment. She fit right in, something that had been a struggle in Goodfield. Walker joined them after a few minutes.

"If it isn't my favorite new friends. Glad you could make it."

"What are you filming today?" Maggie asked.

"We're shooting a scene where we have a high-speed chase weaving in and out of the rows of shipping containers. It ends with Shelby's big stunt. She's going to jump over something like four containers."

"Five," Shelby corrected him.

"That's right. Hector decided to add that

last one on Monday. It's going to be a fun day. I hope you all have a good time."

As much as Ben wanted to not like Walker, he couldn't do it. Walker was more and more likable each time they met. He wondered why Shelby hadn't settled down with someone like him. They seemed compatible in so many ways.

"Doing a big jump like that sounds pretty dangerous," Maggie said.

Shelby finished her bite of pie. "It's not too bad. We have a really excellent team and crew. They put safety first. Always."

"Have you ever been scared driving a car?" Ben asked.

"Not that I can think of."

"Not even after the accident?" Ben sounded a bit too much like his mother for his own liking. He didn't want her to think he was judging her. "It's cool if you haven't been."

Shelby's shoulders seemed to tense. She poked at her pie but didn't take another bite. "Well, I told myself a long time ago that I was going to learn how to drive cars better than anyone else in the world. That way, there would be no risk to me or anyone in the car with me. The more I know about driving, the more control I have, and the less fear I need to feel." She lifted her eyes and met Ben's gaze head-on.

Someone shouted through a megaphone. "We need drivers on set. Drivers on set."

"That's my cue. You guys come with me and I'll show you where you can safely watch."

It had felt illogical for Shelby to become a stunt driver when a car accident had caused her to leave town and Ben behind. Her explanation, however, made perfect sense given what he knew about her. If there was anything she hated, it was not being in control. Too much of her childhood had been dictated by this judge or that caseworker. Too many foster parents did what they wanted regardless of what was best for her. When Shelby got the chance to be the only one in charge, it shouldn't have surprised him that the first thing she did was learn how to master her own recklessness.

Shelby led them to some folding chairs that had been placed well behind the cameras. Once on set, Ben was surprised to see there were ten times the number of people behind the scenes than in front of the camera. Shelby got into the Aston Martin from the other night. Ben was taken aback that she didn't have to wear any extra safety gear.

Walker was part of this stunt as well. He climbed into a matte black Ford Mustang that Ben's dad would love. He would know what year the cars were and all their specs.

"I'm so nervous," Maggie said. "I know she's got this, but my heart is racing."

Ben's anxiety was pretty high, too. This was all planned and plotted out, but working for the sheriff's office had taught him one thing for certain—accidents happened when you least expected them.

Two other cars pulled up and there was some discussion with the director. Shelby gave a thumbs-up. She, Walker and the two other stunt drivers took off and then turned around to get in position a few hundred yards away. The SUV with the crane camera on top looked in position to run alongside them. There were three other cameras set up along the path.

The guy Shelby had pointed out as the stunt coordinator was on a walkie-talkie. He gave the director a thumbs-up. Someone clapped the slate and seconds later, Walker and Shelby hit the gas. They shot down the straightaway, weaving back and forth, barely missing each other, like some kind of wild orchestrated dance. Fake gunshots rang out. The Aston Martin suddenly came to a hard stop. Ben's heart thudded as the car behind it pulled up hard and fast. Was this part of the stunt? The driver chasing Shelby had to swerve with only seconds to spare, causing the car to skid and crash into one of the storage containers on the right side of the lane.

"Was that supposed to happen?" Maggie asked, clutching her scarf.

Based on the fact that he and Maggie were the only ones concerned, he guessed it was.

"I think so," he replied, taking a deep breath through his nose to try to calm himself.

They did the same stunt three more times but without the car behind hitting the storage container. Each time, the crew spent several minutes setting up cameras in different areas in order to capture the scene from multiple angles. Shelby somehow stopped in the same exact spot every time.

"One more time," the director said. "This time with the camera over the Aston Martin."

It took twenty minutes to get everything just right. Shelby backed her car into position and the rest of the team completed the setup for the final shot.

With everyone ready, the production assistant clapped the slate board again and the director called for action. Shelby and Walker took off and did their little dance. Ben held his breath at the point where Shelby hit the brakes, but the car behind her wasn't as precise this time and swerved a second too late, knocking the back end of the Aston Martin and pushing her in the path of the car chasing Walker. That driver was unprepared for the obstacle and hit Shelby on the right side and sent her spinning.

Ben didn't think, he ran toward the damaged car.

CHAPTER EIGHT

TIMING WAS EVERYTHING in Shelby's profession. Everyone needed to be in sync or there were consequences. Big ones.

There was a distinct ringing in her ears and her head hurt. She took a deep breath and closed her eyes, trying to listen to her body to see if she detected any injuries. Things seemed fine. Nothing was broken.

"You all good, Shelby?" Hector asked over the radio.

Medics were always on hand and would need to check her for a head injury. She waited for the stunt crew to come get her out of the car. When the door opened, she wasn't expecting to hear Ben's voice.

"Shelby, can you hear me?"

Her eyes flew open. "What are you doing?" She tried to unlatch her seat belt.

"Don't move. Let the EMS guys check you out first."

"Sir, you aren't allowed to be here," someone said.

"Where's security?" Hector sounded annoyed. "Buddy, what are you doing? You can't be here. You need to go back over there."

"It's okay, Hector. He's with me," she said, getting her seat belt off. Even though Ben had told her to stay put, she knew she was fine. She started to get out of the car.

"What are you doing?" Ben was just as annoyed. "Can you please wait for them to make sure you're okay?"

"I'm okay. I got a little jostled, that's it."

"Who is this? Did you hire your own security or something?" Hector asked.

Ben and Hector hadn't been introduced yet. "Just a friend."

One look at Ben and she knew he was beyond concerned. She hadn't meant to scare him. The EMTs were on the scene. One of the paramedics asked her some questions and assessed the damage. Hector and his team gave their attention to the banged-up car.

"Good thing that was the last take for this stunt. We only have one more of these babies," Hector said, patting the hood.

"You're sure you're all right?" Ben asked, still completely focused on her.

"I'm sure. I'm sorry for worrying you. This is all part of the job."

"I guess you forgot that you might be in control of your car but the other guys are in control of theirs."

She had given him a false sense of security. "Trust me, these guys are the best. Sometimes things go a little sideways, but we're trained to handle those mishaps. When he clipped me, I was ready to take the second hit. We prepare for every scenario, even the bad ones," she assured him.

"You gave me a heart attack," he admitted.

"I'm sorry. You should go tell Maggie everything is fine."

He sighed but did as she asked.

"Is that your new boyfriend?" Hector asked when he came back over to check on her.

She shoved his shoulder. "Are we going to be able to do the next shot?"

"Yeah, Dave already has them setting up the cameras and marking the pavement." Hector gave her a fist bump. "Glad you're good. You nailed that scene every time. I can't believe Gary blew it."

"Happens to the best of us."

"Sorry, Shelby!" Gary, the driver who had

knocked her off course, came jogging over. "You good?"

"All good."

"I thought I had it. I was one beat off."

"How's Johnny?" The driver who'd rammed into her was still in his car, talking to a paramedic.

"All good," Gary replied.

"I thought that was going to be the best take," Walker said, strolling over to check in.

"It would have been."

"You should have seen how the good sheriff sprinted to get over to you. Security didn't even have a chance to react because he was lightning fast. He was ready to come to your rescue. It was cute."

Shelby narrowed her eyes. "Stop talking or I'm going to sideswipe you next time."

"Don't threaten to use my cars to hurt each other," Hector said with a scowl. "Not funny."

"I was kidding. I would never."

"Yeah, right."

Walker chuckled. "I'm glad you're okay. I'm also glad the sheriff was here to prove once again why he is the hometown hero," he teased.

I will crush you, she mouthed so Hector couldn't hear.

Walker sauntered away laughing. "I'm going to make sure Miss Maggie is all right."

THE CREW WAS able to finish two more stunt scenes before they switched to close-ups of the actors behind the wheel. Shelby didn't have any more close calls. The second Aston Martin pulled slightly to the left, but she was able to make adjustments.

"I can't believe how long your workday is and how little actually gets done. Does it get boring doing the same scene over and over?" Maggie asked when Shelby rejoined them.

"I know it might look repetitive, but it takes a lot of concentration to make sure we stay consistent with the earlier takes. For the actors, sometimes they redo a scene over and over in different ways so the director and editor have options."

"Well, I had a blast. I loved every minute of it," Maggie said.

"Almost every minute," Ben added.

"True, I wasn't a big fan of your car crash. Not part of my blast."

"I'm glad you guys were able to enjoy most of the day. You're welcome to stay a little longer if you want. You could have another snack. They bring out new options every couple hours. Who knows what's available now. Someone in food services makes these rice crispy treats that are to die for."

Ben seemed tense and she got the distinct impression he was ready to leave. "What do you want to do, Maggie?"

"Whatever you want to do, Benjamin."

"You don't have to stay," Shelby said, giving him a way out. "If you need to get home, I understand."

"Are you done for the day?" Maggie asked Shelby.

"I am."

"Why don't you come with us and let me make you dinner? I might not have rice crispy treats, but I do have lemon cookies."

"You still buy lemon cookies?" They had been Maggie's special treat when Shelby lived with her. She used to hide them in the cabinet above the microwave. Shelby thought Maggie did that because she underestimated her ability to snoop. One thing Shelby learned while being in the foster care system was if she didn't learn how to scavenge the good stuff, she didn't get any good stuff.

Maggie wasn't like the other foster parents, though. When she caught Shelby sneaking into her stash of lemon cookies, she went to the store and bought a box that she labeled with Shelby's name and placed front and center in the pantry. Shelby would never forget that kindness.

"Of course I do. I have to be careful, though. Gotta keep this girlish figure." Maggie had her hand on her waist and gave her hips a little shake.

Shelby smiled. Being around Maggie didn't feel as heavy as being around Ben. When Shelby had finally called Maggie after taking off, she had been nothing but supportive. She hadn't made Shelby feel guilty for leaving. She had offered her support and guidance as Shelby navigated the world on her own. Maggie had even flown out to California once for a visit. One thing Shelby would never regret was keeping in touch with her.

"I would love to join you for dinner."

"You, too, Benjamin."

Ben startled. "Oh, I can't, Maggie. I promised to take my parents out for dinner since their kitchen is still under construction. I figured tonight was a good night since I was going to be in the neighborhood."

"Even better, your parents can come, too. I still owe your dad for the ride a couple weeks ago."

Shelby's stomach dropped. Eating with Maggie sounded splendid, eating dinner with the Harpers sounded like torture. "I don't know that the Harpers want to see me, Mags."

"Why wouldn't they want to see you?" Ben's eyebrows pinched together.

How could Ben not know how his parents, especially his father, really felt about her? "Your parents have always thought of me as a troublemaker. Not sure I've given them reason to think I've changed. Especially not after what happened at Buck's."

"My parents have fond memories of you. They would love to catch up."

Shelby remembered things very differently. Had Ben forgotten how tense things were even before the accident? After the accident, Mr. Harper had made his feelings very clear to Shelby. "I'm just saying, if they can choose their company, I'm not sure I'm at the top of that list."

"I'm sure my dad would love to hear about all of the different cars you've gotten to drive. He would have been in seventh heaven if he had been here today."

Talking to Mr. Harper about cars seemed like a recipe for disaster since she had promised him she would never show her face around him or Ben again. "I suppose you know them better than I do."

"Then it's settled," Maggie said with a clap. "Let's have a dinner party."

Shelby would call this dinner a lot of things. A party was not one of them.

Ben took them to the grocery store and then dropped the two of them off at Maggie's while he went next door to extend the invitation to his parents. Shelby held on to the slightest bit of hope that Curtis Harper would decline. Ben could insist that his dad would be delighted to catch up. Ben, however, had no idea the things his dad had said to Shelby that had helped push her to leave town ten years ago.

"Maybe you should wait to hear back from Ben before you cook up all that chicken," Shelby suggested.

"Curtis won't refuse me. Can you help me by cutting up the peppers and onions?"

Taco Thursday was a long-standing tradition. Maggie always made tacos on Thursdays. She would change it up every week—chicken, beef, steak, even fish. Hard shell, soft shell, corn or flour. Maggie had a way of putting a special twist on things each time. It was Shelby's favorite day of the week when she lived here.

"Do you talk to the Harpers very often?" Shelby asked, getting out one of the cutting boards. Everything was still in the same place.

"We say hello when we're outside at the same time. Dana comes over sometimes to sit on the deck with me and have a glass of wine or two."

Shelby was happy to hear that they didn't treat Maggie differently because of what happened. It would have been terrible if they had held what Shelby did against her.

"You scared the heck out of poor Ben today."

"One of the first things we learn is how to handle an accident like that. They happen. Our stunts are so technical, it's a lot easier to mess up than it is to nail it. I was totally fine."

"You don't have to convince me. I'm not worried about you one bit, sweetheart. I know you love what you do and because you love it, you'll make sure nothing will prevent you from being able to work until you're an old woman."

"I'm not working until I'm too old. I'm retiring while I still have time to enjoy my retirement."

"Good plan." Maggie turned on the stove and started to heat up her extra-large skillet. "I thought it was kind of sweet that Ben was so worried about you. That man ran like he was being chased by a pack of wild hyenas."

"Ben will always be…Ben." He was about serving and protecting. It was like he was born to be a sheriff even though that hadn't been his plan when they were getting ready to graduate from high school.

"True. He's been trying to keep you safe since the first day you met."

"I'm not some fragile china doll. I can keep myself safe."

"Oh, I know that. You're like titanium. Nothing can break you."

There was a knock at the front door. Suddenly, Shelby felt like her protective shell wasn't thick enough to survive this dinner. The Harpers were probably the only people on the planet capable of slicing through that shield she put up.

"Could you get the door?" Maggie asked as she dumped her cut chicken into the pan.

Shelby wiped her sweating palms on her jeans. Her heart was going to break her rib cage if it didn't relax. She grabbed the doorknob and took a deep breath. Exhaling, she opened the door.

Ben and Mr. and Mrs. Harper stood on the front porch. Mr. Harper held a bottle of wine. Mrs. Harper stepped forward first.

"Hi, Shelby. You look so grown-up. I still pictured you as a teenager." She extended her arms and Shelby felt obligated to give her a quick hug. "How are you?"

"I'm good, thanks. You look like you haven't aged a day since I left. Still the same Mrs. Harper that I remember."

"You're too sweet. Please, call me Dana. We're all grown-ups now."

Shelby was surprised at how their presence made her feel like a kid. She'd been taking care of herself for so long, she forgot what this feeling was like.

"It's funny, I used to call you Dana and Curtis all the time in high school, just never to your faces."

"Why does that not surprise me?" Dana said with a smile. "Now, can I help with anything?"

"I'm sure Maggie would love that."

Ben and Curtis stepped into the house and the air immediately felt charged. Shelby had always been a bit intimidated by Ben's dad.

She had been given a million reasons to not trust men when she was shuffled from foster home to foster home. Curtis had never given her any cause to believe he was like those lowlifes who had mistreated her, but she had spent those six years in Goodfield waiting for him to do so.

Curtis held out the wine in his hand. "Good to see you again, Shelby."

"You, too."

"Ben said it was quite the day on the movie set."

She wasn't sure if he was referring to the accident or the experience in general. She wanted to focus on the positives. "He thought you would have enjoyed it immensely. Maybe you two will have to come out another day just to get a look at the vehicles we brought with us."

"We'd love that," Ben said. "Right, Dad?"

"You know how I feel about cars."

Shelby would take that as a yes. "I think we both feel the same."

"Is it true there was a matte black Mustang there today?"

Walker was so lucky. He always got assigned to the cars Shelby wanted to drive. "There was. It's a gorgeous automobile. They found it in a car show somewhere in the Midwest and convinced the owner to let them use it. The interior is just as cool as the outside."

Ben patted his dad on the back. "You two could probably stand here in the foyer and talk about cars all night, but let's make sure Maggie doesn't need the rest of us to lend a hand."

Shelby led them back to the kitchen. Maggie and Dana were chopping the peppers Shelby hadn't got to and the smell of the cooking chicken was mouthwatering. She found some wineglasses and asked Maggie for a corkscrew.

Ben came up beside her. He was near enough that their arms were touching. Having him this close felt just like this house—it was so familiar, comforting. Ben had always had a kind of calming effect on her, like he was some sort of drug. Her body would relax and her mind could be quiet. She missed a million things about him, but this was the one she missed the most.

"I told you so," he gloated.

He thought because she had carried on a civil conversation with his parents for half a second, everything was good? He was still too much of an optimist.

"The night is very young, Harper. There's still plenty of time for things to go south."

"I'm betting tonight will be a success. And by success, I mean that I will go home tonight without having to put you in handcuffs."

"What would you arrest me for? If things go badly, it won't be my fault."

"My parents promised to be gracious guests. The wild card here is obviously you, but I have faith you'll be on your best behavior."

Shelby elbowed him in the side and tried to keep from laughing. "I'm the only one who can make or break this dinner, huh?"

"My parents have come with open minds and open hearts."

That was hard to believe. Curtis definitely had his mind made up about her. He had since the first day Ben and Shelby met and she convinced Ben to skip school that afternoon. He had told Maggie that he didn't want Shelby to spend time with Ben because she was obviously reckless and a bad influence. Shelby had overheard their entire conversation. It was that night that she decided she wanted Ben to be her friend more than anything in the whole world. He had treated her better than she'd ever been treated and there was something so desirable about doing exactly what Curtis Harper didn't want to happen.

She turned to check on Curtis's where-abouts. He had moved by the sliding door to the deck, watching the sunset over the water. "For sure," she said, laying the sarcasm on thick. "The first thing that pops in my head when I think of your dad is the word *open-minded.*"

Ben chuckled as he opened the wine and poured five glasses. "I have begun believing in the power of positive thinking. If you want something to be true, you simply tell your-self and anyone else who will listen that it is."

Shelby took a sip from her glass. "Yeah, where I come from, that's not called positive thinking. That's called *delusion.*"

The two of them passed out the wine and offered to set the table for Maggie. It didn't take long for Maggie and Dana to have ev-erything ready to go.

Maggie and Ben did most of the talking during dinner, recounting their day on a real movie set. They told the Harpers about meet-ing Hugh and seeing Vanessa on her way to her trailer. They shared how exciting it had been to see Shelby in action, and neither men-tioned the accident. Even though it wasn't the least bit Shelby's fault, she wasn't so sure Curtis would believe that.

Not only was today's accident left out, but thankfully, no one mentioned anything that happened prior to the time Shelby left Goodfield. Shelby was more than grateful for not having to take a trip down memory lane with the two people in town who had nothing but bad memories of her. When dinner ended, Shelby and Ben offered to clean up while Maggie and the Harpers retreated to the family room.

"I told you so," Ben said again.

"Your parents have been very nice. I can admit it." She handed him a freshly washed plate to dry.

"And arresting you hasn't crossed my mind once."

Shelby splashed some of the dishwater at him, making him laugh. It shouldn't have been so easy, but it was. She had feared coming back for so long, she never considered that the experience might be positive.

"I can't believe I actually missed you. I forgot how mean you were," she teased.

"*I* was the mean one? Who used to push me off the dock or do everything in her power to knock me off my wakeboard?"

"Hey, don't blame me because you couldn't stay on your wakeboard. That isn't my fault."

"Oh, you are hilarious." Ben twisted up the dish towel and snapped it at her.

The sound of Shelby's giggles filled the room. Maybe it was the wine, but she hadn't felt this silly and playful in a long time.

"I hope you two are actually cleaning up and aren't going to leave a mess for Maggie," Dana called out from the family room.

"Yes, ma'am. Dishes are almost done!" Ben yelled back.

Shelby pressed her lips together to hold back her laughter. It was like they were kids all over again. Ben reached for the next dish to dry. When they were finished, instead of joining the "grown-ups" in the other room, Ben suggested they go outside. Shelby grabbed her leather jacket and Ben grabbed a couple bottles of beer.

The lake was one of the best things about living with Maggie. There was something so peaceful about the water. Shelby had loved getting up in the mornings and watching the ducks glide across the surface.

As she walked down to the dock with Ben, a mix of emotions stirred inside her. Ben was the best and the worst thing to ever happen to her. There was no one like him, and that made Shelby sad because she knew he couldn't be in her life permanently.

There was a bench at the end of the dock where they used to sit and talk on long summer nights. It was also where Ben had tried to teach her to appreciate the sport of fishing. He had failed. Fishing was not adrenaline-fueled enough for her liking.

"Do you still come over here and fish on the weekends?" she asked him.

Ben shoved his hands in his coat pockets. "Sometimes. I found a spot on the west side that has been lucky lately. The other day, I caught an eighteen-pound bass."

"Impressive."

"You don't think it's the least bit impressive, do you?"

"I really don't know if I should be impressed or not, to be honest. I'm assuming that's a big fish."

"It is. You should be impressed."

"Well, now I am." Shelby took a seat on the bench. Ben remained on his feet. "Do you still water-ski?"

"Nah," he said with a shake of his head.

"Why not? You were so good at it."

"It's just one of those things that…" He stopped.

"One of those things that what?"

"It's one of those things that reminds me of you," he admitted as he looked out over the water. "I just can't."

There was a sharp pain in her chest. She hated that she'd hurt him. She also felt guilty for making things that had brought him happiness too painful to enjoy anymore. She had to remind herself that she would have hurt him worse if she had stayed. Surely, he had to know that. Hadn't she proved in just a few short days what a headache she could be for him?

"I'm sorry that I ruined things for you, but I think not having me around was the best thing that could have happened to you."

Ben's head snapped around. "What is that supposed to mean?"

"You seem to be doing well. You're healthy and happy. You went to UGA like your dad wanted you to, you went into law enforcement, which suits you. You're twenty-eight years old and the sheriff of this freaking county. That's pretty amazing."

Ben's expression darkened. What Shelby said had most definitely struck a chord. "Wow, it's really good to know that since I seem healthy and happy, you don't regret ripping my heart out by disappearing from my life. Glad I could make it easy for you."

He finished his beer and chucked the bottle into the water. Ben never littered in the lake. Shelby wasn't sure what to say. She tried to defuse the situation with humor.

"That was a bad idea. You know you're going to take your boat out tomorrow and search for that sucker."

Ben faced her. His eyes blazed with anger. "I tell you that you ripped out my heart and all you do is make a joke?"

CHAPTER NINE

THE NIGHT HAD been going so well, up until the moment when Shelby acted like she had done him some kind of favor by completely cutting him out of her life and leaving him behind.

"I wasn't trying to make you mad. What I meant by you being better off is that if we had stayed together, I would have ruined everything for you. I had a way of doing that. I've been trouble since the first day we met."

He turned his back on her and stared out at the dark water. He needed to calm down. It felt like his chest had been cracked open. All day he'd been wondering how different things would have been if she had stayed. Maybe the two of them would have ended up in California. She hadn't given him the option of joining her, though.

"I get how you're able to rationalize it now, but I don't understand why you thought that was the right thing back then. We had talked so much about what we wanted, where we were headed. Together. We were supposed to be together. Were we not on the same page about that? I was so sure we were."

"You were ready to give everything up because of me. I couldn't let that happen. Not after what I did to you." Shelby's voice was small. Ben faced her, needing to understand. Her elbows rested on her knees and her head bowed. He wanted to reach out and touch her. Make sure she was real. The last few days were so strange, maybe this was all a dream. He resisted the urge.

"You didn't do anything to me. We were in an accident, Shelby. Plus, I thought we had things figured out. I was fine with deferring for a year so we could start school at the same time."

Ben and Shelby had both applied to University of Georgia in Athens. Ben had gotten in and Shelby hadn't. She had kept it a secret for a bit, but finally had come clean a couple weeks before prom. He had been mad at first, but soon realized that she hadn't said anything because she had been scared that it meant they were going to have to break up.

She lifted her head. "Clearly there was no reason for you to put your life on hold for me.

It was my own fault that I hadn't taken school seriously until junior year."

"The point is you did start to care. I didn't want not getting in to be a setback. I also didn't want to go there without you."

"Ha!" she exclaimed humorlessly. "Like your dad was ever going to let that happen."

Ben could feel his brows pinch together. "He couldn't force me to go."

She laughed again. "Whatever. It doesn't matter."

"Don't do that. Don't shut down. This matters to me. I would have done anything to make things work for you and me. One year was not a big deal."

Shelby covered her face with her hands. "And what if I didn't get in the next year? What would you have done then?"

"I don't know. I would have had to think about it. We would have made a plan, though. Together, we could have figured it out."

"There it is. Mr. Optimistic," she said with a groan.

"Well, sorry for having faith in us. I thought we made a pretty good team. Do you have any idea how much it hurt when you decided to make all the decisions for us?"

She let her hands drop into her lap. "Isn't

it better that I didn't force you to choose between me and going to your dream school?"

"My dream school?"

"Don't act like going to UGA wasn't your number one goal in life. Your whole bedroom was decorated in UGA red and black. You wore more Bulldog shirts than anyone else in Georgia. Your dad and mom went there. It was your destiny."

Destiny? The only thing that had felt like destiny was being with her.

"I wasn't giving up that dream. I was only delaying it."

"I know you felt like you had to be there for me, but I would have held you back."

"So you just left? You thought taking my choices away from me was the best plan?"

"Yes. But not because I wanted to hurt you. It wasn't a choice I made out of spite. It was because I cared about you."

It was amazing how quickly her mind had changed. The way Ben remembered it, the two of them spent a lot of time talking about what they should do. They had considered all the possibilities and both agreed that taking a year off together was the best plan. He recalled that she had been happy with that decision up until the accident. After the accident, everything changed.

Ben rubbed his eyes with the heels of his hands. When Shelby left, he had been so confused. Her behavior had made no sense. They had been in love. He had known he wanted to spend the rest of his life with her. In his memory, she had wanted those things as well.

"I can't believe this is the first time you're telling me you felt that way. I remember having several conversations with you about what we should do. We were always on the same page. I'm starting to wonder if you meant anything you said to me those weeks leading up to prom."

"I never lied to you."

"When did you change your mind? After the accident or before? Did you use the accident as a way to take off, knowing I couldn't physically follow you?"

"Absolutely not!" Shelby sat up and wiped a tear from her cheek. "The accident was proof of what everyone else already thought about me. I was bad news. I was a danger—to you, to whoever got close to me. It made me realize that asking you to wait for me was the wrong thing to do. You had a life plan and I was a clueless foster kid with nothing to offer you in return."

"Shelby, come on. You know how I felt about you. The only thing I wanted was you. You weren't a danger to me." Far from it. She was his heart. When she left, she destroyed him.

"Think about it, Harper. First, you tell your parents that you want to defer for a year. Your dad goes ballistic. Your mom cries. They stage an intervention to tell you all the reasons you should go to Athens. You didn't listen, though. You stood your ground because you thought being with me was more important than your education and your career."

"I was only going to take one year off!" It was so frustrating that he had to explain that to her. She was the one who was supposed to understand. "It wasn't like I was giving up on college for you. I didn't want to leave you behind. You had been left behind by everyone who was supposed to love you. I didn't want to do that to you."

Shelby closed her eyes. More tears rolled down her cheeks. She stood up and placed her hands on his shoulders. "I can never explain to you how much it means to me that you cared about me that much. I didn't deserve it, though."

He wiped her tears with his thumbs. "You did," he said, wanting more than anything to kiss her. She was his one true love, and no one else would ever compare.

She pulled away. "I don't know why you think that. Look at how I repaid you for caring about me. I dared you to steal your dad's Chevelle to drive us to prom and you did it to make me happy. I didn't care about the further damage that would do to your relationship with your dad. I'm sure I begged you to let me drive because that was all I ever wanted to do. I loved speed. I loved danger. We both know that I drove it way too fast. That I didn't think about you or what could happen to you. I took risks with both our lives just like the first time you let me drive that car."

"You don't know what happened. For all we know, that deer bolted out in front of us and you had no time to react."

"You're right, neither of us knows what really happened, but I think we both can guess based on my history. Your dad had been very clear that the police said I was driving too fast and, based on the skid marks, I was distracted when I came up on that deer. It was like I never saw it."

Ben couldn't remember anything about that day. Neither could Shelby. All they knew was what people told them. Topher had said the two of them left the dance early. The doctors said Ben's injuries were more severe because he didn't have a seat belt on and was ejected from the car. His dad had told him that the deer they hit was so large, the impact had been like hitting a brick wall.

"You didn't cause the accident. The deer did."

"Let's say the cops are wrong. Let's say I was driving safely. I was still the reason we were out on that road instead of back in the school gym like everyone else. I'm sure I was the one who wanted to leave the dance. I don't remember, but I think we both know which one of us wasn't into being social."

"You didn't mean for it to happen, Shelby. It was an accident."

Shelby got up and stood at the edge of the dock. For a second, Ben feared she was going to jump in.

"I almost killed you, Ben. You almost died because I was a careless kid. I was perfectly fine with you stopping your life so I didn't have to be alone. At the same time, I didn't do everything I could to make sure you were safe. I didn't protect you like you always protected me. What we had wasn't an equal relationship. You gave and I took. I don't know why you don't hate me."

Ben thought about what she said. His love for her had been overwhelming. She had been his life. Nothing in the world had been more important to him than she had been. He would have given up school, moved to California, whatever she had wanted. The only thing that had mattered back then was being with her. She, on the other hand, refused to hold his hand in public. She wouldn't let him tell other people they were together. She made reckless decisions even though she knew those decisions could hurt him. Shelby was right. She had been somewhat of a selfish kid. He could never hate her, though. He didn't believe that her intentions were ever to do him harm.

"I don't hate you."

"I hate myself. I hoped leaving would give you a chance to have a better life. I wanted to save you from a future of resentment. I didn't want us to end things hating each other."

Ben began to wonder what life would have

truly been like if she hadn't left. Would he have eventually resented the fact that he didn't go away to school after graduation? Would he have ruined his relationship with his family in order to stay with Shelby? His family was so important to him and Shelby knew that. How would they have supported themselves? Would he have agreed with all of her career choices or would that have driven a wedge between them? For the first time Ben started to look at the whole thing in a very different light.

Shelby stood like a statue at the end of the dock. He didn't want her to hate herself, but he understood why she did. He had been so mad at her for selfishly taking off, when in reality, it might have been more selfish to stay.

"I never could have hated you. I wish we could have talked like this ten years ago."

She mumbled something too softly for him to hear. He only made out what he thought was the word *dad*.

"What?"

"I'm going to head back to the house," she said, rubbing her hands up and down her arms. Nights in southern Georgia weren't very warm at the end of January. "Your mom and dad are probably ready to go."

The wind blew hard in his face. It chilled him to the bone. They could sit out here all night and talk about what they should have, could have, would have done differently, but at the end of the day, the past was the past. There were no do-overs. In a few weeks, Shelby would be leaving again and Ben would have to go back to his normal life. His perfectly predictable and fine life. It rubbed him the wrong way that he knew for a fact life with Shelby never would have been any of those things. She had a way of making the world more colorful.

His mom and dad were ready to say their goodbyes when they came back in. At least his parents had seen that Shelby wasn't the wild rebel that they remembered from years ago. They had respected his wishes not to re-hash anything from the past. He regretted not following his own advice.

"It was so good to catch up, Maggie. We should do it again once my kitchen is finished," his mom said as they stood in the foyer of Maggie's house again.

"We better do it soon. Tiffani says she thinks this house will sell quick once we put it on the market."

His mom nodded. "Well, she would know best. No one sells more houses than Tiffani."

Shelby groaned but quickly made it sound like she was coughing. "Sorry, I had a throat tickle," she said.

"It was good to see you, Shelby. I hope the rest of your filming goes well and that you have a safe trip back to California." Ben's mom couldn't stop herself from mentioning Shelby's impending departure from Goodfield.

"Thank you, Mrs. Harper. I mean, Dana," she said, correcting herself.

"I'll have to talk to Ben and see if we can work it out to get that garage tour you were talking about earlier," his dad said.

Ben was surprised to hear his dad was open to seeing Shelby again. He had assumed he was being polite by his response earlier in the evening when Shelby brought the idea up.

"Great. I'll give Ben a few choices and you two can see if any of them work for you. We have a sweet Maserati and this cherry red 1967 Dodge Charger. I can't let you drive any of them, but I might be able to get you a seat in one for a picture."

"That would be amazing. Thank you. Have a good night, Shelby."

Ben gave Maggie a hug. "See you soon, Maggie. Thanks for dinner."

"Anytime, Benjamin."

When he let go of Maggie, he turned to Shelby. He wasn't sure what to do after things had gotten so awkward outside. Did he hug her? Did he simply say goodbye? He remembered she didn't have a ride back to the hotel.

"Can I drop you back at your hotel?" he offered.

"No, I think I'm going to stay for a bit longer. Catch up with Maggie. If that's okay?" she asked Maggie, who was overjoyed with the idea.

"All right. Well, then I guess I'll talk to you later. About the garage visit."

"Right. Sounds good."

Ben decided to go for the hug. It might be his only chance to give her one. Who knew if things would work out for them to connect again before she was done with the movie. He tried to be casual about it, but as soon as it became clear that she didn't mind the idea of an embrace, he wrapped both arms around her. She felt so much smaller than he remembered. Her arms circled his waist and she rested her cheek against his chest. She tightened her hold and his heart melted. He never wanted to let go.

Simple words of goodbye lodged in his throat. She seemed to have the same problem. They stood there, paralyzed by all the things that were left unfinished between them. He understood why Shelby had made the decision to leave without saying goodbye. There was no way he could have let her go back then.

"I missed this more than you know," she finally said, but then abruptly pulled away.

"Have a good night. Don't keep Maggie up too late," he said in an attempt to lighten things up.

Ben stepped outside and followed his parents as they cut across the front yard to their house. Ten years ago, people would have noticed a clear path in the grass where Ben and Shelby had walked back and forth a million times. His dad had complained every time he had to mow the lawn.

"That wasn't so bad, huh?" his mom asked his dad as she opened the front door.

"It's nice to see that she's got a good life. It sounds like she's made a name for herself in that business and not a bad one."

"She's one of the best stunt drivers out

there, male or female," Ben said. "I talked to some of the guys on the stunt crew. They said Shelby rarely makes a mistake. She also is excellent at assessing the conditions and pointing out any potential hazards. They all seemed to respect her."

"I think that's great," his mom said. "I can't lie, I was worried that the world would not be kind to her. Without Maggie watching out for her, without good friends to influence her, I was concerned she was going to end up making a lot of bad decisions to survive."

Ben went on the defensive. "Shelby is the most resilient person I know. Life wasn't going to beat her down. She had survived some of the worst the world had to offer before she got to Maggie's."

"Seems like it all worked out for the best. I think it was a good thing for her and for you that she went her own way," his dad said. He sat down in his leather recliner and picked up the television remote.

After having this argument with Shelby, Ben felt irked that everyone thought the same thing. "I don't know how you can say that. We have no idea how things would have played out if she had stayed."

His dad put his feet up and turned on the television. "I'm glad I didn't have to find out."

Ben's dad had been so understanding at first. Even more than his mom, his dad had seemed to get just how much Ben was in love with Shelby. That understanding didn't last forever, though. When Ben hit rock bottom a couple months after she had left, his dad grew frustrated with him. He had demanded that Ben "get over it" as if it was that easy. He had pushed him to go to UGA and pretended that everything was fine. Nothing was fine, but his dad didn't want to hear about it.

"You guys act like my life has been perfect since she left."

"It certainly could have been worse," his dad said.

"It also could have been better," Ben argued.

"Let's not fight over some alternate reality," his mom interrupted. "Shelby chose to leave and thankfully, she's doing great. You were heartbroken for a bit, but you are also doing great. I would say things worked out just like they were supposed to."

Exactly what was so great about Ben's life? He lived with his brother. In a couple weeks, he wouldn't even have Nick as company. His heart had never fully recovered from losing Shelby. He hadn't been in a serious relationship since and not for lack of trying. He had dated a few very lovely women in college, but he was too guarded, and that never boded well for a long-term relationship. After college, he had been focused on his career and relationships didn't fit into his agenda. His parents had no idea how hard it had been. Sometimes he worried he would never be able to give his heart to someone and that he'd grow old alone.

"Well, I learned tonight that it was the accident that changed everything. It made her believe she was bad for me. Sometimes I wish I had been driving that night instead of her."

Suddenly, he had his dad's full attention. "Don't say that! Why would you say that?"

His reaction seemed a bit extreme. It wasn't like there was a time machine handy to allow him to go back and change anything.

"I'm just saying if I had been driving, she wouldn't have to live with all this guilt. Can you believe she still feels guilty? She told me today that she became a stunt driver so that she would never be out of control behind the wheel again."

"I feel terrible," his mom said. "I wasn't

there for her after the accident. She got out of the hospital so quick, and that's where I was camped with you. I was surprised she didn't come to visit you. I didn't realize she was struggling with so much guilt. I wish I could have eased her mind."

"Can we talk about something else?" his dad barked. "Shelby's alive and well. She knows Ben is thriving. She has nothing to feel guilty about anymore. Leaving town was the right thing to do. If you two want to continue obsessing over this, can you go to the other room? I'm trying to watch my show."

Ben wasn't aware his dad had a show. He also disagreed that there was only one right and one wrong way Shelby could have handled things after the accident. He didn't want to argue anymore, though.

"I should get home. I'll talk to you guys this weekend."

"Hey," his dad said, stopping Ben in his tracks. "I don't think we should go to the garage. When Shelby sends you some dates, tell her we can't make it. I think it's best that she finish her work and be on her way."

Ben's confusion left him speechless. What had changed in a matter of minutes?

"Why wouldn't you want to go?" his mom

asked. "You love cars and she's giving you a chance to see some of the coolest ones."

"I don't want to go. Can't a man change his mind?"

"Why—"

"Mom, it's okay. If he doesn't want to go, we don't have to go. I'll see you later, Dad."

His mom walked him out. "Was that weird or was it just me?" she asked him.

"Are things at work okay? Is it the stress of not having a kitchen?"

"He's been in a strange mood all week. I'm not totally sure what's going on," she said, closing the door behind them and lowering her voice. "I would hope it's just a coincidence that he started acting like this when he had to take Maggie to go bail out Shelby, but I'm beginning to think having Shelby back in Goodfield may have riled up some old feelings."

"What kind of feelings?"

"Honey, Shelby reminds him of how close we came to losing you in more ways than one. She reminds him of that time when your whole future was in question. We didn't know if we could get you to go to school. Then, you two got in that terrible accident and we almost lost you. That was scary. I think seeing

Shelby makes your father remember how bad things almost got."

"And by bad you mean I almost delayed getting my college diploma by one year?" That was how silly this all really was. One year.

His mom frowned. "The unknown was scary."

"Shelby thinks you guys don't like her. She's really going to think that if Dad doesn't go visit the set."

"We have never not liked her," his mom said. Ben gave her a pointed look. "Well, your dad wasn't a huge fan when she first got to town, but she grew on him. He felt terrible when she ran away. Do you know he used to get up in the middle of the night that whole summer and check to make sure you were in your bed? He was so afraid you were going to run after her and we would lose you both."

There was good reason for that. Ben had considered searching for her, only he had no idea where to begin looking. Shelby had no social media to track, no cell phone he could call. He did remember feeling like his dad was watching him like a hawk. He also thought there was no way Shelby would stay away forever. She would miss him too much and come back, begging for his forgiveness.

"I really thought she would come back. And I sure didn't think it would take ten years."

"Neither did we. Your dad used to blame himself for her running away and for your depression after she left. I don't know why he felt so responsible, but he did."

"So what you're saying is give Dad a break. Seeing Shelby makes him feel sad and guilty. That's why he doesn't want to visit the set?"

His mom shrugged. "That's my guess. You know what I want, though? I just want you to be happy, honey. Do you know that tonight was the first time I've heard you really laugh in forever? That was my favorite part of the evening. Your happiness means everything to me."

Ben wanted to be happy, too. The biggest problem was when he pictured himself truly happy in the future, he was married and a dad and the woman standing beside him was Shelby. He couldn't imagine anyone else in that spot. Since that was never happening, it made happiness feel pretty out of reach.

CHAPTER TEN

"ARE YOU SURE you want to move?" Shelby asked Maggie as they sat at the kitchen table, finishing off that second bottle of wine. "I mean, you have great neighbors and this is such a beautiful location." Shelby felt overwhelmingly nostalgic. "Not to mention all the memories."

"It's been a wonderful place to live for the last thirty years. My husband and I did make a lot of great memories. I fostered some amazing kids here, like *you*. But it's time for me to find a smaller place. There is a family out there who is going to be so happy here."

Maggie hadn't always been alone. Her husband, Greg, had been a Goodfield firefighter and, according to Maggie, one of the funniest and most charismatic men she'd ever known. The two of them had tried for years to have a family, but learned that it wasn't meant to be. Instead of giving up, they decided to become foster parents. Before Shelby, Maggie had fostered dozens of kids with her husband over the years.

About five years before Shelby came to live with Maggie, Greg died while fighting a four-alarm fire in the Goodfield Library. Widowed and heartbroken, Maggie stopped fostering and planned to live out the rest of her years alone. That was until a certain caseworker, who knew about Maggie from years back, gave her a call and begged her to help out with a particularly challenging child who had bounced from home to home and was about to be put in a residential treatment center if she couldn't find someone to take her.

That child had been Shelby and, for some reason, Maggie had agreed to open her home and her heart back up. It had been the luckiest thing to ever happen to Shelby. One of her greatest regrets was that she had caused Maggie so much trouble.

"I know I haven't been around, but knowing you were here made me feel connected still. When you leave, I can never come back to this house."

Maggie's eyebrows lifted. "I didn't realize you were so attached to this place."

"It's the only place that ever felt like a home to me. I don't think I tell you enough how much I appreciate everything you did for me."

"I was happy to do it. After Greg died, I never imagined myself taking on another kid in need. We had been foster parents, a team. He made the kids laugh like you can't believe. He was so caring and compassionate. I didn't feel like I could be enough for someone on my own."

"I'm sure Greg was amazing, but you don't give yourself enough credit. You have this way of letting kids know you're there without being in their face. You were firm but fair. I had never experienced that before. You're also pretty hilarious when you want to be."

Maggie wagged a finger at Shelby. "Well, sometimes I think you were laughing at me and not with me."

Shelby chuckled. "Sometimes I was. But never in a mean way," she quickly explained. "I laughed because you made it safe to laugh."

Maggie's expression softened. "I am glad I was able to do that for you. You had been through enough before you got here. All I wanted to do was show you that the world wasn't always a bad place."

Getting choked up again, Shelby bit down on her lip and took a deep breath through her nose. "You did. I want you to know that you did that for me."

Maggie stood up. "Come here and give me a hug. I know you hate them, but you seemed to like the one Ben gave you, so now it's my turn."

Shelby gave Maggie her hug. It was the least she could do. Maggie pulled back and took Shelby's face in her hands. "I hope there's much more happiness in your future, sweetheart."

"I hope so, too."

Maggie sat back down. "Well, I think we both know that Benjamin had a lot to do with why you were happy here, too. How did things go tonight?"

Shelby tightened her ponytail and then shrugged, not knowing what to say.

"You two were having a good time while you were cleaning up. Why do I get the feeling something happened when you guys went outside?"

"It's weird to me that he doesn't understand why I left. I could have ruined everything for him. You'd think he'd be glad I took off."

"He was in love with you, Shelby."

She had been in love with him as well. She hadn't said it. Not out loud. Inside her head, she had said it a million times. Maggie had changed Shelby's life, but Ben had changed her heart. There had been so much barbed wire wrapped around that thing, it was amazing he didn't get hurt sooner.

"I understand that, but it's been a long time and those feelings must have faded, changed. For some reason, he takes offense to the fact that I see he has a nice life. It makes him mad when I say I made the right decision by leaving town. He's got a good life, right?"

One of Maggie's shoulders shrugged. "I think he has a pretty good life. It was a big deal when he was elected as sheriff. I was so proud of him. I also think you may be overestimating how much his feelings have changed. How much have your feelings faded and changed?"

That was a question Shelby couldn't answer. The truth was embarrassing. She had spent the last ten years trying to get over Ben Harper and had failed spectacularly. Even when she had a great guy like Walker, willing and able to love her, she couldn't make herself give him her heart.

"I am not a kid anymore. I understand what Ben and I had was puppy love, naive teenage love. We had no idea what was real. We lived in the Goodfield bubble. Things would have changed as soon as he chose me over going to school. He would have ended up resenting me."

"I think Ben would have gone to school eventually. He was trying to protect you. When he found out you didn't get into the same school as him, he didn't want you to feel abandoned. That's just who Ben is."

"We were dumb teenagers. I think almost everything that happened back then can be explained by that one fact."

Maggie shook her head. "You two were a lot of things. Dumb was not one of them. I think you were both in love and scared to death. Him of hurting you and you of not being worthy of him. When the accident happened, I think fear won out."

Maggie was so right. Shelby believed she hadn't been worth it. He had deserved better. He had deserved to go to school and become something great. And he did that. He was sheriff. He was an amazing leader and protector of the entire county. If she had stayed, the only person who would have benefited was Shelby. That was so unfair to the rest of the world.

"The past is the past. I can't go back and

change things. All I care about is making sure that I don't do any harm while I'm here."

Maggie smiled sadly. "Why are you always so hard on yourself?"

"I stayed with this one family when I was ten. I only lasted about a week. When they called the caseworker to tell her that they couldn't keep me any longer, I heard the dad say something about a disease. He said he couldn't risk keeping me and letting whatever it was that was wrong with me rub off on his biological kids."

"What? You know that's not true. There is nothing wrong with you. That guy was not qualified to be a foster parent if he couldn't handle the adjustment issues that happen with all foster kids when they first come into a home. He was the problem. Not you."

That might be true if that one guy was the only person who thought that way, but he wasn't. Ten years ago, Mr. Harper had practically said the same thing after the accident that almost killed Ben. Just thinking about that conversation sent a chill down her spine.

Shelby had gotten out of the hospital before Ben had because his injuries were so much worse. She had asked Topher to take her back to visit Ben as she hadn't seen him since the day of the accident, a day she couldn't even remember anymore.

Mr. Harper was in the hallway when she arrived holding a balloon that she bought downstairs in the gift shop. He had been standing outside Ben's room on his cell phone. The first part of the memory was a little fuzzy. She couldn't remember if he had already been mad or if seeing her was what had caused him to see red. The only crystal clear part of the memory was the way he had looked at her as she approached the room. It was like she had been a disease. A disease he didn't want anywhere near his child.

Mr. Harper had been quick to tell her that day that she wasn't welcome at the hospital. He and Ben's mom had decided that only family could come visit until Ben was feeling stronger. Shelby had known better than to argue after everything that had happened. She had handed him the balloon and turned to leave, but Mr. Harper had stopped her.

Hopeful that he had somehow changed his mind, Shelby had spun around only to have him usher her down the hall and into a small waiting room area. The conversation they had in that tiny room with the navy blue couch and the TV playing an old game show would forever be engrained in her memory.

Mr. Harper had been the one to make it clear that there was only one way forward after the accident. Since Shelby was the problem, that solution was that she needed to go away, as far away as she could manage. It had only taken a couple sleepless nights for California to be the answer. Two weeks after prom and the accident and three days before her high school graduation, Shelby took off with some clothes and all the money she'd been saving from her part-time job.

"It's sweet of you to say that, Mags. You have always seen something in me that I'm not sure is there. Still, it's nice knowing someone believes in me."

"It's there, honey bun. It's there."

"Do you mind if I stay here instead of the hotel for the rest of the shoot? I feel like since this isn't going to be your home much longer, I'd like to actually say goodbye to it this time."

"There is nothing that would make me happier! What else do you need from me?"

"You don't happen to have a car hiding in your garage, do you?"

THE ENTIRE TIME Shelby lived with Maggie, the old woman drove this huge, white Buick sedan. People could see it coming from a mile away. It had been five years old when Shelby first arrived. She'd lived with Maggie for six years and ten years had passed since Shelby left. Shelby assumed there was no way Maggie still owned that car. Except she did.

"What in the world is that?" Walker asked the next morning when Shelby pulled up in front of the hotel and rolled down the window.

"It's my new ride."

"I'm not sure you are allowed to refer to that thing as a *new* ride."

"Maggie hasn't driven it in a year. I think I need to get an oil change. I was shocked it even started."

Walker shook his head. "Something tells me that thing needs more than an oil change. Did you put new gas in there?"

Not only had she filled the tank with fresh gas, but she added some windshield wiper fluid and air to all of the tires.

"I spent the last half hour at the gas station doing my best to get it ready for the road. So will you come with me to get an oil change before we have to work today?"

"Will you buy me something to eat while we wait for them to do an overhaul on this beast?"

Leave it to Walker to need to fill his stomach before they headed to set where there would be enough food to feed all of Goodfield. "Sure," she said with a shake of her head.

He got in the passenger's seat. "Let's roll. It does roll, right?"

"You are so funny. I'm laughing so hard, my stomach hurts."

"How was your night? Did you and the sheriff enjoy dinner with Maggie?"

"I enjoyed dinner with the sheriff, Maggie and the sheriff's parents."

"Oh my, it was a real reunion."

"I survived. That's all that matters. Did you do anything other than play video games in your room?"

"I'm pretty sure since you weren't logged on to play with me, I got put in a game made up of mostly middle schoolers. I had to turn off the chat because I was about to call their parents."

Shelby laughed. "You're the Xbox Grandpa."

"When did I get so old?"

"You've been old for a while. Haven't you seen those gray hairs in the mirror?"

Walker flipped down the sun visor and opened the mirror, checking his hair.

"It's so easy sometimes," Shelby said with a giggle.

They had two and a half hours before they needed to be on set. They dropped the car off at the local express lube and walked across the street to the diner where Shelby waitressed when she was in high school.

Kelly's Diner was a local favorite. A lot of regulars came to eat there every week. They had their special tables, their special waitresses and their favorite meals. Weekends were the busiest days, but there was something about Friday mornings that brought people to Kelly's as well.

Shelby wasn't sure if anyone she used to work with could possibly still be there, but right away she recognized the hostess. Maribelle had been standing in that same spot on Shelby's last shift at Kelly's.

She didn't seem to know who Shelby was at first, but recognition dawned on her face after welcoming them and confirming there were only two in their party. "You look so familiar. How do I... Is your name Shelby?"

Shelby nodded. "I can't believe you remember me. I worked here over ten years ago."

"I never forget a face! Shelby Young, right? I totally remember you. You used to be the Wilsons' favorite waitress. They were so sad when you left. Their little girl just got married last weekend. Can you believe it?" Maribelle was a talker and a bit of a gossip. Shelby had fond memories of her, though. She had always been kind and helpful.

"We were just talking about how old this guy is on the ride over here and now I'm sure that I'm the one who's old."

Maribelle laughed. "I wish I was only as old as you, sweetie. It's good to see you. Let's get you a table."

As soon as they walked into the dining area, Shelby laid eyes on Ben, who was seated at a table with none other than Tiffani and Nick. Of all the diners in the world...

"Walker, Shelby, hey!" Nick called out, causing Tiffani to look up from her menu and frown.

Shelby gave Ben a wave while Walker shook hands with Nick.

"Hey, there. If it isn't the heavyweight champion of Goodfield. How's the hand?"

"Not too bad. It's not like I had to get a

cast. This thing is barely noticeable, right?" Clearly Nick was trying hard to downplay his injury for Tiffani.

"It's noticeable," she spat.

"Why are you two in town instead of on set?" Ben asked, changing the subject.

"I'm borrowing Maggie's old Buick while I'm here and I took it in for an oil change. I'm staying with her until I have to go back to California."

Ben's eyes went wide. "You are?"

"Great, so you'll be on the road and in the house I'm trying to sell," Tiffani lamented.

"Would you two like to sit near your friends?" Maribelle offered. "We could even put these two tables together, if you like."

Everyone answered at once.

"Sure!" Nick said.

"No way," Tiffani said.

"That's okay," Shelby said.

"Great!" Walker said.

"Let me help you," Ben said, getting to his feet.

Maribelle froze, unclear whose direction she should follow.

"We don't want to impose on your breakfast," Shelby said. "We can sit at a separate table."

"It's fine." Nick gave Tiffani a pointed look. "We're just talking about the bachelor party. Something tells me that Walker has been to some fun bachelor parties before. Maybe you can help my brother."

"What makes you think only Walker has been to fun bachelor parties?" Shelby asked. "I'll have you know that I have also been to a few myself."

"Shocking," Tiffani replied under her breath.

"Since I'm hosting this party, I think we know it won't be anything like the parties you two find fun," Ben said, helping Maribelle put the two tables together.

Walker pulled over a couple chairs. Shelby sat between Ben and Walker on one side while Tiffani and Nick were on the other. "You would think that, Sheriff, but I have yet to be arrested at one. I can't speak for this one, though," he said, thumbing in Shelby's direction.

Shelby didn't find him nearly as entertaining as he found himself. The waitress came by and asked if anyone wanted some coffee to start. Tiffani's patience frayed.

"We're on a tight schedule. Can the three of us put our order in? We'll be doing separate checks anyway."

"I already know what I want," Shelby said. "I used to work here, remember?"

"I'm betting you guys have pancakes and sausage, right?" Walker asked. The waitress nodded. He handed her the menu without even looking at it. "Then I'm set as well. Pancakes with a side of sausage for me, please."

Shelby smirked at Tiffani, who looked ready to lose her cool. Her inability to control things now that Shelby had arrived must have been driving her mad.

"We don't need separate checks. Breakfast is on me," Nick offered.

"You don't have to do that," Shelby said, uncomfortable with the idea of Nick footing her bill.

"For once I agree with Shelby," Tiffani said.

"It's fine. Please, let me treat."

"Don't argue with this guy, Shelbs. He has a mean right hook," Walker joked.

Since Tiffani didn't want Nick to treat, Shelby decided maybe it wasn't such a bad idea. Everyone put in their order. Shelby tried to control her expression when Tiffani made seven different substitutions to her meal. Customers like her were the reason Shelby never wanted to go back to waitressing again. Once all the orders were in, the waitress seemed more than happy to move on.

"So what's this about you staying with Maggie?" Ben asked.

"Being there last night made me realize how much I missed the place. I decided since she's letting it go, I should make the most of this last chance I have to spend some time there."

"You know you won't be allowed to be present when we have showings and we're having our first open house next Sunday," Tiffani warned her. "You can't be there when that's going on either. You'll also have to clean up after yourself when there are showings. A messy home is a bad first impression for buyers."

"Good to know," Shelby replied. It annoyed her that Tiffani assumed she would leave her clothes on the floor or forget to make her bed. Shelby wouldn't sabotage things for Maggie if selling was what Maggie really wanted.

"I think having you around will be really nice for Maggie," Ben said. "I noticed how full of life she was yesterday spending the day with you."

"Is she not usually like that?" Shelby asked, concerned about his word choice.

Ben shrugged. "She has her good days and bad days. It's hard being alone and it's not easy getting old."

"I hate getting old," Walker said. He nudged Nick. "I don't look that old, do I?"

"No way, man, You don't look a day over thirty."

"What? I'm not thirty! I look thirty?"

Shelby held her hand up for Nick. He deserved a high five for that one.

"Kidding! I'm kidding," Nick said as he slapped her hand.

"I don't mean to be rude," Tiffani said, being totally rude if anyone asked Shelby. She flipped open the notebook on the table in front of her. "But we really do have things we need to discuss. You know, the whole purpose for this breakfast?"

"Sorry, honey. I know you're worried about the plans for the bachelor party, but you have to trust that Ben has come up with a great idea."

"Why are you worrying about a party you aren't even invited to?" Shelby asked. Weren't there a million things for her to be concerned about? The bachelor party seemed like something she could take off her plate.

"I'm not worrying, Nicholas," she replied,

ignoring Shelby altogether. "I would just like to know if there's anything I can do to help. Ben is the sheriff and he's a busy guy. I don't want anything to fall through the cracks. I want you to have the best bachelor party ever because you deserve it." She leaned over and gave him a kiss on the cheek.

Nick swooned hard. "That is so…" *Nauseating?* Shelby thought. "…sweet of you," he said, giving her a kiss back.

Shelby could not wrap her head around how these two had come together. Seeing them be lovey-dovey wasn't helping.

"Nick is my only brother," Ben said. "This is probably the only bachelor party I get to throw. I also want it to be the best. I promise that if I need your help, I will ask for it, Tiffani. You have my word."

It was as if she wasn't even listening to him. She started checking things off on the list in front of her. "So I know that it's next Saturday. You have already decided on a guest list, which you will send to me today, and those people have been informed to meet at the golf course at one."

"That's right."

"After golf, you are going to your place to play cards. Where is dinner going to be?"

"I was thinking we would check out the festival in town, stop by the booth that sells Frank's wings."

Shelby loved Frank's. They had the best chicken wings in the world. Shelby, Ben and Topher used to go there all the time in high school.

"Festival food? Wings?" Tiffani frowned. "That's what you want to have for dinner with all of Nicholas's friends?"

"Again, you aren't going to be there, so what's it matter where they eat?" Shelby asked.

"You're not going to be there either, so maybe stay out of this," Tiffani snapped.

"I love Frank's. It was my idea," Nick interjected, pulling Tiffani's attention away from Shelby. "It sounds like Ben has it under control. Let's put the list away and just enjoy breakfast together." He kissed her again and Shelby wanted to bolt from the table.

Tiffani closed her notebook and opened up a packet of artificial sweetener for her coffee.

"Hey, Ben, we should add Walker and Shelby to the guest list," Nick said. For a guy who got in people's heads for a living, he seemed oblivious to the fact that Shelby's mere existence drove his fiancée completely mad. "You guys will still be in town next weekend won't you? Shelby knows how to golf. What about you, Walker? You ever go out and hit the links?"

Before Walker could answer, Tiffani interrupted. "Honey, I don't think it's a good idea to change the guest list after it's already been finalized."

"We don't want to cause any trouble," Shelby said, trying to take the high road. "I think Tiffani is worried that we'll get you in another fight. Hanging around with me, you might end up with a shiner like Walker's, Nicky."

"Don't call him that," Tiffani said with a sneer.

"That's his nickname. It's been his nickname since forever."

"When he was a child. He's a grown man."

"Ladies," Nick tried to interrupt.

Shelby couldn't hold back. "Is it because he's a man or because you don't like it? I know that he doesn't particularly like Nicholas, yet you call him that."

"What would you know about what my fiancé likes and doesn't like to be called? You haven't lived in this town for a decade."

"Okay, whoa, whoa, whoa," Ben said,

reaching for Shelby's hand. "Let's take it down about ten notches, shall we? Shelby, come step outside with me for a second."

"Why do I have to go outside? All I did was call him Nicky."

"Oh, that's not all you did and you know it." Tiffani's voice held fire. "His hand is broken because of you. You sure are good at breaking the Harper boys, aren't you? Almost killing one of them wasn't enough for you?"

Shelby glared at Tiffani. "Excuse me?"

"Okay, maybe we should step outside," Nick said, pushing back on his chair to stand up.

"No," Ben said. "We're going to go cool off outside for a second. Right, Shelby?"

Shelby didn't answer, but she stood up without breaking eye contact with Tiffani. Ben walked behind her as they went to the diner's entrance. Shelby pushed the door open with a little extra gusto and started pacing back and forth on the sidewalk.

"I'm going to give you a couple minutes and then we'll talk."

"I don't need to talk. Actually, you know what I really don't need? I don't need Tiffani Lyons telling me who I can or can't hang out with. I also don't need Tiffani to tell me how to act at Maggie's house or to insinuate that me driving a car somehow makes everyone in this town unsafe. And most of all I don't need Tiffani to remind me of the damage I caused when we got in that accident."

"Tiffani was wrong to say that to you. She is getting married in two weeks and it's making her a little on edge. She thrives on being in control of her world and you, my friend, thrive on doing whatever the spirit moves you to do in the moment. You two are complete opposites."

"Oh, and I suppose my way of doing things is the bad way. I should be more like her, right?"

Ben stayed perfectly calm. "I never said one of you was good or bad. You're just different. Just because she likes to know what's going to happen every minute of every day doesn't mean that you have to. It's what works for her. The way you live your life, appreciating the spontaneous moments, is what works for you."

Shelby put her hands on her head and took some deep breaths. Ben always knew the right thing to say. He was always able to defuse her bomb. She calmed down and stopped pacing.

"How can you let that woman marry your

brother? He is a happy, easygoing guy. He's smart and funny. He could literally marry *anyone*!"

"I have to keep telling myself that he's happy with her," Ben weakly asserted. Shelby could tell that he wasn't fully on board with this marriage.

"She is going to make him constantly question everything he does because she loves to make people think that she deserves to have an opinion about everything, even things that have nothing to do with her."

"Listen," Ben said, putting his hands on her shoulders. "I don't totally disagree, but I also don't like telling anyone who they should or should not be in love with."

Shelby knew why he felt that way. The only reason he had agreed to keep them a secret was because they both feared people would convince him he shouldn't be with someone like her. Too bad for him that no one did. "This is your brother and the biggest commitment of his life. If you think he's making a mistake, shouldn't you at least say something?"

He shook his head. "I don't know."

"You want to be supportive, I get it, but what if she makes him miserable and you didn't voice your concerns when you had the chance?"

"Listen, I'll think about talking to Nick, but I need you to be on your best behavior for the rest of breakfast. You were letting her push your buttons."

"She's so good at it. It makes it hard not to push hers back. What can I say?"

"You can say that you're sorry for letting things get heated. You are here to eat your breakfast and spend some time with old friends. You are not here to cause trouble."

Shelby knew he was right, but that didn't mean she wanted to listen to him. Being levelheaded was hard. She had been working on it, but it still sometimes evaded her.

"Fine. She better apologize after I do."

"She won't. You know she won't. She will probably pretend that she needs to think about whether or not she can accept your apology just to see if she can get you all fired up again and point the finger at you for being the bad guy."

Shelby kicked the ground. "Oh, she'll totally do that. I am not going to give her the satisfaction."

"That's what I wanted to hear." He reached for her hand. As soon as he wrapped his hand around hers, Shelby's whole body relaxed. His touch was even better than his words at getting her to calm down.

"Remember how you used to hold my hand when we went through the haunted corn maze every Halloween over at Granger Farm?" she asked. "You told me it was because you were scared, but I knew you could tell that I was terrified but would never in a million years admit it. You acted like you were afraid so you could take care of me. That was pretty amazing of you."

He feigned surprise. "You were scared? No way."

"You've always made me feel safe. Just being around you helps me relax. I don't know how you do it."

He tightened his grip on her hand. "I'm happy to help. You ready to go back in there and eat some breakfast?"

"Ready as I'll ever be. Why did Nick have to fall in love with Tiffani Lyons? There are so many people in this world. Lovely, wonderful women. He couldn't ask one of them to be his wife?"

"We Harper boys have a bad habit of falling for who everyone else thinks is the wrong girl, I guess."

Shelby wished she could tell him he was wrong, but he wasn't. Nick and Tiffani were as bad for each other as Shelby was for Ben.

They went back inside to find Walker and Nick laughing about something. Since when had they become best friends? Shelby let go of Ben's hand and stood behind her chair.

"Tiffani, I'm sorry I lost my cool. I'm here to have some breakfast and catch up with old friends. I don't want to fight with you and I'm sorry if I made you feel like I did."

Tiffani's mouth fell open as if she couldn't believe that an apology could come out of Shelby's mouth. Nick gently elbowed her and she snapped her mouth shut.

"Don't you have something you want to say, Tiff?" Nick asked.

Shelby wasn't about to hold her breath. Tiffani probably wouldn't accept her apology and she sure as heck wasn't going to apologize for being rude.

Tiffani blew a breath out of her nose. "I'm sorry for being so tense. Wedding planning has made me a little anxious. I didn't mean to take out my anxiety on you."

Shelby glanced out the window behind Tiffani to see if pigs were flying.

Ben put his hand on her back to get her

attention. "That's understandable. Isn't it, Shelby?"

"Yeah, understandable." She pulled out her chair and sat down in complete disbelief. What kind of trickery was this?

The waitress brought the food and everyone was too busy stuffing their mouths to talk. Shelby didn't trust Tiffani. One apology wasn't going to change that. They had a long history of not liking one another. Just because Nick fell into her trap didn't mean that Shelby would.

As everyone was finishing up, Ben got a text message and had to excuse himself from the table to make a call. Walker excused himself to go to the bathroom and Nick went up front to pay the bill, leaving Tiffani and Shelby alone at the table.

"I don't think you need to stress too much about your wedding," Shelby said. "I'm sure it's going to be perfect. You don't do things any other way."

Tiffani dabbed her lips with her napkin. Her expression hardened. "Do not speak about my wedding. Do not think about my wedding. I plan to do everything in my power to make sure you have nothing to do with my wedding. You ruin everything you touch, Shelby Young. You should have stayed away."

Just like that Shelby lost any doubt. She was not going to let Nick marry Tiffani.

CHAPTER ELEVEN

WHY DID THINGS have to go haywire at work at the same time things in Ben's personal life were chaotic?

"Was anything else vandalized?" Ben asked as he stared at the red spray-painted message scrawled across the billboard his dad made him buy for the election. Someone had painted a mustache and pointy ears on his head. The word *pig* was sprayed over the word *hero.*

"The mustache and ears showed up on one of Shannon Gertz's billboards. You know the lady who sells insurance," Deputy Simon said. "There must have been some bored teenagers running around last night."

"Seems like a good time to take this thing down. It should have been gone a while ago."

"I can ask some kids I know up at the high school to see if they've seen anything posted on social media or heard anything. Kids today like to film themselves doing everything, even things that can get them in trouble."

"See what turns up. I'll make a call to get this down." Ben didn't have time for this nonsense. He needed to write end-of-the-month reports today and finish three performance evaluations as well.

This was not how he wanted to start his shift. His morning had already been tense enough thanks to Shelby crashing his breakfast meeting with the bride- and groom-to-be. He'd never understood why Tiffani had it out for Shelby. Shelby had been rough around the edges when she came to Goodfield, but for the most part, she had been quiet and kept to herself. She'd hardly been major competition for Tiffani. Shelby despised attention from people other than those close to her. She'd had no interest in dethroning Tiffani.

Something about Shelby still rubbed Tiffani the wrong way, though. She acted like Shelby's arrival in town sixteen years ago and then her disappearance had made some kind of monumental impact on her life. Shelby was right, Tiffani had a way of making everything about herself. At least she had apologized. Shelby might disagree, but maybe Tiffani could be better than they both thought.

The office wasn't very busy when he arrived. He reminded the deputies that roll call was in ten minutes. Today, he planned to finish his paperwork and spend the rest of his evening shift on the roads, keeping the streets safe from Friday night drunk drivers.

"I heard someone decorated your old billboard," Mitchell said, popping his head in Ben's office.

"You got some information about who might have done something like that?"

"No."

"Then I guess there is nothing to talk about. Is there, Deputy?"

Mitchell glowered at Ben before leaving without saying another word. If Ben didn't think Mitchell had better things to do with his life, he might be his number one suspect.

After roll call, Ben shut his door and got to work. He told everyone not to bother him, but around five o'clock, there was shouting outside his office.

"Miss, you need to calm down."

"Calm down? You bring me in here after she assaulted me and you want me to calm down?"

"*I* assaulted *you*? That's fresh."

Ben knew those voices. He held on to his doorknob and said a prayer that he was wrong. As soon as he opened the door, he knew his prayer had not been answered.

"What is going on?"

Shelby's eyes were wild with rage. "She did this, Ben. I sure hope you don't think she's changed because Nick made her apologize at breakfast. She didn't mean it. She doesn't regret being a *jerk*!"

"The only jerk in this town is you. You have serious issues. Issues no one here wants to deal with. Why don't you go back to where you came from? No one wants you here." Tiffani's hair was disheveled, her clothes dirty.

"Separate these two in the interrogation rooms, and someone needs to debrief me immediately."

Lieutenant Frye followed Ben into his office. "We got a call about a domestic disturbance outside a house on Lake Street. When I got there, those two were screaming at each other and before I could intervene, they started shoving. One of them tripped over a landscaping rock and they both fell, tumbling down this little hill. I tried to mediate, but they wouldn't stop yelling at each other, so I called backup and we brought them in for disturbing the peace."

Ben pinched the bridge of his nose. This

was ridiculous. "Let me talk to them. I would like to kick them both loose from custody. We don't need to make this bigger than it already is. I'll see if I can calm things down."

Ben went into the room with Shelby first. She was sitting at the table with her hands handcuffed behind her back. He pulled out his keys and removed the cuffs.

"Three times. That has to be some kind of record."

"This was not my fault," she began.

Ben held up his hand to stop her. "Don't even try to go there. I don't want to play that game. Just tell me what happened so I can tell you that you're both to blame and let you go."

She glanced up at the ceiling and sighed. "If you've already made up your mind, why should I bother telling you what happened?"

He started to stand. "I can go ask Tiffani to tell me what happened if you don't want to."

"Sit down," Shelby snapped.

Ben slid back in the seat. "What happened?"

"I finished work today and went back to Maggie's. We were sitting outside when she got a call that Tiffani wanted to come by to go over what needs to be done before the open house on Sunday."

"Okay, how did that lead to the yelling and wrestling match on the front lawn?"

"Tiffani came over and immediately started judging everything. She told Maggie she needed to take down this and put that away. She made comments about how my room smelled and how Maggie should consider cleaning the bedding before the open house, like I left some kind of stink all over the place."

"Maybe it wasn't as personal as you think. This is Tiffani's job and she's very good at it. She sells a lot of houses."

Shelby's eyes flashed with anger. "If you're going to defend her, you might as well go get her version of the story because mine doesn't matter."

"I'm not defending her. I am explaining that so far, you've told me that she made some suggestions to make the house more attractive to potential buyers. I get that you took offense, but it doesn't mean she meant it that way."

"Well, maybe this will convince you. We went outside and she had to remind me one more time that I wasn't allowed to be at the house on Sunday while the open house was going on. I told her that I had no intention of causing Maggie any trouble. And do you know what she said to me?"

Ben was afraid to find out. "No idea."

"She said, 'You've never been anything but trouble for that poor woman. No wonder she didn't adopt you when she had the chance.'"

Ben took a deep breath and had to rein in his own emotions. He knew he was only getting one side of the story, but it was hard to believe Tiffani could ever justify saying something so mean.

"You know that Maggie—"

Shelby stopped him. "I know how Maggie feels. I know if I had wanted her to, she would have adopted me in a heartbeat. It's the fact that Tiffani would think it was okay to throw something like that in my face, not even knowing why Maggie didn't do it."

"I don't understand why she hates you so much," he said, shaking his head.

"I don't even care that she hates me. She can hate me all she wants, but why does she have to be such a—"

"Okay, I'm going to go talk to her. I want you to sit in here and do your best to calm down. I know that you're mad and you have every right to be, but I need you to take some deep breaths so I can get you out of here faster."

Shelby's eyes were welling with tears. She tried to wipe them away before they could fall. Ben got up and knelt next to her. He pushed her hair back over her shoulder so he could see her face. It killed him to see her so hurt, so demoralized.

"Listen, Tiffani doesn't know the first thing about the relationship you have with Maggie, so she makes assumptions. I know Maggie loves you like a daughter. Always has. You told me a long time ago that you only worry about what the people you care about think. Everything else is just noise. Tiffani is just noise."

Shelby sniffed and turned her head away from him so she could swipe at more tears.

"I know." Her voice was rough with emotion.

"I'll be right back and we'll get you out of here, okay?"

Shelby nodded her head.

Ben stood up and strode out of the room. He needed to tread carefully. This was his brother's fiancée. Maybe Shelby was right, maybe Nick needed to know Tiffani wasn't the kind of person he thought she was. She had hurt the person Ben cared about more than anyone in the world. Shelby's life had been a series of rejections and there had been too many people who had made her feel like she wasn't good enough.

None of those people had been right about her, though. Shelby was smart, resilient and brave. He needed to remind Tiffani that making people feel small didn't make her big. It only made her look weak and petty.

Ben entered the second interrogation room, and Tiffani jumped to her feet. "Thank God you're finally here. You need to get me out of these handcuffs. Can you believe that cop had the audacity to put me in handcuffs?"

"I can't do that just yet, Tiffani. Sit down."

"What do you mean you can't do that? You're the sheriff, aren't you? You can do whatever you want."

"I am the sheriff and that means I don't get to do whatever I want. It means I need to follow rules and be a leader by example. I need you to sit down."

Tiffani sat down with a huff. "Your brother is going to be really mad that you held me here like some kind of criminal when I was the victim here."

"Did you know that Shelby was only five

years old when her biological mom died of cancer and her dad decided he couldn't raise a kid on his own?"

"What?" Tiffani's face showed her confusion. This wasn't the conversation she expected.

"Did you know that she was encouraged not to cry about missing her mom because it made her first foster parents feel bad? Did you know that some of the kids in the homes she was sent to called her trash because the system made her use black garbage bags to move her personal belongings?"

Tiffani's gaze dropped to the table between them. Ben wanted her to understand that what she did was cruel.

"Were you aware that she once had foster parents who refused to feed her for days if she looked at them disrespectfully? I'm still not sure how someone looks at someone disrespectfully, but they ended up punishing her for it multiple times until someone at school noticed she was hoarding food at lunch and asked her about it. She also hates teddy bears because the case workers used to give her one every time they had to move her to a new house because someone thought a stuffed animal would somehow make the feeling of being unwanted hurt less."

Tiffani stayed silent.

"Did you know any of that?"

She lifted her head. "No," she whispered.

"No, you didn't. You know why? Because Shelby never wanted your pity or your sympathy. Shelby's whole life has been about survival. She puts on a front to keep people away because most people have not been kind. They judge her for things out of her control and they use their words as weapons. You were not kind today, Tiffani, and your words hurt someone I care about."

Tiffani dropped her head again. He couldn't tell if he was getting through or not.

"And for the record, Maggie was the first person who made Shelby feel like she wasn't a burden. Maggie made it okay to make mistakes because mistakes can be forgiven. Maggie loves Shelby and Shelby loves Maggie. They didn't need labels and they didn't need papers to tell them that they were family. What you did today by insinuating that Maggie ever felt any other way was out of line."

"I get it. I was unkind, but so was she and she put her hands on me. I want to press charges for assault."

Was she serious? After everything he just told her, she wanted to file charges?

"Have you not listened to a word I said?"

"I heard you. You have always been blinded to who she is, Ben. You're falling all over yourself to do her bidding, just like you did as a kid."

Ben took a deep breath before he said something he would regret. "If you file assault charges against her, I will have no choice but to detain you for disturbing the peace. Understood?"

Tiffani's eyes went wide. "Are you kidding me? You're going to arrest me?"

"It's really up to you. I can release both of you or you can press charges and I can hold both of you."

If steam could have come out of her ears, Ben was sure it would have. "This is a travesty of justice."

"Does that mean I can let you two go?"

Tiffani closed her eyes. "She wins again. Can you call Nick and ask him to pick me up?"

"I can."

Ben didn't need to call Nick. He was already there with Maggie. Ben brought them both into his office.

"Are you charging them with anything?" Nick asked.

Ben shook his head. He needed to have a serious heart-to-heart with his brother. There was no way that someone as compassionate as Nick would be okay with the way Tiffani was handling this situation. "We're going to send them both home."

"Thank you," Maggie said. "I don't know what happened. I ran inside to get a pen and notebook to write down Tiffani's suggestions and, the next thing I know, they were screaming at each other. Someone must have called the police. I suspect it was Carl across the street. He's always minding everyone's business on our block."

"Well, the good news is no charges are being filed. We have one problem, though. I can't release them both to you two. I assume you came together."

"Why not?" Nick asked.

Ben wanted to say that he refused to subject Shelby to Tiffani any longer, but he had to be careful and wait until he was home to delve into the real issues with Nick. "They need to stay separated. Emotions are still running high."

"Have you had them sit down with each

other and work things out like adults?" Nick clearly had blinders on.

"I'm not a mediator. And honestly, I don't think there's a mediator on this planet who could get those two to see eye to eye."

"Oh come on." Nick sat forward in his chair. "Can I mediate so I can take them both home? I think it would do them good to be heard and come to a resolution."

"Like I said, I don't think it's a good idea."

Nick wouldn't let up. "I'm sure Tiffani would feel better if she knows Shelby has her temper under control."

Ben had exerted all of his restraint. Tiffani had crossed a line and he wasn't about to let everyone think that what happened was Shelby's fault. "And I'm sure that Shelby would feel better if she knows Tiffani actually took enough time to reflect on why being cruel is not okay before she has to see her again."

Nick's forehead creased and a line appeared between his brows. "Whoa, are you saying that they're here because of something Tiffani said?"

"I am, and I think we need to have a real long conversation about what happened here today when I get off work. Right now, you need to trust that I have everyone's best interest at heart, and it is in everyone's best interest to not put Shelby and Tiffani anywhere near one another."

"I want to talk to Shelby," Maggie said. "Can I do that while you get her released?"

"Sure. Nick, you're welcome to wait with Tiffani as well."

"I'd appreciate that."

He put Maggie in Shelby's room. "I'll be right back. I just need to clear things up with the officer who brought you in, then I can take you and Maggie back home."

"Thank you, Benjamin," Maggie said.

Shelby pressed her lips together, still fighting her emotions. He gave her a wink to let her know he understood. He opened up Tiffani's door next. Nick rushed past his brother and Tiffani ran into his arms.

"Are you okay?" he asked, holding her close.

Tiffani didn't answer. Ben prayed she would be honest with Nick about what happened even if it meant she had to admit to being wrong. He didn't like the idea that she might manipulate his brother into thinking that she was the victim of the big, bad Shelby Young.

"I'll finish things up with the paperwork and then you two will be free to go."

"Thank you," Nick said. Tiffani remained silent, but made eye contact. She had to know that he would set Nick straight if she wasn't truthful. He hoped he could convey that through a look.

Once Ben handled the procedural stuff, he released Tiffani first. When they were gone, Ben offered to take Shelby and Maggie home. They were both quiet in the car.

"Do you want me to pick up some dinner?" Ben asked. "We could stop anywhere you'd like."

"I don't want to be in the back of a police car any longer than I have to be," Shelby replied.

"We have some leftovers to eat," Maggie said. "We'll be fine. Thank you."

He pulled into Maggie's driveway. "Can I talk to Shelby for a minute?"

Maggie looked over her shoulder for Shelby's consent.

"It's fine. I'll be right in, Mags."

"Thank you for the ride, Benjamin," Maggie said, getting out of the car.

When she shut the door, Ben turned around

so he could see Shelby face-to-face. "Did you tell her what happened?"

"I told her it was stupid and not worth me explaining. I offered to go back to the hotel to make things easier on her, but she doesn't want me to go. She's always a glutton for punishment."

"Spending time with you is not a punishment. Maggie hasn't been this happy in a long time." He wanted to tell her he felt the same way. Spending time with her in any circumstance other than this was something he'd choose without a second thought. "You should stay here if you want to stay here. Don't let Tiffani dictate how you live your life."

"Trust me, I won't."

"Mind if I ask why you didn't tell Maggie what Tiffani said?"

"Because she would fire her," Shelby replied like it was obvious.

"You're worried about Tiffani losing her commission?"

"No, I'm worried about the stress it would put on Maggie to have to find a new real estate agent. She doesn't need that right now."

Of course, Shelby was looking out for Maggie. "Well, that's nice of you."

"I don't think Tiffani would learn a thing

from losing the sale of one house. I do think she'd wake up if, say, your brother didn't marry her in a couple weeks. I'm going to—"

"*I'm* going to talk to him tonight," he warned. "You don't need to do anything."

"I guess I just cross my fingers extra hard that you get through to him. Nicky is smart, I keep telling myself. Can you let me out of here?"

Ben got out and opened the door for Shelby. "Nick's a good person who should be with a good person."

"That's what they used to say about you."

Ben frowned. "You're a good person, Shelby."

She made a face to show she didn't believe him. "Thanks for the ride, Harper. Let's hang out again when you aren't at work."

He got back in the car and watched her walk up to the house. If there was a way for him to eliminate this need she had to always paint herself as the bad guy, he would.

Ben's phone chimed with a text. His brother had sent him a message.

Call me ASAP

CHAPTER TWELVE

"YOU'RE NOT GOING to leave, right?" Maggie said as she set the table.

"I'm not leaving tonight."

"I don't know why you and Tiffani were fighting, but if it would help, I can hold off on selling the house until you have to go back to California. She wouldn't need to come over for any reason."

Shelby didn't want Maggie to feel like she had to fix this for her. She shouldn't have to protect Shelby from the likes of Tiffani.

"I promise not to cause you any trouble, Mags. When Tiffani needs to be here to do her job, I will stay out of her way."

"Since when do you and Tiffani not get along?"

"Since I was twelve," Shelby answered plainly.

Maggie cocked an eyebrow. "I knew you weren't friends, but I didn't realize you were enemies."

"I am an acquired taste. Not everyone likes me. Tiffani has never liked me. She has always looked down her nose at me like how dare I exist in the same space as her. Today, I wasn't able to let her nastiness roll off my back like I usually do."

"She seems so sweet. She's marrying Nick Harper. He's a doll. I can't imagine she would treat you like you don't belong."

That was exactly how she treated Shelby. "I've been dealing with people like Tiffani my whole life. They act one way in front of some people and different around people like me."

"People like you?"

The corner of Shelby's mouth lifted. "Super cool, amazingly witty and slightly sarcastic people like me."

Maggie laughed. "My favorite kind of people."

A knock on the door spoiled their fun. Shelby offered to answer it. Ben stood on the porch with his sheriff's hat in his hands.

"Missed me already?"

"Nick is on his way over to talk to you. He wouldn't tell me why. I assume either Tiffani told him the truth and he wants to apologize or she wasn't totally truthful and he wants to hear your side of things."

Shelby's stomach churned. "Since we're making assumptions, I am going to assume it was assumption number two. What if I don't want to give my side of the story? Is he going to make me?"

"You know Nick. He's always been the peacekeeper. As soon as he got his counseling license, he believed he was some kind of superhero put on this earth to help resolve all the problems in the world."

Nicky, Nicky, Nicky. He was such a good guy. Maybe if he hadn't been blinded by Tiffani's phony smile and her Georgia peach facade, he would see her for the controlling attention fiend she really was. Maybe telling him exactly what happened was the perfect way to show Nick what Tiffani was truly made of.

"You know what? I'd be happy to talk to him."

Ben studied her carefully. He was unlikely to believe that she had no issue with having this conversation.

"Don't treat this like a joke. He'll be taking this very seriously."

"What if your brother got a real glimpse

of who Tiffani is? What do you think would happen?"

"I don't know." That was what probably worried him. Ben didn't like going into anything blindly.

"Benjamin? Did you want to stay for dinner again?" Maggie called from the kitchen.

"No, Maggie. I needed to tell Shelby something. I won't be staying. Or should I?" he asked Shelby.

"You don't have to stay on my account. I can handle your shrink brother."

Ben looked anything but convinced.

"He's not staying, Mags!" Shelby shouted while staring Ben straight in the eye. "What do you want me to do? Not talk to him? Tell him to come back later? I think Nick is making the biggest mistake of his life by marrying her. She is not the right person for him. I know that. You know that."

"Then I'm going to stay and tell him that he needs to leave you alone. For his sake and yours. You don't need a reason to dwell on any of the things Tiffani said to you today."

"Always coming to my rescue. Doesn't it get exhausting?"

"You gave me a lot of years off, so I have to make up for lost time."

Shelby loved her independence, but sometimes she yearned to be cared for. Ben had been that person when she was in high school. She could let her guard down around him because she knew he wouldn't take advantage of her vulnerability. No one had ever made her feel like that—not before Ben or after.

"It means a lot that after everything I put you through, you still choose to have my back."

"You're a hard habit to break."

Shelby couldn't stop her brain from imagining what it would have been like if she had stayed. Part of her wanted to believe that there could have been a happy ending for the two of them. It was a fantasy she didn't dare let play out too long. The one that ended with them starting a new life together and getting married.

Shelby opened the door a little wider. "If you're not going to go back to work, why don't you come inside?"

Maggie was busy reheating last night's leftovers. "You are joining us! Shelby, set him a plate."

"No, no, I'm not eating dinner. My brother is on his way over to talk with Shelby and

I felt like I needed to stay to help keep the peace."

"I'm not sure a sit-down between you two is a good idea," Maggie said to Shelby. "You always do better after you get some sleep and have time to think about what happened with a clear head."

"I agree," Shelby said. "Make sure you tell Nick that when he shows up. For some reason he thinks he can erase years of animosity with one conversation."

"For being such a smart boy, he sure isn't using that brain of his, is he?" Maggie asked rhetorically.

Ben leaned against the kitchen counter and folded his arms across his chest. "My brother has always been an optimist."

"You both have that fatal flaw," Shelby said, poking a fork into a piece of chicken in the skillet and blowing on it before putting it in her mouth.

Ben scrunched up his nose. "I do not."

"Raise your hand if you have ever uttered the words, 'every cloud has a silver lining.'" She stared hard at Ben, knowing he had said that about a million times. "How about 'things have a way of working themselves out'?" He'd said that close to a billion times.

"Then there's 'don't worry, can't you see the light at the end of the tunnel?'" A real favorite of the sheriff, to be sure.

"Are you done?"

"Who said 'it can only get better'? Was that you, Harper?" She pointed her fork at him. "Because I swear that was you."

"You are so funny. Do you ever get tired of laughing at your own jokes?"

"Never," she said with a smirk.

"Oh my, how I have missed your banter," Maggie said, bringing the food to the table. "I used to think you guys were so cute together. Little did I know, all those playful wisecracks were really your way of flirting."

Shelby chewed her food while doing everything in her power to not make eye contact with Ben. Was Maggie implying their conversation tonight was also flirtatious? Was she right? Shelby didn't want to make going back to California any more challenging, and if she kept opening up her heart to Ben, he would be in big trouble.

The ring of the doorbell abruptly cut off the debate inside her head. She groaned because those chicken fajitas were even better the second night and would be cold by the time she and Ben convinced Nick that he couldn't have this conversation with her tonight.

"What's the plan, Harper? Are you going to tell him that I don't want to talk to him about Tiffani?" she asked. "Or do I have to do it?"

"Let me try first."

While Ben went to the door, Shelby attempted to get as much food in her mouth as possible. If she was going to be forced to stand up for herself, she wanted to do it on a full stomach.

Maggie set her own fajita down and went to run some interference alongside Ben. Shelby couldn't hear exactly what they were saying, but she definitely heard Nick say something about being confused and needing Shelby to explain. The dread that had already taken residence in her body rooted itself deeper.

Two more bites and Shelby was finished. She took a swig of water to wash it all down and went to the door, hoping the battle had been won for her and that Nick understood if he pushed her to talk, he wouldn't like the things he was going to hear.

"I get it. I know that she's probably mad, but I need to understand," Nick said to Ben and Maggie.

"Maggie, why don't you go finish your dinner before it gets cold? I've got this," Shelby said, giving Ben a look that told him she could handle this on her own. "What's up, Nicky?"

"Can we…" he motioned outside "…talk outside?"

Maggie left them with her parting thoughts. "There's nothing wrong with letting people sleep on it, Nicholas. It gives them a better chance to see things from the other person's perspective."

It was a good argument for not wasting their time tonight. At the same time, Shelby didn't need a good night's sleep to see this from Tiffani's perspective. Miss High and Mighty could take her perspective and—

"Or I'm happy to have this conversation wherever you'd like, Shelby. I didn't realize my brother was going to try playing bodyguard."

"I'm not her bodyguard. Shelby has always been able to take care of herself. I just thought you would listen to your big brother's wise words of advice and let this go for tonight."

"I appreciate your advice, but I just got in a huge fight with the woman I am supposed to marry in a couple weeks. I came all the way over here, Ben, so I can make sense of what happened today."

Shelby thought that little revelation would have made her feel better than it did. The words had been coated in so much disappointment and sadness, she felt kind of guilty.

"Come on, Nicky. Let's go talk outside. We can sit on the deck and hash this all out."

"Thank you," he said, giving his brother an I-told-you-so sneer.

Shelby really did feel protective of Nick. He was the little brother she never had. He had been picked on growing up for the opposite reasons that she had. People thought he was an easy target because he was smaller and younger than they were. He was too smart, so it wasn't "cool," it was nerdy. She couldn't remember if Tiffani had been mean to him. Knowing Tiffani, she probably didn't pay any attention to Nick back then. He would never have been allowed in her circle.

"I really appreciate you talking to me. I'm hoping things aren't as bad as I think they are."

They had walked around Maggie's house and ended up on the deck. They both took a seat on the cushioned chairs Maggie had out there for bird watching with her friend Sandra.

"Nicky, you are one of my most favorite

people in the world. I know I've been gone
a long time and have no right to an opinion,
but I need to tell you that the woman you're
planning to marry is not a nice person."

"I get why you think that. She was out of
line today—at breakfast and I'm assuming
this afternoon."

"She insinuated Maggie didn't adopt me
because I didn't deserve to be adopted, Nicky.
If that's not out of line, I don't know what is."

Nick's face fell. "She said that? You didn't
deserve to be adopted?"

"Pretty much." Shelby wondered if Tiffani understood what a low blow that was to
someone who grew up the way Shelby did.

"Oh man." Nick held his head in his hands.
He lifted his head and looked her in the eye.
"I am so sorry. I can't believe she went there
to try to hurt you."

"I don't know why she hates me so much.
But she does."

"She doesn't hate you. Tiffani lashes out
when she's insecure or jealous."

Shelby burst with laughter. "Jealous? Of
me? Why in the world would she be jealous
of me?"

"I don't think you realize how people see

you. Or at least, how they saw you when you were in high school."

"Your brother used to call me Trouble and he was my best friend. I have a pretty good idea that everyone else had similar opinions of me or worse." They all thought she was weird, damaged, no good.

Nick laughed. "You were definitely trouble, but that wasn't always seen as a bad thing. Some saw that as being brave and tough. I think people like Tiffani were jealous of the fact that you didn't care what other people thought about you."

Shelby shook her head. "Tiffani used to tell me back then that it's weird I don't care."

"Just because she says one thing, doesn't mean she actually believes it. Tiffani's mom really messes with her head. I know she would give anything to not care so much about what other people think."

He was trying to use his psychological mumbo jumbo to make her feel bad for Tiffani. Shelby didn't want to feel bad for her.

"I don't really care why she said the things she did. It should matter to you that she said them, though."

Nick rubbed the back of his neck the same way Ben did when he was upset. "I'm not okay with the way she lashes out. It really bothers me that she used your foster situation against you, that's just plain wrong. I want to believe that she's not that kind of person."

"I can't lie, Nick. The Tiffani I remember said stuff like she did today all the time. It's part of the reason I came over to talk to Ben when I thought he was the one marrying her. I really hope you are going into the marriage with your eyes wide-open."

"I thought I was. I hope I am. I don't know. Sometimes she puts this wall up, and I don't feel like I can ever get all the way through."

Tiffani grew up in a home with both her biological parents, was given everything she ever asked for, and had more friends than Shelby had fingers and toes. There was no way that Tiffani felt the need to build walls to keep people out. She didn't need to. People didn't think she was no good because she was a foster kid. People had never asked her to pack up her stuff and get out.

"Maybe it's not a wall. Maybe it's your supersmart brain telling you something isn't right."

Nick shook his head. "I don't know. I have a lot to think about."

"You should talk to Ben. Listen to what he says. We both know he's got good advice."

Nick stood up and stretched. He stared down at the lake behind the house. "Speaking of my brother, I feel like maybe we need to talk about that, too."

"Your brother? Why do we need to talk about Ben?"

Nick turned to face her. "Come on, Shelby. I need to know what your intentions are. I am the one who will be here picking up the pieces again if you choose to leave and not come back."

"What if he doesn't want me to come back? Why do you assume I have all the control?"

Nick laughed and sat back down across from her. "Are you serious? Are you really going to act like you haven't been the one in control of your relationship from the start? My brother has always followed your lead."

He wasn't wrong. Ben had let her dictate the rules. Things were different now, though. She didn't have a right to ask anything of him.

"All I've ever wanted is for him to go on with his life and be happy. He'll be able to do that if I stay away. Won't he?"

"As a counselor, I had to get good at discriminating between people who are truly happy and people who act like they're happy so no one worries. My brother has become an expert at acting since you left."

A guilty wave washed over her. What would it take to get Ben to realize he was better off without her?

"I think he refuses to believe we weren't meant to be together because I left before it got bad, but it would have gotten bad."

"And I think you ran because you refused to believe things *wouldn't* get bad."

Shelby did have a way of sabotaging everything good in her life. Mr. Harper's chat with her in the hospital had affirmed that she would definitely ruin Ben's life if she stuck around. She had decided back then not to take the chance he was wrong.

"That's a nice thought, Nicky, but I didn't need to stick around to find out that me and Ben living happily ever after was a fantasy. Why is it that your dad was the only one who got it?"

Nick's face scrunched up. "My dad?"

Shelby didn't mean to bring Curtis into this. "I want Ben to be happy. If he wants me to stay out of his life, I will."

"And if he wants you to stay in his life, you will?"

Shelby swallowed hard. "I don't know. He would really need to convince me that's best for him."

"What's the worst that could happen?"

Was she really supposed to answer that? The one thing Shelby never had a problem doing was coming up with worst-case scenarios.

"I think a lot of bad things can happen," she replied.

"Like what?"

Shelby tried to think of something specific, but came up blank. "I don't know," she said, flustered. "Bad things could happen. Trust me."

Nick's smile broadened. "Or good things could happen, right?"

Shelby had a hard time admitting that because hoping for good things made the letdown when they didn't happen that much worse. "Sure, but not as likely as something bad happening."

"Why do you do that?" Nick's forehead creased.

"What?"

"Give the bad more weight than the good?"

Finally, an easy question. "Experience," she answered.

Nick nodded. "You've been burned a million times. I get it. I work with kids who have had experiences so similar to yours. You know, I went into psychology because of you."

"Because you wanted to make sure there weren't any more kids like me running amok here in Goodfield?"

She made him laugh again. "That's not how you inspired me."

"How did I inspire you exactly? I sure wouldn't have recommended you go into the field. I was never a big fan of psychs. I hated how they messed with my head."

"That is exactly why I wanted to do it. Not to mess with kids' heads," he quickly clarified. "I wanted to do the opposite. I wanted to give kids like you a real ally. I wanted to be someone they could trust because I saw how much you needed that growing up. If you had learned to trust, maybe you wouldn't have run away."

Her trust issues had a lot to do with the choices she made even today. She didn't trust others not to hurt her or trust herself not to do some hurting.

"You're probably right," she said, nodding her head.

"Can you do me a favor?" he asked.

"Maybe." Shelby knew better than to commit before knowing what she was committing to.

"Trust Ben. My brother isn't going to hurt you, Shelby. He would rather die than hurt you. Remember that when you're deciding what to do when your job is done here."

Nick didn't understand that she wasn't worried about getting hurt by Ben. Her biggest fear was hurting him again. The giant lump in her throat made it impossible to put into words what she was thinking. Shelby nodded her head and blinked to keep the tears at bay.

"And one more thing," Nick added. The way he looked at her convinced Shelby he could see right through her and read exactly what was on her mind. "Trust yourself. You aren't a bad person, Shelby. Believe that."

CHAPTER THIRTEEN

NOT KNOWING WHAT they were saying out there was making Ben lose his mind. He was spying. It wasn't very respectful of their privacy, but he didn't care, because he needed to make sure that Shelby was okay. If at any point during this conversation between her and Nick she seemed distressed, he planned on walking out there.

"Who's talking now?" Maggie asked from the kitchen table. She hadn't joined him at the window, but she was just as curious as Ben was.

"I think she is. I can tell she's nodding and he's smiling. That's got to be good, right?"

"Nicky's not going to say anything to upset her. He knows better than that."

Ben wanted to believe that. He wished he knew what Tiffani had told Nick before he let Nick talk to Shelby. That would have eased his mind a bit. He lifted the slats in the blinds again.

"They're hugging. I think they're done." Ben slipped into the chair next to Maggie so it looked like the two of them had been minding their own business the whole time. He grabbed a napkin and a lemon cookie off the plate she had on the table.

Shelby and Nick came in through the back door. Ben resisted the urge to ask a million questions.

"Everything resolved?" Maggie asked.

"Resolved? I'm not sure we can call it that. We both have things to think about," Nick said.

"Lemon cookie?" Maggie offered.

Nick happily accepted. Shelby shook her head and sat down next to Ben. He tried to read her expression. She didn't look particularly happy. She gave him a half smile. Her eyes were red, though. Had she been crying? Like so many times before, he wished he could snap his fingers and make the rest of the world disappear so he and Shelby could be alone. When it was just the two of them, he could get her to confide in him and there was at least a chance he could make things better for her.

There was only one sure way to get her to himself for a moment. "I should probably get back to work. I am still on duty. Shelby, you want to walk me out?"

"Um, sure." She stood up and followed him to the door after he thanked Maggie for everything and told his brother they would talk at home.

It wasn't until they were outside that Ben dared to question her. "Are you okay?"

"I'm okay enough," she replied.

"I'm sorry if he upset you. You've been through enough tonight."

Shelby shook her head. "He didn't upset me. I feel like I made him feel worse instead of better. He's going to need your help figuring out what to do. I think he's questioning his decision to marry Tiffani."

"Is that all you talked about? Tiffani?"

Shelby's gaze dropped. It was late and the sky was darker than usual. Cloud cover kept the stars and moon from shedding light. Ben wished he could look into her eyes. She thought she was a good liar, but when he stared into her eyes, he could always tell if there was something else going on.

"Pretty much," she replied.

That meant no. "What else did he want to talk to you about? Did he tell you what Tiffani said happened? Was her version the same as yours?"

"Slow down there, Sheriff. Is this an interrogation or were you just checking to make sure I'm okay, because it's starting to feel more like the former."

Ben didn't mean to grill her. His curiosity had gotten the best of him, though. "I'm just worried about you."

"You always seem to be."

"I think we've established that I am still very much attached," he admitted.

Shelby fidgeted, exposing her nerves. "You should be more worried about Nick. This wedding might not happen. He's seriously considering calling things off."

"Oh man. Calling the wedding off would be the hardest thing he's ever done. I'd hate to see him go through that. At the same time, I don't want him to marry someone who can be so insensitive and malicious. I don't want to tell him what to do."

"It's better for him to get out while he can. Before she destroys him."

"Get out like you did." Ben leaned against his cruiser. Was she trying to convince Nick to run away?

The temperature was dropping. Shelby

pulled her hands into her long sleeves and wrapped her arms around herself. "That was different. I was trying to protect you."

"Right. You were protecting me from the horrible future of a life with you."

She had nothing to say to that.

"You know why I don't want to tell him what to do? Because if you let other people tell you who to love or not to love, you can blame them. If you love who you want to love, you have no one to blame but yourself if you get hurt along the way. I learned that when you left."

"You shouldn't blame yourself. You should blame me. It's so Ben Harper of you to let me off the hook."

"You're not listening if you think I was letting you off the hook. What happened to my heart was one hundred percent your fault. I have been mad at you for a long time because you didn't let me love who I wanted to love."

She rubbed her hands up and down her arms. A hardheaded smirk crossed her face. "Well, that's because *I* believe a real friend tells you when you're being an idiot and in a relationship that's going to break your stupid heart."

He lifted an eyebrow. "Wow, are you calling me and my heart dumb?"

Shelby stepped in his direction, making his breath hitch. She took his hat out of his hands and placed it on his head, adjusting it until she seemed pleased with how it looked. The way she regarded him made his knees weak. It was a good thing he was leaning against his car. Being near her was like being on his favorite roller coaster. Up and down and all around.

"When it comes to me, you've always been completely oblivious. It's the only way to explain why you never were bothered by all my flaws."

In his mind, she was perfect. Shelby was exactly who she was supposed to be and he loved all the little parts that made her *her*. "What can I say? I used to listen to my heart and not my head. That was my biggest flaw, I guess."

Shelby shook her head. "That wasn't a flaw. Your heart is so big and so pure. It's the best part of you. I wish I would have taken better care of it, so I could have been worthy of all that love."

Ben pushed off his car and stood tall in front of her. Following where his heart took him, he reached up and slipped his hand against her cheek. "You are so hard on yourself. It's like I remember you being one person and you remember being someone else. You never had to earn my love, Shelby. You just had to accept it."

"I was nothing but trouble. You called me that for a reason."

"What's life without a little trouble now and then?"

Without asking, he tipped his hat up and kissed her, causing his head to explode with memories of some of the best kisses they had shared over the years. This was how it had felt when they kissed for the first time, Valentine's Day twelve years ago. That time, she had been the one who surprised him. Ben was happy to be the one turning her world upside down for once.

Shelby didn't resist. In fact, she kissed him back and grabbed the front of his jacket to pull him closer. Ten years of separation seemed to vanish. It was like they had never been apart. When she was near, he felt whole again.

He brushed his nose against hers when he broke their kiss. "I've waited a long time to do that."

Shelby's breathing was as uneven as his. Her eyes roamed over his face, searching for something. He hoped he could convey how much he wanted her to let him stay in her life.

"Sheriff?" Dispatch called over the radio. "We've got an 11-81 at the intersection of First and Hammond. Are you able to assist?"

Duty called. There was a traffic accident with injuries. "This is Sheriff Harper, ten-four. I'm on my way."

Shelby stepped back and the space between them felt too large. He reached for her hand. "I have to go, but I think we need to talk."

"You Harper boys and your obsession with talking."

Ben smiled, hoping the fact that she was comfortable enough to tease him meant she wasn't completely freaking out. "I liked the kissing part more than the talking if that makes you feel any better."

She gave his shoulder a shove and he imagined her cheeks were pinker than they were a moment ago. "You need to get out of here and go be sheriff."

"We'll talk. Later."

"Go," she said, pulling her hand out of his grasp.

He had never wanted to go to work less

than in this moment, but he was the boss. Blowing off his job was not an option. He kept his eyes on Shelby as he walked around his car. Part of him feared that as soon as he left, she would disappear. Opening his heart to her again meant taking the risk that she might walk away without looking back like she did last time.

The reward and the risk were both huge. He wanted to believe that she was more emotionally mature than when she was eighteen. She wouldn't take off without saying goodbye this time.

Ben drove away not feeling exactly confident. He tried to focus on that kiss.

"Sheriff's here," he heard Deputy Russo say when he got out of his cruiser.

Deputies Mitchell and Russo seemed to have the scene secured. There were two cars involved in the accident, one with significant damage. The ambulance had already responded and the EMTs were talking to one of the drivers.

"Well, well, look who made it." Mitchell strolled over. "Heard your criminal girlfriend needed a ride home again. I don't think we've ever had a woman so desperate for the sheriff's attention that she'd get herself arrested just to spend some time with him."

Mitchell's brazen disrespect could no longer be tolerated. Did he think he was untouchable or that Ben wouldn't have the guts to discipline him for his insubordination? He was about to learn that neither was true.

"When you're finished breaking the code of conduct for disrespecting a superior, you can take over traffic management from Russo." Traffic management was the least popular assignment on an accident scene. Usually that fell on the officer with the lower rank. Ben had no trouble reassigning it to Mitchell given his attitude and behavior.

"I'm interviewing witnesses," he said, unfazed by the comment about the code of conduct.

"Russo, finish interviewing the witnesses. Mitchell is going to take over traffic management." Ben waited for Mitchell to argue so he could add that to the discipline report he was going to fill out when he got back to the office, but Mitchell decided to keep his mouth shut.

Shelby was not a criminal and he was not going to let anyone call her that. The last thing he needed was for the outside world to make it any more difficult for them to figure things out. That was too similar to high school for his liking. Shelby had refused to go public when they were in high school because of people like Mitchell.

That would not happen again. Not when he was this close to convincing her to let him in.

AT THE END of his shift, Ben signed the disciplinary report on Mitchell. He was going to request that Mitchell complete a two-day training course and five hours of counseling to address his authority issues. Ben could have just given him a warning, but he felt he had been too easy on the guy from the start and a message needed to be delivered.

"Have a good night, Sheriff," Russo said when Ben came out of his office.

"You, too, Deputy."

"Hey, I just wanted to say that I don't think it's cool how Mitchell talks to you. I know there are some guys in the department who are still loyal to Bowden, but I think you should know that there are a lot of us who are happy you're the sheriff in these parts now. You lead by example and not just talk. I appreciate that about you."

Ben was humbled by the compliment. "Thank you. That means a lot."

"I just know that sometimes the negative voices are louder than the positive. You need to know that there are positive ones out there."

"I appreciate that."

Ben headed home feeling a tiny bit better about things. As soon as he got in his driveway, he texted Shelby to see if she was still awake. After three minutes without an answer, he slipped his phone in his pocket and got out of the car. Shelby had been a night owl for as long as he knew her. It wasn't like her to be in bed before midnight.

Nick, on the other hand, was sitting on the couch watching a movie when Ben came inside.

"How was work?"

"After your fiancée caused a public disturbance? It was good."

Nick shut off the television. "Yeah, not her proudest moment."

"I hope that means she feels bad about it."

Nick cocked his head. "Of course she feels bad about it. Do you think she enjoyed getting put in handcuffs and dragged down to the sheriff's office? She did not. She has a reputation to uphold in this community. She knows that didn't look good."

"I sure hope the fact that she embarrassed herself wasn't the only thing she felt bad about. She needs to be feeling bad about the way she treated Shelby. Do you know that after I set her straight about everything Shelby went through in her childhood as a foster kid, she still wanted to press charges against Shelby? It was like she didn't even hear me. She had zero empathy, Nick."

Nick got quiet for a second. "That's not who she is. I don't want to believe that's who she is. I don't know why she has it out for Shelby. Shelby has been pushing her buttons, but that's not an excuse."

"Putting Shelby on the defensive is never a good idea. Shelby's defense is always to go on the offensive."

Nick held up his hands. "I am not defending what Tiffani said to Shelby. It scares me that she can be so cruel."

Ben took off his belt. "It's pretty opposite to the way you treat people."

Nick scrubbed his face with his hands. "I know. I guess I just want to believe she has a reason. There's got to be a legitimate reason for her to lash out like that so we can work through it and she can change."

"I think you need to figure that out before you go through with this wedding."

"I know," he said with a sigh. "I love her. There are so many things I truly love about her."

Ben understood what it was like to see someone differently than the rest of the world did. "I don't doubt that. You need to talk to her again and you need to be sure before you make any final decisions."

Nick nodded and wiped his eyes. "I hope Shelby understands that I am not okay with how things went down today. I like Shelby. I have always liked Shelby."

Nick had hero-worshipped Shelby when they were younger. He thought she was some kind of rebel, fighting the hierarchy like the characters in those dystopian novels he used to read. Shelby wasn't some character, though. She was a real person, with real feelings.

"This is where you tell me that you like Shelby, too." Nick said, snapping Ben out of his thoughts. "And then we talk about what's going on in your love life since mine sucks."

"I have no love life." Ben checked his

phone to see if Shelby had responded to his text. She hadn't and he got an uncomfortable feeling in his gut.

"What's the matter?" Nick said, reading his mood immediately.

"Nothing. It's nothing."

"That sounds very familiar to what Shelby said when she came back inside after walking you to your car. Except she looked like the cat who swallowed the canary."

Ben sat down on the couch next to his brother. He wasn't sure he wanted to tell anyone about the kiss. He was used to keeping things between him and Shelby a secret and old habits died hard.

"She seemed happy when she came back inside?"

"I guess you could call it that. What did you say to her out there? Because when I talked to Shelby, she was going to let you decide how things go from now on."

Ben tensed. "You talked to Shelby about me?"

"We may have had a conversation about you and what her intentions are."

Ben put a hand on his forehead. "Please tell me you did not use those words. Sometimes I think you were supposed to be born before me. You're an old man in a young man's body."

"I probably said something like that. I don't remember. She wasn't too forthcoming, though. My analysis is she's torn. She doesn't want to hurt you. She doesn't want to be hurt. It makes it impossible for her to commit to letting you back in her life."

No one had asked Nick to psychoanalyze the situation. "You do know that I don't need you to interject yourself into this...whatever it is that's going on with me and Shelby. We need to figure it out ourselves."

"And how is that going so far?"

Ben knew if he told his brother that they kissed, it would lead to a million more questions. Ben wasn't ready to let anyone else in on this yet. He didn't need other people's opinions to cloud his thinking. The only person he wanted to hear from was Shelby.

He checked his phone one more time. Still no response from her. It was beginning to bug him that she wasn't replying.

"We're talking, trying to figure out what happened all those years ago. We haven't got to the part about what happens next."

"It's important to clear the air between you two, but don't spend too much time dwelling on the past. Decisions about the present and the future have real consequences."

"I'm handling it, Nick. You don't have to worry about me."

Nick laughed. "Right. I know you, did you forget? And I'm not sure what to be more worried about—if Shelby says see you later, have a nice life or if she says she wants to see where this can go, because I'm not sure what that would look like. You have a life here and she has a life in California."

"I'm well aware of that, little brother. I'm not ready to think about life-altering events just yet. Right now, the most I can imagine is I get to be her friend like Walker is."

"You wish you were as cool as Walker."

Ben elbowed his brother. "You've got quite the bromance going on with him."

"Walker is exactly what I imagined being cool looks like. I've always wanted to be cool, but I have to settle for being the smartest guy in the room instead."

"Wow, how do you fit that head of yours through doorways?"

"It's not easy. Sometimes I have to turn my head this way and then carefully slip through," Nick joked.

Ben loved his brother. One thing he wouldn't

change about the last ten years was how close the two of them had become. Things were destined to change if Nick and Tiffani got married, but Ben knew their bond would stay strong. Would it stay as strong if Ben went to live in California? It would be much harder to stay in touch. Not to mention being a cop out West was nothing like being a small town sheriff.

He wasn't going to California. He couldn't even get Shelby to text him back after they kissed. For all he knew, she was so freaked out that she was booking her flight home.

"You okay?" Nick asked, picking up on his mood.

"I'm fine. Tired. I'll see you in the morning." When he stood up, his phone chimed with a text.

Come outside?

She didn't have to ask twice.

CHAPTER FOURTEEN

SHELBY PACED NEXT to Maggie's Buick while she gnawed on what was left of her thumbnail. Coming here was impulsive. Typical Shelby. At the same time, it was the opposite of what she had wanted to do, which was run. So perhaps this wasn't impulsive but brave instead.

Ben's front door opened and he stepped outside. She watched his head swivel back and forth as he searched for her. When he spotted her across the street, she noticed his lips curl upward. He was happy to see her. Should he be?

"Why didn't you come to the door?" he asked. "You know we're all grown, we don't have to sneak around anymore."

"I'm living with Maggie and you're living with Nicky. I don't think much has changed actually."

Ben flashed her a full-on smile. She loved seeing it. "Did you want me to sneak you in through my window? If we're falling into old routines…" He reached up and tucked the hair falling out of her ponytail behind her ear.

His touch made her whole body tingle. The butterflies in her stomach were having a dance party. It would be so easy to give in to her need for instant gratification. Ben was here. He wanted her and she wanted him. Why not do what she wanted?

Because she did not want to do things the same way as last time. Things ended badly back then. She wanted to avoid a repeat of that at all costs. The only way to do that was to set firm boundaries that she could not cross no matter how beautiful Ben's smile was or how much she wanted to kiss those lips again.

"I don't want to go backward. We need to do things differently this time. Don't you think?"

Ben shoved his hands in his pockets. No more touching. He had much better self-control than she did. "Right. We aren't those kids anymore."

That was exactly right. Shelby was trying hard not to be that selfish, reckless kid. She wanted to prove she could think about some-one other than herself. "As much as I enjoyed that kiss tonight. I think we should focus on being friends. Friends were what we were best at and what I think we could be good at again if we try."

He didn't do a very good job of masking his disappointment. "Whatever you want, Shelby. I am willing to try anything because something is better than nothing."

"Good. Friends it is, then."

"I'm glad we're on the same page."

"How did things go with Nicky tonight?"

"He's confused. He wants to believe that Tiffani is better than her behavior today. Things are rocky for sure."

"Oh man. Can you imagine what Tiffani would do if her wedding got canceled this close to the day?"

Ben frowned. "I don't want to think about it. Nick isn't giving up yet. As far as I know, I am still in charge of this bachelor party, which, as my friend, you need to come to. I think my brother would love it if he could call Walker his friend as well. He told me tonight that he thinks he's the epitome of cool."

"Oh my. I need to make sure Walker never knows that. I wouldn't ever hear the end of it." Nicky didn't look like one anymore, but his infatuation with Walker was proof he was still an adorable nerd.

"I won't tell him if you don't," Ben promised.

"Okay, then we'll be there. I appreciate the invite. We probably shouldn't mention the guest list has expanded to You Know Who."

"What she doesn't know won't hurt her. Is that what you think?"

"That is what I know."

Ben's smile was lopsided. It wasn't as big as it was when he first came outside, but at least he was still smiling. "All right. Well, I should get to bed. I'll see you next Saturday."

Shelby nodded and pulled open the car door. She had successfully resisted the urge to throw herself in his arms and kiss him all night long. That would have made leaving for California in a few weeks a million times harder. She was going to prove she could be trustworthy. That she could guard Ben's heart as well as her own.

GOODFIELD COUNTRY CLUB was a public course that had fast greens, thick roughs and way too many sand traps. The sand was where Mr. Cool was currently stuck for the hundredth time today.

"You would think you'd be an expert at getting out of the sand by now given how many times you've had to hit out of the hazards today, Walker," Shelby said with her hands on her hips. She wasn't used to playing this slow. She didn't do anything slowly. It was against her nature. "If you wanted to go to the beach today, you should have just told me. We could have made other plans."

"Ha. Ha. You're so hilarious." The look he shot her was pointed. "Maybe if you could stop flapping your lips, I could concentrate and get out of this thing."

"Use a slight wrist bend at the top of your swing. You want to have an outside-in swing. It will help with the loft. You can do it. High and soft," Nick coached from the cart path.

"I have no idea what any of that means," Walker admitted. He wiped the sweat dripping from his forehead and lined things up. He swung the club and kicked up a ton of sand. The ball, on the other hand, stayed right where it was.

Walker tossed the club in the air. "I give up."

Shelby covered her mouth to contain her laughter. He wasn't used to not being good at something. She couldn't help but love that he was struggling.

"I feel like we should tell him that Nick thinks he's the coolest guy in the world," Ben said, coming up beside her and whispering into her ear. "He could use the ego boost after this hole."

"No way. This is good for him. Me, too. He bet me five bucks a hole. I'm up to fifty dollars."

Ben chuckled. "You are a piece of work, Trouble."

"Hey, I can't help it that he foolishly believed that he'd be better than me. You'd think he would have learned by now."

"I don't know why anyone would underestimate you. That's for sure."

Shelby had wondered the same thing her whole life. She appreciated that Ben was never one of those people. She was also glad that she hadn't bet Ben because he was currently shooting under par.

"I'm going to take Walker to the clubhouse bar to drown his sorrows. You guys can meet us there when you finish the rest of the back nine?"

"Remember to pace yourselves. We still have a lot of partying to do."

Shelby saluted Ben. "Yes, sir. Pacing. Lots of pacing."

The way he smiled at her made her insides turn to mush. She found herself wanting to stay close to him instead of leaving to console Walker. Being near Ben felt like getting a hole in one.

"Are you going?" he asked, making her aware of the fact that she had been standing there staring at him.

"Yeah," she said, backing away. "I'll see you when you're done."

So much for focusing on being friends. Shelby was the one who asked for the boundary and then was, of course, the one who wanted to cross it immediately. Sending mixed messages was definitely not on the list of ways to protect Ben from getting hurt. She needed to be more careful.

"What kind of evil place did you bring me to?" Walker asked, flipping his hat around so the bill covered his neck instead of shadowing his face. He was sitting in their cart, with a sports drink bottle in his hand.

"The last time I played this course, I was seventeen, we all used Topher's dad's clubs and it was the middle of the night. We didn't even keep score, so I kind of forgot how hard it is. Let's go wait in the clubhouse for the other guys to finish. Unless you don't want to forfeit the rest of the holes."

"I can't take the humiliation anymore and

I need something stronger than this fruit punch."

"That's what I told Ben. Let's go," she said, sliding into the seat next to him.

"What is this town's obsession with Valentine's Day?" Walker asked as they drove over the sidewalk chalk hearts drawn on the cart path. "Do they realize how those of us who are not in love feel having love crammed down our throats?"

"This town loves love. Valentine's Day is its spirit holiday."

"I don't think that's a real thing."

"You know, like a spirit animal. The town and the holiday are one."

Walker laughed, which was what she wanted. "Well, I can tell it's rubbing off on you a little bit. I saw the way you and the sheriff were smiling and awkwardly chatting a couple holes ago."

Shelby rolled her eyes. "Don't start with me. I'm trying to do the right thing while I'm here."

"What's the right thing?"

"I want to be a good friend, not a bad memory. I'm trying to think about how I make other people feel instead of just taking what I want."

Walker kept his eyes forward. "And what is it that you want?"

Shelby didn't feel like answering that question for two reasons. One, she didn't want to admit it was Ben she wanted most. Two, she knew that Walker still had feelings for her and she felt guilty confiding in him about her feelings for someone else.

"I don't know," she lied.

Walker stopped the cart. "I think you know exactly what you want. It's pretty obvious. It's also obvious that he wants the same thing. I don't get what's holding you back. As much as I wish it was me, you have never looked at me the way you look at him."

"You are my best friend."

"Oh, I know. Being friend-zoned is why I hate Valentine's Day."

Shelby cringed. "I'm sorry that I crossed lines, knowing I wasn't in a place to actually commit to you. That wasn't fair."

"Apology accepted. I just want what's best for you, and the sheriff seems pretty impossible to top."

How could she commit to Ben when he had a life in Goodfield and she had a life in Los Angeles? As much as she enjoyed that kiss they shared the other night, pursuing it further would only end with them both having to hurt each other.

"I don't know."

"Boy, Shelbs, if you can't imagine being with Ben, how will you see yourself with anyone?"

Seeing herself with someone like Ben wasn't the problem. Being with Ben was easy to imagine. She just wasn't sure she could live up to the idealized version of herself that Ben had believed in for the last ten years. That was the real issue. She still doubted she was worthy of everything he was willing to sacrifice for her.

"He could do so much better than me, and I've gotten pretty good at being alone."

Walker shook his head. "I think we both need a drink," he said, pressing on the accelerator.

The clubhouse wasn't very crowded, but it was decorated like Cupid lived there. It was all hearts and arrows. The waitstaff were even wearing wings and heart antenna headbands. Walker pretended to gag as they made their way to the bar. Shelby ordered a soda while he got himself a beer. She was not going to cause any trouble during this party. She wanted to prove to Ben and to herself that she could control her impulses.

A group of men took over the stools at the other end of the bar. There were four of them and one looked familiar, but Shelby couldn't place him until she overheard what they were talking about.

"I saw the sheriff out there. He was a couple holes behind us."

"What is your issue with the sheriff again?" another man asked.

"How does a guy like that get elected with barely any experience?"

"You don't want to know. My wife said one of her friends voted for him because he's good-looking. I mean who cares about the safety and well-being of our town? At least the ladies have someone nice to look at." The sarcasm was thick.

"Those billboards were effective," the familiar guy said. "He was the hero who saved those kids from the lake. Like that makes him qualified."

"I heard some kids did a number on the billboard on the northside of town."

"Yeah, I'd like to shake that kid's hand and ask him why he didn't think to do that before the elections instead of months after."

"Well, we all know that Sheriff Bowden wanted you to have that job when he retired. I guess you'll just have to run against this pretty boy next time around. You'll win hands down."

Shelby didn't even hide that she was staring. It took her an extra minute to recognize him out of uniform. He was the other officer on the scene when Ben had pulled her and Walker over that first night.

"Don't say anything," Walker said before taking a swig of his beer.

It was hard to bite her tongue, but he was right. This was going to be quite the test of her self-control.

"You need to distract me or I'm going to cause trouble and I really don't want to. Today is about Nick, and Ben has worked too hard to plan this party for him."

"I got you," Walker said, tipping his bottle at her. He called over the bartender and ordered two more drinks.

It was probably a mistake to drink while offended, which was exactly what Shelby was. How dare these guys bad-mouth Ben. After everything he had done for this town and county, how dare they act like he didn't deserve to be sheriff.

"The guys have to be finished soon. Maybe we should wait for them outside," Walker suggested once the drinks arrived.

"Did you hear he has an old girlfriend in town who has become Goodfield's most wanted?" the deputy said. "She's been arrested like four times since she's been here. That's got to be some kind of record."

Shelby was seething. She had been brought into the station twice and arrested once. The second time she was taken in, she was the victim. She did get handcuffed at Buck's, but was released without being charged. It took an exorbitant amount of self-control not to correct this guy and his exaggerations.

"How am I supposed to make people feel safe in a town where a criminal is the sheriff's ex? What does that say about him?"

"Nothing," Shelby barely muttered under her breath. She wanted to set the record straight. She could do that without causing trouble, couldn't she?

The deputy continued, "I'm not so worried about him running with criminals. It's really just another example of how weak he is. You should see how he kowtows to her. I mean, she's *H-O-T*, hot. Bad girl through and through. We all know our milquetoast sheriff isn't man enough for someone like that. She'd chew him up and spit him out."

Walker grabbed her arm when she got up to go give them a piece of her mind. The deputy who thought he was destined to be the next sheriff was a sexist goon. If Shelby could vote, it would never be for a guy like him.

"Don't," Walker told her in a low but assertive tone.

"He doesn't get to talk about me and Ben like that. I just want to tell those guys what's true and what's a lie."

"You aren't going to convince guys like that of anything. We need to get out of here. Now."

"I think I should be allowed to defend myself."

"Getting into a fight in the clubhouse is not what Nick wants to happen at his bachelor party."

She kept scowling in the other group's direction while they continued to take potshots at Ben. Walker threw down some money to pay their tab and moved to stand between Shelby and the men who had her so enraged.

"Let's go outside so Ben doesn't have to come in here and listen to his fan club."

Shelby didn't want to leave. She wanted to

be able to hear what they were saying about her and Ben. Knowledge was power. Walker was right, though. She wasn't going to keep her cool much longer and she did not want to ruin Nick's day. She also didn't want Ben to hear what they were saying about him. This was her chance to protect him and she had to take it.

She grabbed her drink from Walker and threw the men a last dirty look. One of them made eye contact and nudged the guy next to him. They must have worked for the sheriff's department. They definitely knew who she was. They whispered to each other before informing the rest of their little posse of her presence. The deputy who had been there the first night she and Walker were arrested turned around.

"Well, well. Look who's here. If it isn't the town troublemakers in the flesh. You two behaving yourselves? You haven't stolen any golf carts for a joyride, have you?"

Shelby's whole body was hot. She had heard of the fight-or-flight response but had never experienced the fight part so strongly before. "How could I do that? From what I just heard, I've been too busy running around your mind for the last few days. It's really kinda sad that you think you have to talk about other people to make yourself feel big, little man."

Shelby definitely struck a nerve. Deputy Tough Guy took an aggressive stance. Squaring his hips, he tilted his head and chin forward. "Something tells me that mouth of yours is one of the many reasons you've ended up in the sheriff's office so often."

Walker kept a hand on Shelby, probably hoping that would keep her from lunging for the guy and putting him on the floor like Freddy at Buck's.

"Something tells me that mouth of yours gets punched a lot because it's unfortunately attached to your face."

"Are you threatening a police officer?"

"Shelby," Walker said her name like a plea for peace.

"Everything okay here?" Ben's voice stole all of Shelby's attention.

Ben and the rest of the bachelor party had walked in. Walker let her go.

"Let's get that table outside on the patio. Come on, Shelby." Walker tried to pull her away.

"How's it going, Mitchell?" Ben asked.

"You should keep a better eye on your little

friend here, Sheriff. She's bound to get herself in more trouble when left on her own."

"Sorry, it's my allergies," Shelby shot back. "I'm extremely allergic to liars. They make me violently ill."

Deputy Mitchell seemed to realize that she had been listening to his rant longer than he knew. "What is it that you think you heard, huh?"

"You know exactly what I heard. And you know exactly why my allergies flared up."

"All right," Ben intervened. "I like the idea of going outside. Shelby, let's go." He gave his deputy a quick nod. "Have a great day, gentlemen."

Shelby was suddenly flanked by Nick and Ben, who were eager to get her outside and as far away from the deputy as possible.

"What the heck was that about?" Ben asked.

"I wouldn't trust him to have your back out there for a second. That guy is not loyal to you."

"He was a big fan of the last sheriff. There's a few of them out there."

Shelby hated everyone who didn't see Ben for the amazing person he was. "Well, that Mitchell guy is bad news. I don't know what his problem is, but he is trying to stir up trouble for you. You need to watch him."

"Don't worry, Shelby. He can't do anything to me."

Shelby wanted to believe that, but she knew how easily people could spin a web of lies that could trap those who weren't paying attention. Her gut told her this Deputy Mitchell wasn't going to stop badmouthing Ben until he got what he wanted. She also hated that he could use her against Ben. It was another reason to keep Ben at a distance.

The bachelor party crew had a few drinks outside on the patio before heading back to Ben and Nick's for a little poker tournament. Shelby was looking forward to taking some more of Walker's money.

"Shoot," Ben said as they were walking to their cars. "I forgot to grab the poker chips from my parents' house when I was there yesterday. Everyone's headed to our house."

"I can stop by and get them," Shelby offered. "No problem."

"You don't have to do that."

Happy to be helpful for once, she insisted, "It's fine. You take Walker and Nick. I'll swing by your parents' and be just a few minutes behind you guys."

"Thank you so much. I'll text my mom, she'll have them waiting by the front door for you."

"Got it." Maybe she could pull off being his friend after all. She was currently doing a stellar job. She didn't get into a fight. She was being helpful. Nick was having a good time and Ben was happy.

Shelby pulled into the Harpers' driveway and jogged up the brick pathway to the front door. She rang the doorbell but instead of Dana, it was Curtis who answered.

"Hey, I'm here to pick up the poker chips for Ben," she said, unsure if Ben had gotten ahold of him to tell him she was coming.

He stared at her like she was the last person on earth that he expected at his door. "Poker chips?"

"He said he was going to text Dana. Maybe she knows where they are."

"She's not here."

"Oh." Shelby put her hands on her hips so she didn't fidget.

"I know where they are," he said, opening the door wider and stepping back as if to make room for her. "I didn't know they were playing cards."

"Yeah, we're going to play cards before we

go get dinner. You should come over and join in for a few hands."

"They don't want the old man there. Come on in. I'll get them for you."

Shelby entered the house, which was totally different than she remembered. The Harpers had done some updating since she had lived next door. The walls that had been covered with wallpaper were now painted a light gray. The carpeted floors had been switched to dark hardwood. The furniture was also new, at least new to Shelby.

Mr. Harper led her through the kitchen, which was under construction. The old oak cabinets were replaced with white ones. They had knocked down the wall that separated the kitchen from the great room. A huge island now stood between the two spaces. There were no countertops yet and the sink was in with no faucet.

"The kitchen looks great. Dana finally has her gourmet kitchen, huh?"

"It's getting there. They should be done this week. Just in time for the wedding."

"You must be over the moon that Nick found someone like Tiffani." Shelby assumed that was mostly because Tiffani couldn't be more the opposite of Shelby if she tried.

Heaven knew Mr. Harper would have done anything to keep his boys from permanently attaching themselves to someone remotely like Shelby.

"Nicky is happy. That's all that matters to me and his mom."

Shelby wanted to laugh. They sure didn't care that Ben had been happy when the two of them were together. But could Shelby have kept Ben happy? Mr. Harper hadn't thought so.

"Hopefully, Ben will be that lucky someday," she said. "I mean, I was told a long time ago that he would be if I wasn't around."

Her boldness seemed to take him by surprise. He cleared his throat. "He's working on it. The election season was busy. Taking over as sheriff is keeping him busy now. Once he settles in, he'll be able to focus on finding someone to start a family with."

Ben just hadn't found the time to meet the right person? Could that really be the reason he was still single?

Mr. Harper disappeared into the office off the great room and returned with the chips in hand. "So how much longer are you in town?"

It wasn't surprising that he was interested. He'd probably like to circle the day on the calendar and start a countdown. He didn't want her to stick around while Ben was looking for someone to fall in love with. "We wrap up the stunts next week, so pretty soon."

He nodded. "It'll be good to get back home, won't it?"

Shelby had never felt at home anywhere. Maggie's was the closest thing to a home. Sadly, it wouldn't be Maggie's much longer. "I'm sure it will."

"Well, you guys have fun." He handed her the poker chips.

"We will." Shelby couldn't get out of there fast enough. She jumped into Maggie's beast of a car and took off for Ben and Nick's.

Someday Ben was going to meet his dream woman. They would get married and have adorable, well-mannered kids. Mr. and Mrs. Harper would be doting grandparents. Curtis would pat himself on the back for helping Ben dodge the bullet that was Shelby.

She was halfway to Ben's when she spotted a car on the side of the road. Not just any car, but Tiffani's red BMW. The car had a flat tire and Tiffani stood in three-inch heels beside it on her phone. Shelby had two choices. She could pretend she hadn't noticed and keep driving or she could stop and help the woman who hated her maybe more than Mr. Harper did. What would Ben want her to do?

"Ugh!" She pulled over and got out of the car.

Tiffani had her back to her. "I don't want to call Nicholas because today is his bachelor party, Mother. Can you just send someone to help me?"

"Flat tire?" Shelby asked to get her attention.

Tiffani's face registered her displeasure in having Shelby come to her rescue. "I'll call you back." She ended her call and folded her arms across her chest. "Yes."

"Do you need some help changing it?"

"Yes."

"Would you like me to help you?"

Tiffani paused. Shelby waited. If she said no, Shelby was getting back in Maggie's car and going to Ben's, where she would not say a word about seeing Tiffani on the side of the road.

"You know how to change a tire?"

Did she really need to ask? "I do."

"Why would you want to help me?"

Shelby sighed. This was taking too long. They could spend all day dancing around the issue. "Can you pop your trunk, please?"

"Why?"

"Because that's where your spare tire and jack are."

Tiffani pressed the trunk release on her key fob, allowing Shelby to get to work. Less than twenty minutes later, Tiffani had a new tire.

"You're all set. You need to get a new tire as soon as possible. Spares aren't meant to be driven on permanently."

Tiffani nodded. "Okay."

Apparently that was all Tiffani had to say about it. Shelby started for her car. "Have a good one."

"I'm sorry," Tiffani called after her, stopping Shelby in her tracks.

"Sorry for what?"

"For everything. For what I said the other day. For being mean, not just the other day but for as long as you've known me. I have been trying to be a better person, but sometimes, I slip back into old habits. Especially when I'm under a lot of stress. That's not really an excuse. It's just an explanation, I guess."

Shelby wasn't sure what to say to that. She wasn't expecting Tiffani to admit she had a flaw. "I guess I can relate to that."

"I have always been jealous of you. You used to walk around like you didn't care what anyone else thought while all I do is worry about what other people think. I am so afraid that people are going to figure out that I'm not who they think I am."

"Who are you exactly?"

Tiffani shrugged. "I'm still trying to figure it out. I want to be the person Nick believes I am. I was not that person the other day, though. I tried to hurt you because I could, which seems like the worst reason to be mean. I don't know why you helped me today. You had every right to drive on by."

"I won't lie and say I didn't think about it, but I guess we have something in common. We both want to be the people those Harper boys think we can be."

Tiffani snorted a laugh. "Your relationship with Ben has always been something out of this world. That was another reason I was jealous of you. I could tell he was completely devoted to you. No one felt the same way about me. Until Nick."

As tempting as it was, Shelby couldn't begrudge her being loved. "What I had with Ben wasn't like what you have with Nick."

"That's because what you guys have is like next level. You came back and fell right back into your special spot, and it wasn't just

Ben. It was Nick, too. They both care about you, and my jealousy came back with a vengeance."

Shelby wasn't prepared for this little detour to turn into a full-out confessional. Tiffani Lyons was jealous of her. Nick had said so, but she didn't believe him. Hearing it straight from the source made it feel pretty real. She didn't know how to tell her there was no reason to be jealous. Tiffani was the one who was going to be in Nick and Ben's lives forever.

Before Shelby could respond to Tiffani's revelation, another car pulled over behind the BMW. Shelby shielded the sun from her eyes as she tried to make out who it was.

The door opened and Shelby's claws came out.

"What do we have here?" Deputy Mitchell asked.

CHAPTER FIFTEEN

BEN TRIED SHELBY's number again. It rang and rang until it went to voice mail. Again. This was getting ridiculous.

"She's not answering my texts," Walker said, stepping outside to join Ben on the front porch. "Should we go looking for her?"

Ben signaled to hold on a second while he pressed the button to call his dad. It would be easier to look for her if they knew if she went missing before or after going over there.

"Hey, Dad. Did Shelby make it over there to get the poker chips?"

"She did."

Ben wished he could feel relieved, but Shelby was still missing. "How long ago was that?"

"Boy...about an hour ago. Maybe a little more. Why?"

"She's not here yet and she's not answering her phone."

"Well, I'm sure there's a good explanation."

There was certain to be an explanation. Ben just feared that it would be something bad.

"Let's hope so," he said before hanging up. "She made it to my parents and left over an hour ago. It takes ten minutes to get here and that's at the busiest time of day."

"Can I borrow someone's car? Someone needs to go look for her," Walker said, anxiously raking his fingers through his hair.

Nick poked his head outside. "No word?"

Both Ben and Walker shook their heads.

"Can you check to see if there's been any accidents?" Nick asked. "You're the sheriff. Can't you find that kind of stuff out?"

"I can." Ben dialed the office. The sergeant on duty answered. "Hey, this is Sheriff Harper. Can you check to see if there have been any accidents reported in Goodfield in the last hour? And if so were any involving a white Buick?"

"No sir, there haven't been any accidents reported in the last hour. There is one thing, though."

"What's that?"

"Mitchell just brought in that friend of yours. The woman who was involved in that domestic dispute the other day. He's having them book her for assaulting him and resisting arrest. She was pretty fired up when she came in. I don't know if she's been allowed to call anyone yet."

Ben was already walking toward his car. "I'll be there in five minutes."

"What's wrong?" Walker followed him to the car.

Ben felt all his worry immediately shift into frustration. "Shelby decided to ruin the day. You can stay here. She doesn't deserve any friendly faces." He got into his car and slammed the door shut. He rolled the window down. "Do not stop the party," he told Nick. "If I'm not back when it's time to go get dinner, go without me. I will meet you there."

"Is she okay?" Nick asked.

"I'm sure she's fine, but don't save her a seat at dinner." Ben hit the gas and sped out of there. He was going to go to the station and read Shelby the riot act. This was exactly the thing that he feared. She couldn't control herself for one day. He was so angry, he wanted to scream.

He barreled into the sheriff's department without greeting anyone. He went straight for the lockup area. Shelby was sitting on a bench in the back corner of the holding cell. She was in one piece. He'd spent the last hour worried out of his mind and she was alive and well. His emotions were all over the place. He was glad she was okay and so disappointed in her for being here instead of at the party. He was angry and sad.

As soon as she saw Ben, she was on her feet, coming his way. "Thank God. Did Tiffani call you?"

He didn't want to know why Tiffani would call him about this. If what happened today also included Tiffani, Ben was going to have a complete meltdown.

"Today was supposed to be about Nick. I know you're still hoping that he won't marry Tiffani, but until he tells us different, we're supposed to support him. All you had to do was stay out of trouble for one day, Shelby. One day! But you couldn't do it, could you?"

The look of pure shock on Shelby's face was disarming. "You're mad at *me*?"

Ben closed his eyes and took a deep breath. Of course, she was going to shift the blame. He opened his eyes and stared her down. "Who else am I supposed to be mad at? Instead of having a fun and relaxing day, I was pacing my front porch thinking you had been in some kind of terrible accident. Walker and

I were ready to drive all over town looking for you. But here you are. Behind bars. *Again*. Because you have no self-control. Why can't you think about the consequences of your actions?"

"You aren't even going to ask me what happened?"

"Do I need to ask? You're in here for assaulting an officer. Something I could tell you wanted to do earlier but we stopped you. Why can't you ever stop yourself from hurting people? Do you enjoy it that much?"

Shelby gasped as tears filled her eyes. Ben didn't want to hear her excuses, so he got out of there. He knew exactly how she would play this. Mitchell deserved it. He was being a jerk. As if someone's bad behavior justified her bad behavior.

Ben was mad at her and mad at himself for ever believing it was a good idea to welcome her back into his life. To think he had wanted more than friendship! Shelby didn't know how to be in a real relationship. She would have to grow up and she was incapable of that.

"Where's Mitchell?" Ben asked one of the other deputies.

"He's in the break room, I think."

"I want a copy of the arrest and incident logs on my desk right away." Ben stormed off to find Mitchell in plain clothes, calmly drinking a can of soda and chatting it up with one of the officers on duty.

"I want your arrest report on my desk ASAP. Do you understand?"

Mitchell leaned back in his chair. "I'm off duty, Sheriff. Do I really need to write that up today?"

"If you were on duty enough to arrest someone, you are on duty enough to complete your paperwork."

"So let me guess, you're here on your day off to figure out how to get your girlfriend out of trouble again? I'm starting to question your integrity, Sheriff. You seem to be willing to hold certain people to a different standard than others."

Ben didn't appreciate the accusation. "I have no intention of getting anyone out of trouble. I am here because there was a report that one of my deputies was assaulted. I take that quite seriously."

"I would hope so. How can we trust our fearless leader if he doesn't have our backs? I know a lot of men and women in this office who would feel the same."

Ben was done protecting Shelby from herself. The only way she was going to learn was from suffering the consequences. "I am here to make sure everything is done by the book so justice is served. Get started on that report."

He went back to his office where a copy of the arrest log was waiting. According to it, Shelby was being charged with misdemeanor battery of a peace officer and a felony charge of obstructing an officer, which was a big deal. That meant she had assaulted him during the arrest as well. She could end up in jail.

Scrubbing his face with his hands, Ben dealt with the mix of emotions wreaking havoc inside him. He had to remind himself not to feel bad for Shelby. She had brought this on herself. That thought only pushed the anger he was feeling over the edge and into rage.

How could she do this? All she had to do was pick up the poker chips. The log stated that the incident occurred on Hilltop Road, less than two miles from his house. Why was she out of her car at that point? There was nothing around there. It wasn't like she would have been getting gas or running into a store to pick something up.

Ben pinched the bridge of his nose. He needed to manage his feelings so he could think more clearly. Why did Shelby ask if Tiffani had called? Was Tiffani there? Was she fighting with Tiffani and then Mitchell rolled up to break it up? He needed that arrest report to understand. If Mitchell was charging her with battery against a peace officer, he had to be performing his duties as a deputy. What was he doing there?

Maybe he needed to listen to Shelby's side of the story. He wasn't sure he could stomach it, though. He'd wait for Mitchell's report. Glancing outside his office, he could see Mitchell at his desk, clicking away on the keyboard of his computer. He would be done in less than an hour.

Ben stood up and moved to the window. He took a closer look at the deputy. Mitchell didn't have a hair out of place. His face was unblemished. No bruises. No cuts. Ben's gut told him that if Shelby had assaulted him, there would have been evidence. A black eye, a bruised cheek, something. Maybe she had hit him below the belt. That was the only explanation and also quite possible.

Ben snatched his phone off his desk and called Tiffani. He had to know how she was involved in all this. If Shelby had done something to Tiffani, there was no way he and Shelby could ever be friends again. Ben had to be loyal to Nick and if Tiffani was his wife, that meant Ben had to be loyal to her as well. The call went straight to voice mail. Was no one answering their phone today? He texted her to call him as soon as she could.

The desk sergeant led an older gentleman in a gray suit into one of the interrogation rooms. Ben stepped out to see what was going on. That was when he spotted Tiffani standing at the sergeant's desk.

"Tiffani," he called to her.

She seemed stressed, fidgeting with the purse in her hands. Her eyes went wide when she realized Ben was there. He waved for her to come back. She glanced around before pushing open the swinging half door that separated the front desk area from the work area.

"What are you doing here?"

"Something tells me you know exactly what I'm doing here. Come talk to me," he said, leading her back to his office.

"Miss Lyons," Mitchell said with a strained tone. "I was just about to contact you to get your statement. Could I have a word with you?"

"I need to speak with her first, Deputy," Ben asserted.

"You're the one who wanted me to finish this report as soon as possible. I don't know how I'm supposed to do that if you talk to my witness before I do. Let's not forget I'm off duty. I shouldn't even be here."

Tiffani moved closer to Ben. He could sense she was completely unnerved. Her breathing was labored and she didn't take her eyes off Mitchell.

"My conversation won't take that long. Why don't you finish up everything else and then you can talk to Miss Lyons?"

"I'm a little concerned that because of your personal relationship with the offender that you might ask Miss Lyons to tell a certain story," Mitchell said, causing everyone else in the office to stop what they were doing to pay closer attention to what was unfolding.

"Are you seriously accusing me of witness tampering?"

"I brought my lawyer," Tiffani said from behind Ben. "So don't get any ideas."

Ben spun around. When had everyone lost faith in him? Tiffani was about to become family and she doubted his integrity? Had being friends with Shelby damaged his reputation that much?

"I'm not going to make you say anything that's not true, Tiffani. I just wanted to talk to you about what happened."

She was still staring at Mitchell and that was when everything clicked. She wasn't informing Ben. She was warning Deputy Mitchell. One of the officers in charge of the detainees ushered Shelby into the office area and led her to the interrogation room where the older man was waiting. The lawyer. The lawyer Tiffani brought *for* Shelby.

"Come with me," he said, guiding Tiffani over to the same room.

"This is not proper procedure," Mitchell complained.

Ben pointed a finger in the deputy's direction. "You finish your report and don't forget that you are obligated to state the facts."

He knocked on the door and pushed it open.

"Sheriff. My name is Dennis Falls, Esquire. I am here to meet with my client. I was told we would have privacy."

"I just have a few questions for your client and Miss Lyons. It's good that you're here, Mr. Falls."

"Just remember, you are not obligated to say anything," Mr. Falls informed Shelby.

Tiffani's bottom lip was quivering. "Ben, I don't know what is going on."

"You don't know what's going on?" Shelby asked her. "Were you and that deputy in on this together?"

"What? No!"

Shelby shook her head, clearly unwilling to believe anything Tiffani had to say. Ben may have figured out what Tiffani was doing, but Shelby still didn't trust her. She turned on the lawyer. "And who hired you? Did Walker send you over here?"

A crease appeared between Mr. Falls's bushy eyebrows. "Miss Lyons called me and asked me to come. Her father and I are good friends."

Shelby's glare shifted back to Tiffani. "What are you up to?"

"I didn't know what else to do but find you a lawyer. You have to sue that deputy for false arrest or police misconduct. I don't know what, but he should be the one arrested, not Shelby."

Shelby was stunned into silence.

"Why didn't you just call me?" Ben asked.

Tiffani threw her hands up. "I don't know.

I guess I was trying to protect Shelby. I didn't want you to think any of this was her fault. I was trying to get her out of here before you heard she was taken in. I guess I was too late."

"Someone needs to explain to me what happened because I have never been more confused," Ben said.

"What does it matter?" Shelby jutted her chin in his direction. "I'm just a careless sadist, who loves hurting people. Why would you want to hear my side of the story?"

Her anger was justified. Ben felt the weight of his guilt for not hearing her out. "I lost my cool. I should have let you explain. I'm sorry about that."

"You're sorry about that?" Shelby's jaw tightened. "I have nothing to say to him. I don't have to say anything, right?" she asked her lawyer.

"You do not."

"Shelby, I understand why you'd be mad at me, but I want to help you. I can't do that if you won't tell me what happened."

Shelby sat stoically, refusing to make eye contact with him.

"I'll tell you," Tiffani said. "Shelby helped me change a flat tire and that's when your deputy pulled over. He started making some pretty rude comments. He knew that I had been brought in the other day with Shelby and thought that I shared his ill-feelings toward her. He tried egging her on, provoking her to fight him. He said he just needed her to give him one reason to arrest her."

Ben's bad shoulder was aching. He gave it a rub. Mitchell had pushed all of Shelby's buttons. He couldn't completely blame her for falling into his trap.

"So she hit him." He didn't ask because he knew.

"Wow." Shelby stood up. "Can I go back to my holding cell? I can't listen to this."

"What?" Ben couldn't believe she was still angry. "Tiffani is standing up for you right now."

"It's not Tiffani I can't listen to. It's you. In your mind, I always make the wrong choice. I didn't realize how much you've become like your father. I guess I should have known you'd start to see me that way."

"She didn't hit him, Ben," Tiffani said. "She didn't do anything. She tried to go back to her car and leave. He's the one who put his hands on her."

Ben felt his mouth fall open.

"Oh, you weren't expecting that, were you, Sheriff?" Shelby said with a sneer.

Ben was wrestling with a new anger. "Did he hurt you?"

She sat back down on the metal chair. "Not as much as you did."

CHAPTER SIXTEEN

"You can sign right here for your personal effects." The sergeant slid the clipboard across the counter.

Shelby scribbled her signature on the line and handed it back. All she wanted to do was get out of this place. This town. This state. She wanted to be as far away from everyone who lived in Goodfield, Georgia, as possible.

"My car?"

"Your car?"

"I was pulled over on the side of the road when your deputy attacked me. Is my car still there or did they impound it?"

"I'm going to have to check. Hold on a second." He picked up the phone and made a couple calls.

Shelby looked at the clock on the wall. So many hours wasted because of a bad cop.

"I can drive you to your car if it's still there," Tiffani said. She was sitting on the bench where Maggie had sat the first night Shelby had been dragged into this station.

Shelby could barely believe that of all the people who could have gone to bat for her, it was Tiffani who came through and saved the day.

"You've really done enough, Tiffani. You should go home."

She stood up and smoothed the wrinkles out of her tunic shirt. "It's okay. I don't want you to think that you have to deal with all of this on your own."

That was where she was wrong. Shelby had learned a long time ago that the only one she could count on was herself. She had been foolish to believe that Ben was different from all the rest. She had spent so much time thinking she was unworthy of him, but maybe it was the other way around.

The sheriff was busy dealing with his lying deputy. Once the truth had come out, Ben had tried to apologize. He had tried to convince her of his remorse. She didn't care that he was sorry. He had believed the worst. It didn't seem fair that what finally pushed him over the edge wasn't even her fault. He had unleashed all of his resentment over her recklessness when she had finally reined it in.

It didn't matter what Ben thought. When she was back in California, she wasn't going to be subjected to his judgment ever again.

"Okay," the sergeant said, hanging up the phone. "It seems that the car wasn't called in, so no one has picked it up yet. It should be exactly where you left it."

Shelby took the manila envelope filled with her personal items. "Thank you." She turned to Tiffani. "I can call for a ride."

"I can take you to your car." Ben's voice cut through her.

She glanced at him over her shoulder. "I'd rather walk."

"Shelby." He dared to sound exasperated.

"I can take her," Tiffani said as if it was up to Ben who was going to give her a ride.

Shelby headed for the exit. "I don't need a ride. I can take care of myself."

Unfortunately, Ben and Tiffani followed her outside. "I know you're mad at me, and you have every right to be," Ben said. "I'm begging you to let me take you to your car, so I can start to make it up to you."

"I am under no obligation to make you feel better, Harper," Shelby snapped.

"I know you're not. But I'm hoping you'll

show me a little grace and let me do one thing right today."

She searched for a ride on the app on her phone. There wasn't anyone in the area and the first ride couldn't get there for over twenty minutes. She couldn't stand out here with Ben for that long. A ride to the car would be much shorter.

"Fine." She dropped her arms to her side. "Thanks again for everything, Tiffani. I hope you and Nick have a good life. You got a really good guy and maybe he didn't do so badly either."

"Thanks. I feel guilty. If you hadn't stopped to help me, you wouldn't have gotten into this mess."

"It was not your fault. Deputy Jerkface was the only one to blame."

Tiffani agreed with that and headed off to her car. Shelby walked beside Ben like she was on a death march. This ride was bound to be worse than when she had to sit in the back of his police car a couple weeks ago.

"I want you to know that I am going to make sure he loses his job," Ben said when they got in the car.

Shelby didn't respond. Ben could try all

day to make this better and it wasn't going to work.

"I hate that I hurt you."

She stared out the passenger window and stayed quiet. She hated that he'd hurt her as well. Talking about how much they both hated the same thing wasn't going to make anything better.

"I was so scared something had happened to you when you didn't come back to the house. I imagined all the worst-case scenarios."

"Yeah, then you showed up to the station like you wished I had been in a terrible accident. Sorry I disappointed you by being alive."

"I would never want anything to happen to you."

"Right, but on the other hand, I... What did you say? I can't stop myself from hurting others."

"I didn't mean that," he said. "I was mad and I should have taken a minute to cool down before I talked to you."

"Hey, you just finally agreed with me and your dad. Don't feel bad about it."

"Why do you keep bringing up my dad?"

Shelby was done with all this. If she could

go back in time, she never would have convinced Walker to go drag racing with her that one night. Then she never would have shown her face in Goodfield and this little reunion never would have happened.

"You know he was scared to death when you ran away," Ben said. "My mom thinks he felt responsible because they weren't able to be there for you because all their attention was on me."

Shelby shook her head. "You have no idea."

"My parents considered you one of the family, Shelby. They were very worried about you."

"Your dad told me to leave, Ben. He sat me down and explained that every bad thing that had happened to you, and would happen to you in the future, was because of me."

Ben pulled over and slammed the car into Park. "What are you talking about?"

"It doesn't matter. Can we please get to the car so I can pack up my stuff at Maggie's?"

"You're telling me that my dad told you to leave? He suggested it?"

"He reminded me that I was eighteen and that I could go anywhere and do anything. And that if I really cared about you, I would get as far away from you as possible. Why do you think I picked California?"

"I don't believe that. My mom told me how upset he was when you were missing. I remember him offering to help Maggie find you and bring you home."

Shelby was tired. Today was officially one of the most exhausting days of her life. She didn't have the energy to argue with Ben about who said or did what. "You can believe whatever you want, Harper. Can we just keep moving in the direction of Maggie's car?"

"No one wanted you to run away."

"Keep telling yourself that."

Ben got quiet but drove back onto the road. Maggie's car was still on the side of Hilltop right where Shelby had left it. She got out of the car as soon as he came to a stop. She didn't even bother to say goodbye. As soon as she unlocked her car, she realized that she had his poker chips. When she turned around to get Ben's attention, she found him standing right behind her.

Shelby nearly had a heart attack. "Goodness, don't do that."

"We can't end things like this," he said, his voice raw with emotion. He could not deter her. She had to hold her ground.

She reached in the car and pulled out the poker chips. She pushed them against his chest. "Have a great life."

"I was mad and I said things because I was mad. You know how I feel about you."

She pushed the poker chips against him again. He took them from her and she reached up and touched his cheek. "Let's just call this a clean break. No hard feelings. I really do hope you have a great life. It's time we let each other go. Goodbye, Ben."

He leaned into her hand. Shelby could see the pain in those blue eyes. He wasn't lying about being sorry. He might have been lying to himself about not meaning what he said back at the station, though. Sometimes people were the most honest when they lost their filter.

Shelby left him there and got in Maggie's car. At least this time she wasn't running away without saying goodbye.

MAGGIE WAS SURPRISED to see her when she walked into the kitchen. "What are you doing here? I thought this bachelor party was going to go late into the night."

"Well, I guess you could say I ran into a little trouble and my night came to a sad end."

Maggie's brows pinched together. "What happened?"

"I don't know if I have the energy to talk about it, Mags."

Maggie got up from the table and went to the cabinet with her lemon cookie stash. "You come sit down and have some cookies. We'll get some sugar in you and maybe you'll feel more like talking."

"Thank you for being you and for always having my back. I know I wasn't easy to live with, especially in the beginning. You never held my attitude against me and you always made me feel like if I messed up, I'd get another chance to make things right the next time. I don't know how you knew I needed to hear that message."

Maggie gave her a half smile. "When you've been around as long as I have, you learn a thing or two."

Shelby's phone chimed with a text. She had messaged Walker that she was not rejoining the party and that if he needed her, she could pick him up when he was ready to go. He told her he would get a ride and not to worry about it.

I'm coming over.

"Who was that?" Maggie asked.

"Walker is on his way over. I think I might pack up and go back to the hotel with him. We are almost done shooting and I'll be leaving soon."

Her face fell. "Already? I thought we had a little more time left."

"I don't think I can stay here anymore. Not with the Harpers right next door. Ben and I had an intense falling-out tonight. I don't think I could handle running into him again. I need to go back to the Starlight and be done with Goodfield."

"I'm shocked. I thought you and Ben finally reconnected. That things between you were good."

Shelby had thought so, too. Today it became clear that Ben didn't trust her. He would never trust her. "The best thing for me and Ben is to remember the good times and move on. I need to move on."

Maggie covered Shelby's hand with hers. "I don't understand, but I'm going to trust that you are doing what is best for you, my dear."

"Thank you." Shelby's voice broke with emotion.

Within minutes of his text, Walker knocked

on the door. He wrapped Shelby in a big hug as soon as she let him in.

"I should have gone with you to get the poker chips. No one would have harassed you if I had been there."

"It doesn't matter. I just feel bad that I ruined the day for Nick. I hope he's not too mad at me."

Walker pulled back. "Mad at you? He's not mad at you. He's furious with that cop. He's sorry that you had to go through that today. Everyone was."

"How was Ben when he rejoined the festivities?"

"Not very festive. He looked like someone ran him over. He said that he messed up and that he didn't think there was anything he could do to make it better."

He wasn't wrong. There wasn't anything he could do. The damage was done. Truthfully, it had been done long before today. The facts were that they had been trying to patch this sinking ship with duct tape and there was nothing but icebergs up ahead. It was time to jump ship, plain and simple.

"I need to go back to California. As soon as possible."

"That's it? You're done trying?"

"I'm done."

"I'm sorry. I have to admit, I kind of dig those Harper brothers. I think we all could have been friends."

"Hey, I'm not going to stop you from being friends with whoever you want to be friends with. You know that Nicky thinks you are the coolest person he's ever met? He told Ben you were the epitome of cool."

Walker put his hand on his heart. "You're killing me here, Shelby. Nick is a good guy, but I can't keep in touch with your people if you aren't keeping in touch with them. It would be too weird."

"Choosing me over the Harper brothers kind of makes me feel like a big deal. Thank you."

Walker pulled her in for another hug. "I'll always choose you. That's what best friends do."

As much as it meant to her for Walker to say that, it was also a painful reminder that she would never have that kind of friendship with Ben ever again.

"Ben still wants to be your friend."

Shelby pulled away this time. "Ben lashed out at me today in a way I have never seen before. He was so sure that I had gotten in a fight, he didn't even give me a chance to explain my side of the story. It was so easy for him to believe that I was to blame for what happened. If Tiffani hadn't stepped up and had my back, I probably would have been charged with a felony. I could have ended up in jail."

"Way to go, Tiffani. My boy Nick knows a good woman when he sees one. Who would have guessed that you and Tiffani would be parting on better terms than you and Ben?"

"Not I, my friend. Not I."

There wasn't anything else to say. Walker shared some cookies with Maggie while Shelby gathered her things. It was time to put this place in her rearview mirror for good.

When their ride arrived, Shelby put her bags in the trunk and hugged Maggie long and hard. It wasn't until they were pulling away that she noticed Ben getting out of his car next door.

CHAPTER SEVENTEEN

Ben watched as the car carrying Walker and Shelby drove out of sight. Was that really how this was going to end? He wanted a different answer than the yes his head was telling him.

Too many thing were wrecked today—his relationship with Shelby, his brother's bachelor party and his faith in himself. Standing outside his parents' house, he figured he might as well confront his dad about what Shelby said happened over ten years ago. If he was going to blow everything up, might as well get it over with.

"You sure you want to do this?" Nick asked, getting out of the car. He had confronted Ben about what was going on after dinner and made the decision to end his party early. He was the one who said they should clear the air with their dad sooner rather than later.

They could hear the television playing in the great room, which meant their dad was still awake. Their mom was in the kitchen.

"Hey," Ben said, causing her to jump.

"Hey. What are you two doing here? Is everything okay?"

Ben had the poker chips in hand. They were his excuse for coming over but not the real reason. "We brought Dad his chips back."

"Did you guys have a good time?"

"It started off great," Nick said. "It ended... not so great."

"I had a deputy so determined to undermine me, he falsely arrested Shelby and ruined the whole day."

"What? Shelby got arrested again?"

"Shelby was illegally detained." Ben could feel the vein in his forehead pulsing. "She didn't do *anything*."

His mother put a hand on his arm. Her face etched with concern. "Honey, relax. I understand."

Their dad entered the kitchen. "What's going on? What are you guys doing here so late?"

"They wanted to return your poker chips."

"I also need to talk to you," Ben said, wanting to get this over with. "Shelby told me something today and I need to know if it's true."

He expected his dad to look confused, but

that wasn't the expression on his face. He glanced at Nick and then their mom before returning his gaze to Ben.

"You need to understand that everything I did, I did because I wanted the best for you and I couldn't let you ruin your life over some first love teenager baloney."

Ben grabbed on to the kitchen chair beside him to keep from falling over. "So it's true? You told her to leave? You told an eighteen-year-old kid to run away from home?"

"What?" his mom said. "Your father wouldn't do that. Is that what Shelby said?"

"I didn't tell her to run away. I told her to stay away. To stay far away from you. I didn't know she would take that to mean she should leave town."

His mom's eyes were round as saucers. "You did what?"

"He was planning on giving up everything for her. When Nick told me that Ben had been talking about getting married, I couldn't let that happen."

"You told Dad I wanted to get married?"

Nick held his hands up. "Let's not forget I was fifteen years old. I hated that everyone was fighting all the time. Mom and Dad were so confused about why you didn't want to go to UGA. I probably thought it would be best if I explained why you didn't want to go."

"You knew that they were dating before the accident?" his mom asked his dad. "Why didn't you tell me?"

"You already suspected that there was more going on there. If you knew the truth, you would have encouraged their little teen romance and our son would have thrown his future away."

Ben was furious. "So instead, you told her to go away."

"I've already said I didn't think she'd pack up and move across the country. I thought if she believed she was driving when the accident happened, she'd break things off. I felt terrible when she ran away. That's why I offered to look for her. I didn't mean to hurt Maggie and you the way that I did."

Ben sat down, unable to hold himself up anymore.

"Hold up," Nick said. "Why did you say if she *believed* she was driving? Why would you need to make her believe it?"

His dad sat down at the table as well. He covered his face with his hands. Ben didn't like where this was heading. His whole body was vibrating.

"Shelby wasn't driving. Ben was. I was the only one that the police told. Your mother and Maggie were busy talking to doctors. Since it was my car, I was the only one who got the accident report. I didn't file with the insurance company. No one had to be questioned. The police didn't issue any tickets even though Ben wasn't wearing his seat belt. They figured he had been through enough. I just thought if she believed she had been driving, she would see that she wasn't right for Ben. She wouldn't argue with me because—"

Ben slammed his fist on the table. "Because she'd feel so guilty about almost killing me? You were fine with her punishing herself by running away and leaving behind the only people who ever showed her some love and compassion?" Ben wanted to break something. He wanted to scream and tear apart everything he could get his hands on. "Shelby has spent the last ten years hating herself because she thought she hurt me. If you wanted her to think she was bad for me, you accomplished your goal. She definitely left after the accident because she thought she was a bad person. I can't believe you would do that to someone. Especially someone like Shelby.

After everything she had been through in her life."

Nick and their mom stood in astonished silence. His dad hung his head and cried.

"I am not proud of what I did."

Ben got to his feet. He couldn't be in this house anymore. He couldn't look at his own father for one more second. "I don't know how I'm going to forgive you for this. I feel like I don't even know who you are."

"Ben," Nick called after him as he headed for the front door. "Ben, stop."

"I can't be here. I need to get as far away from that man as possible or I am going to end up spending the night in jail."

"Give me the keys. I'll drive us home."

Ben pulled the keys out of his front pocket and placed them in Nick's hand.

"Let me say goodbye to Mom and then we can go."

Ben nodded and yanked open the front door. He stood on the front porch with his hands behind his head. He couldn't slow down his breathing no matter how hard he tried. He had never been so angry, so disappointed, so disgusted.

When he thought about how Shelby had beaten herself up for what happened. How she'd spent the last ten years learning how to control a car because she thought she was the one who'd lost control that day. They had never questioned what they had been told. They had trusted the adults to be honest.

He needed to tell Shelby the truth. He owed her that much.

"Ready to go?" Nick asked, coming outside.

"I wish Shelby was still next door. I have to tell her the truth."

"This is something you definitely need to do in person. Text her about meeting up."

Ben hesitated. "She hates my guts. I don't know if she'll even talk to me."

Nick tugged on his hair. "I can't believe Dad lied about something so big. I can't believe he lied for so long."

Ben was stunned as well. Things could have been so different if his dad had been honest. "I really did want to marry her. I was saving up to buy a ring. I would have had enough after I worked that year we were going to take off."

"I'm sorry things didn't work out the way you planned. I'm sorry that Shelby has felt she was to blame this whole time. It's not right."

"How am I supposed to get past that? How do I forgive him when what he did hurt Shelby so bad?"

Nick put his hand on Ben's shoulder. "I don't know. I hope he does what he can to make amends to you, to Shelby. Heck, he owes Maggie an apology, too."

Ben couldn't imagine what his dad could do to make things better for any of them. Ben didn't even know how he was going to get Shelby to forgive him.

"Maybe I shouldn't tell her. Maybe I should let her go back to California and forget all about us. She's so mad at me, she won't be beating herself up anymore. She'll be able to go on with her life. Knowing the truth might only make her feel worse."

Nick shook his head. "I don't know, Ben. I'm not sure if this is the kind of secret you want to keep."

Ben needed to think about it. Shelby would be leaving town soon. He didn't have a lot of time to decide.

CHAPTER EIGHTEEN

"THAT'S A WRAP!" the director announced.

There was an eruption of applause. The car stunts were complete, which meant that it was time to leave Georgia and head back to California. She was going to book the next flight to Los Angeles that she could find.

"Friday night wrap party. Perfect timing," Walker said. "I don't know about you, but I am ready to party."

Partying wasn't exactly on Shelby's to-do list. Getting away from everyone with the last name Harper was. "I'm going to the hotel, so I can get on my computer and find me an early morning flight back to the City of Angels."

"Oh come on. You, of all people, deserve a fun night. How am I going to enjoy myself when I know you're sitting alone in the hotel?"

"I feel like you'll figure it out because you do not need to worry about me one bit. I am going to shower, order room service, pack and go to bed."

"Shelby!" A production assistant waved a hand to get her attention. "Shelby Young?"

"Yeah."

"We've got someone trying to get past security." The man pressed the button dangling from the cord attached to his headset. "What was the name again? You're breaking up." He waited for an answer. "Someone named something Harper wants to talk to you. Do you want us to send them away or do you want to go to the checkpoint and sign them in?"

Seriously? She was so close to getting out of here and Ben had to show up now? Of course, she had been easy to find today. It had to be all over the news that they were shutting down sections of the highway to film scenes today.

Walker gave her that you-know-what-you-have-to-do look. She closed her eyes and took a deep breath in and out.

"I'll head over to the checkpoint."

Walker gave her a thumbs-up. "You need me to come with you?"

"I got this. I'm sure he's just here to tell me one more time that he's sorry for assuming I would do what I usually do but didn't that one time."

Shelby had resolved her feelings about what had happened between her and Ben. He really hadn't done anything wrong. Why *wouldn't* he think she assaulted that deputy? When had she ever given him any reason to believe she could control her emotions or think before she acted? Never. Ben had done what his dad had been waiting for him to do for the last ten years: see Shelby for what she was.

She fixed her ponytail and headed for the checkpoint. She was still dressed as the movie character. Thank goodness she had a jean jacket to cover up the crop top. This was a good look on Vanessa. Shelby wasn't a fan of showing so much skin in real life.

"Shelby Young. I'm here to sign in Ben Harper," she said when she got to the security checkpoint.

"Ben Harper?" The security guard flipped through the papers on his clipboard. "Not Ben Harper."

"*Curtis* Harper," a voice said from the other side of the checkpoint table. Curtis took off his sunglasses and gave her a chagrined smile.

It took every bit of self-control Shelby possessed not to make a run for it. It was bad enough when she thought she had to face Ben one more time, but Curtis? That was torture.

Shelby signed him in and waited while the security guard handed him a visitor's pass.

"You're all set," the guard said, letting Curtis through.

"Thank you. Hi, Shelby."

"What can I do for you, Mr. Harper?"

"I was hoping I could have a couple minutes of your time."

"If you came to get a garage tour, you're going to be disappointed. I needed to set that up ahead of time. I can't get you in there today."

"No, no. I'm not here to see the cars. I'm here to tell you something."

If he was there to thank her for cutting ties with Ben, she might just have to tell him to take a long walk off a short dock. She did not need his gratitude.

"Well, lay it on me," she said, sliding her hands in her back pockets. She wanted to get this over with and send him on his way.

Curtis scanned the area. There were crew members milling around, cleaning up the set. "Is there somewhere we can go that's a bit less public?"

This part of filming had taken over a whole block in downtown Atlanta. The crew weren't allowed in any of the buildings. Shelby pulled him into a vacated alleyway. "Mr. Harper, I don't have a fancy trailer or anywhere that isn't buzzing with folks trying to do their jobs. Whatever it is that you need to tell me, you can tell me right here."

He slipped his sunglasses back on and scratched the back of his neck the same way Ben did when he was nervous. "I'm not even sure I know how to say what I need to say. I probably should have put some thought into it before heading over here. Nick and Tiffani get married tomorrow and the weekend is going to be insanely busy. You said this week was your last week. I knew today was probably my only chance to come and talk to you face-to-face."

"Well, here I am. Sometimes the best way to say something is to just say it."

Curtis nodded his head and stared down at his feet. "I did a really terrible thing to you after that accident and I am here to be accountable for my actions."

"Mr. Harper, I really don't need to rehash the past. We are all moving forward. I will be out of your life in less than twenty-four hours.

I have no intentions of staying in touch with Ben. We have cut all ties. Hopefully he gets on with his life. I know I plan to."

"You weren't driving, Shelby. You weren't the one who was driving when you and Ben hit the deer."

Shelby cocked her head to the side. She must have misheard him. "Excuse me?"

"I told everyone that the police found you in the driver's seat, but that wasn't true. Ben was the one driving. I told you different because I believed that if you thought that you were the one behind the wheel, you wouldn't argue with me when I encouraged you to stay away from Ben. I was betting on you feeling guilty and hoped that you'd break things off with him so he would go to school as planned."

Shelby felt dizzy. It felt like she was standing on a merry-go-round. She leaned against the brick wall behind her. "I wasn't driving?"

Curtis shook his head. "I was scared. I was afraid Ben was going to make permanent decisions based on temporary feelings. I didn't realize that those feelings were much more permanent than I thought."

"I wasn't driving." Shelby couldn't remember that day to save her life. Practically the whole day had been wiped from her memory. The only thing she recalled was looking at her dress in the closet the night before prom and then being in an ambulance after prom. Everything in between was covered in a dense white fog. She had trusted the adults to fill in the gaps. She had trusted that Mr. Harper had told her the truth because he was Ben's dad, and Ben never lied. Apparently, his dad did.

"What I did was wrong. It was unforgivable. I made the assumption that you would move on and forget all about Ben. I didn't think about how that guilt would stick with you. I didn't think about how losing you would impact my son."

"Does Ben know?"

"He does, and he's not speaking to me because of it. He's beyond disappointed in me. Disgusted might be a better description. I don't blame him. I wouldn't blame you for feeling the same. I was wrong, and if I could go back, I would do things very differently."

Shelby didn't know what to say. There weren't words for how she felt right now. And any words that might slip from her lips would not be appropriate for her to say while she was on the job.

"Ben has been in love with you since the

day you came to Goodfield. He was twelve years old and you were the most exciting thing to ever happen to him. I ruined that. He's been successful. He finished school and he got a job. He ran for sheriff and he won. But my son doesn't laugh or smile the way he did when you were in his life. He doesn't love anything or anyone the way he loved you. I took something from him that I can't give back, and I am going to have to live with that."

Hot tears flowed down Shelby's face. Her chest ached worse than it did that day she packed her bag and bought a train ticket to Denver, the first stop on her escape route. And she'd been running for reasons that didn't actually exist.

"To top it off, I did the same to you and that was unbelievably unfair. I could justify my actions by saying I thought I was doing what was best for Ben, but I knew what I was doing wasn't the best for you. I will forever be sorry for that."

"I don't forgive you," she choked out.

Curtis wrung his hands. "I don't expect you to. But I do hope that you won't hold my bad behavior against Ben. I don't want my lie to be the reason there's a wall between you two any longer."

"Goodbye, Mr. Harper." Shelby took off running. She didn't have a clue where she was going, she only knew she couldn't stand there another minute and listen to anything that he had to say.

BAGS DIDN'T PACK THEMSELVES. Shelby folded her clothes and stuffed them in her suitcase. Her movements were robotic. She was on autopilot because if she switched her brain on, she would probably be curled up on the bed, sobbing herself to sleep. There was no time for a pointless emotional breakdown. She needed to be ready to leave tomorrow.

A knock on her door startled her. She checked the peephole, unwilling to be blindsided a second time today. Walker was in the hallway, bouncing anxiously on the heels of his feet.

She pulled open the door. "I'm not going to the party. I told you."

"I heard from Chris who heard from Johnny who heard from Sarah that you left location today in tears. What happened? What did Ben do?"

Shelby shook her head. "It wasn't Ben. It was his dad."

Walker slipped past her and into the room. "What happened?"

Shelby tried and failed to stay emotionally detached as she sat on the bed and told Walker everything.

"Are you going to talk to Ben?"

"Why? What will that accomplish?"

"Shelby, it wasn't your fault. His dad lied to keep you two apart. You aren't the bad guy. You're the good guy. You deserve to be happy."

"So what does Ben have to do with that?"

Walker cocked his head. "Don't do that. Don't act like that man isn't the one. I have wanted to be the one for so long, but when I saw you two together I understood why I wasn't. You've been so worried about messing things up and being bad for him because of what happened all those years ago, but it wasn't your fault. It wasn't your fault, Shelby. You don't have to be sorry about anything anymore."

"I'm going home tomorrow, Walker."

Walker took her by the hand. "You can go back to California, but I hope you'll think long and hard about what you should do before you go."

Think was all Shelby did the rest of the night and into the wee hours of the morning. She hadn't caused the accident. She hadn't been driving. The reality of that made her happy and infuriated at the same time. Mr. Harper had manipulated her to get what he wanted with no thought for what she and Ben had wanted.

If she had known the truth, she never would have left. She would have figured out a way to be there for Ben in the hospital. She would have been there to help him get back on his feet. She would have loved him through it all.

They could have been happy.

Shelby was done pushing her feelings aside. She was done apologizing for believing someone like Ben could love her. He could love her. He did love her. Then and maybe now. There was only one way to find out for sure.

CHAPTER NINETEEN

Valentine's Day—Present Day

"Do you have the list?"

"I would not be a very good best man if I didn't have the list the bride wrote me." Tiffani's list was one page long, front and back. It was folded up into a little square and tucked in the inside pocket of Ben's tuxedo jacket in case he needed to reference it.

"She'll be very happy to hear that."

"I want nothing more than for Tiffani to be the happiest person in the world today."

Nick smiled and patted his brother on the back. "Me, too, brother."

It was wedding time. After everything Tiffani had done to help Shelby, Nick had no doubts that she was the right woman for him. Ben wasn't going to have to work too hard to get him where he needed to be.

"Have you seen Mom and Dad?"

Ben had been avoiding his father as much

as possible, which hadn't been easy this week as the wedding approached. Ben hadn't allowed his father to speak more than a couple of words to him. Mending their relationship was going to take time. What his dad did was inexcusable. His mom shared that they had spoken to Maggie a couple days ago. Maggie was sadly disappointed in his actions, and her biggest concern was how Curtis planned to make things up to Shelby. Ben had no idea how his dad would ever accomplish that. Shelby's life had been irrevocably changed because of what he did. There was no making amends for that.

"I have not."

"You're walking Mom down the aisle, right?"

Ben patted his chest. "That's what the list says."

The wedding coordinator came into the back room. "Okay, gentleman, we are ready for you to line up."

This was it. Nick's big moment. Ben was happy for his little brother, but there was a tiny part of him that was jealous as well. Nick and Tiffani met, fell in love, got engaged, went through a rough spot and came out okay on the other side. They had persevered. Ben and Shelby weren't as lucky.

He had heard on the news that *Ready, Set, Go 4* wrapped up production yesterday in Atlanta. That meant Shelby was going back to California. For all he knew, she might have gotten on a plane the second she was done filming. He wouldn't blame her for getting out of town as fast as she could. She didn't even know the worst of what had been done to her.

Ben had decided not to tell Shelby what his dad did. After weighing the pros and cons, he felt that it was best to keep the secret. Not to protect his dad but to protect Shelby from knowing that someone she had trusted betrayed that trust in the most egregious way. He feared what that would do to her, how it might ruin any chance she had at letting people into her life. It was also his father's cross to bear. If Maggie and Shelby were going to find out what happened, it should come from Curtis, not Ben.

The wedding coordinator had Ben follow her after she placed the rest of the groomsmen in their spots at the front. His mom waited anxiously at the entrance.

"You look beautiful, Mom."

"Thank you, sweetheart." She adjusted his boutonniere. "I don't know how the single ladies will stop themselves from falling head over heels in love when they see you walk down that aisle."

Ben smiled but inside, he felt nothing. There wasn't anyone in this church he wanted to fall in love with him. The only woman in his heart was probably halfway across the country by now.

On their cue, his mom took him by the arm and they glided down the aisle toward his dad, who was already seated. Ben didn't make eye contact. He kissed his mother on the cheek and took his place next to his brother.

After the bridesmaids and the little flower girl made their way down the aisle, the whole congregation stood as the music changed and Tiffani and her dad made their entrance. Nick's eyes were wet as soon as he saw her. That man did not take his eyes off her until she was at his side. Even then, he was completely mesmerized by her. Ben was happy for his brother. He wanted nothing but the best for Nick, and Tiffani had proven herself to be worthy of him.

The minister began the ceremony. Ben's last responsibility was to give Nick the ring.

After the vows and the pronouncement of them being husband and wife, Nick got to kiss his bride. As the wedding party began their procession out, a loud screeching noise came from outside.

Tires squealing and the revving of an engine stole everyone's attention. All eyes were on the large windows lining both sides of the church in order to catch a glimpse of whatever was making that noise out in the parking lot. That was when Ben saw the flash of yellow. The Maserati slid sideways, spun and stopped perfectly between two parallel-parked cars.

Gasps and shocked exclamations filled the church. Ben's heart leaped inside his chest. He was pretty sure it wasn't Walker making that kind of entrance.

"You don't need me anymore, right?" he asked Nick, who quickly shook his head. Ben ran down the aisle and outside.

Shelby opened the car door and stepped out. Her dark hair was down, cascading over her shoulders. She was wearing a blue dress that hugged all her curves. "I was hoping they'd send the sheriff out to investigate."

"Are you here to report a stolen vehicle?

I've seen this one before and I have it on good authority that it is not yours."

"It is not mine, but can you hold off on arresting me for a minute so I can get through what I want to say?"

Ben did not intend to arrest her today. Ever, if he could help it. "Go ahead."

"So I've done a lot of thinking since your dad came to see me yesterday."

"Hold up. My dad came to see you yesterday?" Ben had no idea. His excitement turned to worry. If his dad told her the truth, she might not be here for the reason he was hoping for.

"He did. He told me I wasn't driving on prom night. I didn't hit the deer."

Ben nodded. His throat was tight, but he managed to speak. "It was me. All this time, it was me. And I cannot begin to tell you how sorry I am that he did that to you. I am really struggling to understand and to figure out how I can ever forgive him for lying about something that had such a huge impact on your life and mine."

Shelby stepped closer to where he stood. "I had a feeling you were going to say that and you know what?"

Ben braced himself for the worst. "What?"

"I am so sick and tired of you and me always being sorry. I think it's time you and I stop apologizing. I am not sorry for making you break curfew when we were kids. I am not sorry for pushing you in the lake so you'd have to take your shirt off."

Ben laughed as all the worry he felt a few moments ago completely disappeared.

"I am not sorry for being happy that you wanted to choose me over going to college. I am not sorry for coming back to town and hunting you down to make sure this wasn't your wedding day. I am really not sorry for being in love with you. Nor am I sorry that I think being with you would make me the happiest I have ever been."

Ben's heart felt like it was ready to burst out of his chest. Shelby was right. There was a certain kind of freedom in not being sorry.

"Wait, what did you just say?"

"That I'm not sorry?"

"No, the other part. The part about being in love with me."

Shelby flipped her hair back over her shoulder and bit down on her bottom lip. "I said I'm not sorry for being in love with you. I have been in love with you for a very long time."

"Like how long exactly?"

Shelby giggled. "Are we really going to do this?"

"Hey, I feel like facts are important. How long are we talking here?"

"Pretty much since you pulled me out of the lake the first and only time I got you to play hooky with me."

Ben nodded his head as his heart skipped and jumped and threw up rainbows. "Wow. That's a long time."

"I realized last night after talking to your dad and then Walker that I deserve to be happy. I don't get to feel happy a whole lot, but I do when I'm with you. So here I am, kind of crashing your brother's wedding to tell you that we don't have to be sorry anymore. Maybe we should try being happy."

Ben scratched the back of his neck. "Well, I am not sorry for being so damn happy that you are not sorry. I am also not sorry that you are the only person I have ever and will ever be in love with. And I would do anything to have a chance at being not sorry with you for a long, long time."

Shelby closed the distance between them and held his face in her hands, kissing him without an ounce of fear. Ben wrapped his

THE SHERIFF'S VALENTINE

arms around her waist and pulled her against him. Being free from remorse and regret made kissing her a million times more satisfying. Why hadn't they thought of this sooner?

"Are you coming to the reception? Or do I need to find someone else to give the best man speech?" Nick asked, interrupting their moment. Tiffani and Nick stood side by side, smiling ear to ear. Husband and wife.

"I'm coming, but I'm bringing a last-minute plus-one."

Usually, this was when Ben would apologize for not following the rules or doing what was expected. One thing Ben would never do again, though, was apologize for loving the woman in his arms.

EPILOGUE

February 14—Two Years Later

SHELBY PULLED OVER on the side of the road as soon as she noticed the red and blue lights flashing behind her.

"You've done it again. We are going to be so late," Walker said with an exasperated sigh.

"If we're late, it's going to be your fault for not putting us on an earlier flight." She readjusted the rearview mirror and tried to see who she was going to have to sweet-talk to get out of this. A smile broke across her face the moment the officer stepped out of the car behind her.

"What are you smiling at?" Walker looked over his shoulder. "Ah!" He turned back around. "I see what's going on here."

Shelby rolled down her window.

"Do you have any idea how fast you were going back there, miss? I clocked you going seventy-five in a forty-five. That's thirty miles over the speed limit. You know that automatically qualifies you as a Super Speeder in the state of Georgia, right?"

Shelby rested her elbow on the open window. "First of all, Officer, I am a Mrs., not a miss." She wiggled her left ring finger with the diamond band on it. "Second of all, of course I am a Super Speeder, I don't want to be late for my nephew's christening. Third, you better kiss me because I have missed you something bad while I was away."

Ben didn't hesitate. He tugged on the handle and pulled the door open. "I'm gonna have to ask you to step out of the car for that kiss, ma'am."

Shelby didn't resist this arrest. She jumped out of the car and into his arms as quickly as she could. She kissed her husband properly.

"I missed you," he said when they finally came apart.

"Next movie is being shot here, so I'll be home every night."

"That's the way I like it."

That was the way Shelby liked it as well. She tried her best since they got married to choose jobs that kept her close to home. It was a good thing that more and more movies and television shows were being filmed in Georgia. It made living in Goodfield not only possible but convenient.

Shelby and Ben lived in Maggie's old house. Shelby had bought it two years ago when she decided to give being happy with Ben a real try. She was done walking away from things she loved and she loved that house almost as much as she loved the man she shared it with.

It took some time to warm up to the neighbors, though. Well, one of them at least. Shelby, Ben and Curtis were finally on speaking terms. Ben's dad had done all he could to make amends. If Shelby expected people to forgive her for her past indiscretions, she had to learn how to be forgiving in return. She wasn't completely over how Curtis had changed the course of her life, but she was willing to let him be a part of this new life she was leading.

Ben, on the other hand, still struggled with letting go of his resentments. He was getting there, and Shelby knew that father and son would find a way to move past all this eventually. They had begun fishing together on Sundays. It was a start. Ben's heart was too big to shut his dad out forever.

"Can you two cut it out? We're going to be late to my godson's christening."

"Um, he's our godson," Shelby corrected. "Nick told you you could be the backup godfather if for some reason Ben couldn't fulfill his duties."

Walker waved her off. "Potato, patato. Let's go."

"I'll see you at the church?" she asked Ben.

"I've got to run home and let Trouble out, but I'll be there. On time, so don't get any ideas of taking over, Mr. Reed."

Walker grumbled in the passenger's seat. Something about being cooler than Ben ever could be. He was hilarious.

Trouble was Ben and Shelby's golden retriever puppy. An early Valentine's Day gift from Shelby to Ben. She liked the idea of him always having a little trouble in the house even when she was away.

"And you, Mrs. Trouble," Ben said, pulling her closer for one more kiss. "I'm letting you off with a warning this time, but you better slow it down."

She tapped him on the nose. "You love being married to a Super Speeder. Don't even lie."

"I love being married to you period."

The feeling was mutual. Shelby didn't know what she had done to deserve this man, this life, but she was going to thank the good Lord every day and would never apologize for allowing herself to enjoy each and every moment.

* * * * *

HARLEQUIN SELECTS COLLECTION

Visit
ReaderService.com
Today!

As a valued member of the Harlequin Reader Service, you'll find these benefits and more at ReaderService.com:

- Try 2 free books from any series
- Access risk-free special offers
- View your account history & manage payments
- Browse the latest Bonus Bucks catalog

Don't miss out!

If you want to stay up-to-date on the latest at the Harlequin Reader Service and enjoy more content, make sure you've signed up for our monthly News & Notes email newsletter. Sign up online at ReaderService.com or by calling Customer Service at 1-800-873-8635.